Nicola Moriarty is a Sydney-based novelist, copywriter and mum to two bright, kind (and remarkably strong-willed) teenagers. In between various career changes, becoming a mum and completing her Bachelor of Arts, she began to write. Now she can't seem to stop. Her previous works include the bestselling novels *The Fifth Letter* and *You Need to Know*.

nicolamoriarty.com.au
facebook.com/NicolaMoriartyAuthor
@NikkiM3 (Twitter)
@nicmoriarty (Instagram)

Also by Nicola Moriarty

NICOLA MORIARTY

Every Last Suspect

HarperCollins*Publishers*

HarperCollins*Publishers*
Australia • Brazil • Canada • France • Germany • Holland • India
Italy • Japan • Mexico • New Zealand • Poland • Spain • Sweden
Switzerland • United Kingdom • United States of America

HarperCollins acknowledges the Traditional Custodians
of the lands upon which we live and work, and pays respect
to Elders past and present.

First published on Gadigal Country in Australia in 2024
by HarperCollins*Publishers* Australia Pty Limited
ABN 36 009 913 517
harpercollins.com.au

A catalogue record for this book is available from the National Library of Australia

ISBN 978 1 4607 6100 7 (paperback)
ISBN 978 1 4607 1407 2 (ebook)
ISBN 978 1 4607 4585 4 (audiobook)

Cover design by Hazel Lam, HarperCollins Design Studio
Cover image by Adobe Stock
Typeset in ITC New Baskerville Std by Kirby Jones
Printed and bound in Australia by McPherson's Printing Group

MIX
Paper from
responsible sources
FSC
www.fsc.org   FSC® C001695

For Mum,
who is effortlessly wise
and endlessly kind

And for Ally,
who is one hell
of a warrior

PROLOGUE

A ceiling fan spins lazily above the bed, but it does little to shift the thick blanket of heat in the room. A cupcake sits on the table, the red paper liner peeled away from one side where a large bite has been taken and crumbs spill out. A line of ants have begun their relentless march towards their prize. Above the table, an old movie poster has been pinned to the wall, the edges curling. Outside, the rain falls steadily. It's been raining now for days with no signs of easing, but the downfall offers little relief from the heat. Instead, it intensifies the humidity. The air is thick and damp.

In the middle of the floor, a petite, dark-haired woman lies face down; she's on the edge of consciousness. Blood seeps from a gash on the back of her head. Her breathing is shallow and rattly.

If someone were to enter this room, it would become swiftly apparent to that person that this woman is dying. Unfortunately, though, no one knows she's there … or at least, no one who's going to come looking.

Harriet

You can feel it. Your grip on this world is slipping away. It's like you're ready to give in to the deepest sleep you could ever imagine. Your head is pounding, pulsing like your brain has expanded to twice its size and is trying to escape the constraints of your skull. Worse than that is the sensation of liquid trickling through your hair and pooling in your ear, before winding its way down the curve of your cheek to your chin to drip on the carpet. The thick liquid muffles and distorts sound, but it does more than that. It tells you that the wound on the back of your head is severe. It tells you that you're losing blood. Steadily. Relentlessly. You can only lose so much blood before you reach the point of no return.

Maybe you have an hour left, maybe two. Without help, you are *going to die.*

But there is no hope of help. No one knows you're here. Hell, you don't even know where 'here' is.

You think you're ready to give in to that deep slumber, don't you? Well, guess what? You can't. Not yet.

You open your mouth, attempt to swallow to clear your throat, ready to call out. For God's sake, you need help! But you can't seem to make your voice work. It would be pointless anyway; you don't think anyone would hear you, not over the sounds of the driving rain.

Okay, so no chance of moving, no chance of getting up and finding help. And no chance of alerting someone to the fact that you're here.

You really are going to die, aren't you?

It seems impossible that one minute you could be here, feeling, breathing, touching, seeing – and the next, you could be gone. What's that going to be like? To simply cease to exist? It won't be like anything, strictly speaking. If you don't exist, then you don't … exist. No more feeling, breathing, touching, seeing. No more listening, tasting, moving, loving. No more hating. No more hurting.

What are you going to do with the time you have left? The answer is obvious. You're going to figure out who it was that hit you. You're going to work out who murdered *you. And maybe, when you have the answer, you can find a way to leave a clue. To make sure this person pays for what they've done. You're going to have to start with a list.*

Who could hate you enough that they want you dead? Surely there can't be that many people – you're not a bad person! Of course, you've made mistakes, but no one is perfect.

No, there has to be a reason. A motive. What's happened recently? What's changed?

The first person is obvious: Karen, Tallulah's mum from school. You know why she's top of the list. You know what you did.

Number two is harder. You don't want to put her on this list, but you have to. Victoria. Your best friend. But then, she's much more than that, isn't she?

Who else? You could consider colleagues from work; a client that feels like they were short-changed. Or your sisters-in-law – they never thought you were good enough for their brother.

No, you don't think any of those people would have real motive.

Besides, there's one major player you're ignoring, and you must acknowledge the possibility.

Number three: Malek, your husband. Everyone knows that the first person the police check out is the spouse. It just seems so incomprehensible. After all, it's Malek! Your Malek. Your gentle giant. Your kind and doting husband who allowed you to coax him around to your way of thinking about how a marriage should work. And it did work! You have the perfect relationship and you both get exactly what you need.

You're trying to imagine it. Malek, with his powerful, five-eleven frame and his broad shoulders and his muscular arms. Would he? Could he? Could he genuinely swing a blunt instrument at the back of his wife's head and take her down? Leave her here to die?

The thing is, as gentle as Malek seems, there's that fiery temper underneath. The nasty clash with Ollie Cook back when he was playing in the Jersey Flegg Cup is proof of that. If you pushed him too far ...

You're going to have to move him to the top of the list.

SUSPECT ONE

the husband

CHAPTER ONE

Malek

Friday, early morning

Malek hadn't woken with heart palpitations like these in months. Maybe longer. He reached one hand across the bed, but found only sheets and empty space. Typical. Had he really expected Harriet home last night? He grabbed his phone off the bedside table with his other hand and checked for a message from her. Yep, he was right, she'd stayed over at Victoria's. He dropped the phone and tried to slow his shallow breaths. Spread one hand across his gut and placed the back of the other on his forehead. It was slick with his sweat.

Come on, pull it together.

He closed his eyes and focused on the rhythmic sounds of the rain drumming on the roof, allowed the steady white noise to fill up his mind and push everything else out. Slowly, his breathing started to calm as he felt the rise and fall of his stomach. He slid his hand up to his chest and noted that the hammering of his heart was already dissipating.

That's it. Just don't slow all the way down to nothing.

He wasn't sure if it was a dream that had set him off. He had no way of knowing, he'd never been the type to remember his dreams. But sometimes he thought he could feel the floor giving way beneath his feet. It was ridiculous that an incident that hadn't even actually happened to *him* could still do this to him all these years later. Seventeen, in fact. Seventeen fucking years!

Some random woman at a party had sat down opposite him once, taken his hands in hers, leaned in close, breathed what seemed like an entire bloody loaf of garlic bread into his face and said earnestly, 'Survivor's guilt is a real thing, Malek.' Apparently, Harriet had told her all about his panic attacks. Years of having good manners drilled into him by his mother meant he'd been too polite to tell the woman where to stick it, but later he'd snapped at Harriet, 'Why do you always feel the need to tell complete strangers about my private business?'

Besides, the problem with that woman's assessment was that he wasn't a survivor. You had to have taken part in the near-death experience in order to have survived it. So, what was his excuse?

He'd quickly forgiven Harriet for oversharing. All she had to do was tip her head to the side and flutter her eyelashes at him and he was putty in her hands. Did all beautiful people wield that kind of power over the general population? Although to be fair, Harriet really was next-level attractive. High cheekbones, soft full lips and that cheeky sparkle in her eyes that somehow hinted at danger and pleasure all at once.

It used to be known as their serendipitous moment – that incident from seventeen years back. The catalyst for his romance with Harriet. Well, the catalyst for him to take it to the next level, anyway. The story they told at dinner parties. *Did you know I once saved Malek's life?* And while Malek understood why Harriet would be so keen to share such an enthralling story, it often left a sense of uneasiness in the pit of his stomach to know that people were salivating over something that had been a tragedy for others.

Even Malek's mother, Maryam, believed fate had brought Harriet and Malek together, that she was destined to save his life. Malek had to admit, over the years he had started to see Harriet as his lucky charm. Not that this was the basis for his love for her. That sounded wrong, like she was a rabbit's foot or a horseshoe that he wanted to carry around in his pocket. Instead, it was like an extra layer to their relationship that enhanced his love for her. Smaller things had happened. Things like narrowly avoiding a parking ticket because Harriet asked him to go back to the car to grab her sunglasses. Or winning two grand on the pokies because Harriet said, 'Let's sit at that one so I can see the Rihanna concert on the TV at the same time.' They would have seemed like nothing more than fortuitous coincidences if they were standalone incidents, but piled one on top of the other, it really did seem like there was something divine about Harriet's effect on his life. Of course, the flames of this theory were fanned by Maryam's insistence that Harriet truly was her son's guardian angel.

Eventually though, when Harriet realised that Malek's panic attacks weren't subsiding with time, she stopped telling the story. She understood that constantly reliving the night she 'saved his life' wasn't helping and instead she became his rock. Any time he had one of his panic attacks, she would talk him through it, remind him to breathe, reassure him that he was safe, that she was there with him. She would squeeze his hands and rub his back and stroke his forehead until he was calm again.

But she wasn't always there. So he'd learned how to soothe his panic-stricken mind and body by himself.

As his heart finally returned to its usual rhythm, he slid his hand down from his chest to feel the more gentle rise and fall of his stomach, then, after a moment's hesitation, further. He was awake now. And alone … He lifted his head to glance at the bedroom door and make sure it was shut. It was. He figured he may as well. At least this would make for a better start to the day.

*

Malek stood in front of the mirror with his towel tied around his waist and his toothbrush clenched between his teeth. He tensed his abs and turned side-on. His rounded gut lifted slightly with the tensing, but it didn't change the fact that his stomach was what it was: a beer belly. He turned back to face the mirror and lifted his arms instead, clenching his biceps. They still bulged but there was too much fat over the muscles for there to be any real definition. He'd always been a big guy, broad shoulders and chest, above average height – 5 foot 11 to be precise – and he was a powerhouse on the footy field.

Not as big as the front-rowers, but he was solid, the perfect build for a half-back. Sometimes it took three blokes to take him down in a tackle. But he never used to feel overweight. His frame had carried his 90 kilos well. Now he saw a similar number if he stepped on the scales, but the weight sat on different parts of his body.

'Dad, what are you even doing right now?'

Farrah appeared behind him in the mirror. Malek kept his arms clenched and turned to face his daughter. 'Did you know I used to have a six pack?' he asked, his voice mumbling around the toothbrush sticking out of the side of his mouth. 'And huge, I mean, *huge* biceps.'

Farrah tipped her head to the side. Her dark hair was pulled up into a high ponytail and for a moment Malek could see nothing but Harriet in her face. But when she said, 'They're still pretty big,' Harriet seemed to vanish like a ghost, and it was just Farrah again.

He dropped his arms and slapped his stomach. 'But this,' he said, taking the toothbrush out of his mouth and leaning forward to spit into the sink. 'Where did this come from?'

'It's fine,' Farrah said. 'You're still fit. You used to be an *actual professional athlete.*'

'You're very kind, habibti, but you know I was only semi-professional. And that was a long time ago now.' He rinsed his mouth and replayed those words through his mind. *You know I was only semi-professional.*

Mal, don't forget you played at a semi-*professional level.*

Fark, when had Harriet's words permeated his brain and become his default? The description was accurate, but it was also splitting hairs. Because he *had* made it to a professional level. It was just that his injury had hit at the wrong time – right when he was about to sign the contract. Harriet wasn't being unkind when she said that, just pragmatic. Besides, she'd been a huge support to him when he'd had the injury. He wouldn't have made it through that dark time without her.

Malek wiped his face with the hand towel and turned to look at Farrah again. 'I wish you could have seen me back then,' he said. 'I wish I could describe to you the way it felt when I played footy for hours and hours. The adrenaline I got from it. It was the only thing I was any good at and it made people want to know me, made them want to talk to me, or just be around me.'

'I've seen some of the old footage of your games on YouTube, Dad. Like, it's terrible quality but I can still tell how good you were. And people do want to talk to you. I like talking to you. Are you … okay?'

Malek realised he'd worried his daughter and gave her a quick smile. 'Of course, sorry, kid, I was just being sentimental. Shit, what time is it? Are we late?'

'Uh, yeah, that's why I came to get you. Did not expect to find you flexing in front of the mirror.'

'How long until the bell?'

'We have twenty-five. And it's still raining, so traffic will be bad.'

'All good, we can make it, meet you downstairs.'

Farrah turned to walk away and then stopped. 'Dad?'

'Yeah?'

'Where's Mum this morning? Did she stay at Victoria's again?'

Malek hesitated. 'She did. One too many wines.'

'Dad ... don't you think —?'

Malek could hear the wheedling tone in her voice, and he cut her off. 'What I think is that *you* don't need to get involved.'

He saw Farrah's face drop and felt bad for snapping. He tried to soften his voice. 'But I do love that you care. Now go. Otherwise we *will* be late.'

Farrah disappeared as Malek left the ensuite and closed the bedroom door. He was glad she'd been the one to catch him examining his own body in the mirror instead of Harriet. His wife would have laughed at him. Maybe prodded his stomach, told him it was his own fault for drinking too many beers. Which would have been fair, really. He needed to get back into shape. Maybe he could take up boxing again. Would that be okay on his knee? He used to love boxing to keep fit back when he played footy. Back before his knee blew out and cost him his one and only chance at turning his favourite sport into a *real* career.

These days professional players trained differently. It was more about technical skills and tactical drills, HIIT sessions and plyometrics. But back in the late nineties when he played, his coaches just wanted him to be strong and aggressive. He remembered doing sit-ups while medicine balls were thrown at his stomach to toughen him up.

What time did the gym open on weekday mornings? If he joined up, would he have enough time to take a class a few mornings each week before driving Farrah to school? Or maybe Harriet could do school drop-off sometimes on her way to her first appointment?

He picked up his phone from the bed to look it up, then immediately remembered that he didn't have time to stuff around, Farrah was going to be late if he didn't move it. And she was right, everyone drove like shit in the rain. It had been pouring down all week, although it didn't offer any relief from the summer heat. Instead, it just made the air humid and thick. It felt like they were living in tropical Far North Queensland instead of Western Sydney. The estate they lived in had been built on a hill surrounded by old wetlands. He still remembered the way the real estate agent had made him feel like a moron for questioning the suitability of the land and the possibility of flooding: 'Mate, engineers much smarter than us have deemed the area safe to build.' Guys like that always underestimated his intelligence when they found out he was an ex–footy player. They assumed that the bigger the muscles, the smaller the brain. Just because he wasn't the intellectual type, didn't mean he was completely clueless.

Case in point: Right now, there were several flooded 'unfloodable' roads to the south and the east of the estate and the rain wasn't showing any signs of easing. At least the school was in the opposite direction and so far, no houses were in danger. But Malek still felt like grabbing that snooty-nosed agent who'd made him feel stupid and shoving his face in the muddy flood waters. *See, ahbil! It was a* valid *concern!* he would say as the agent spluttered.

Maybe he was feeling a tad too aggressive this morning. It was probably just the memory of that agent making him feel inferior, the same way Harriet sometimes did.

As soon as the thought entered his mind, he shook his head. Where had that come from? Harriet didn't make him feel inferior. They were partners.

He chucked the phone back down and made a mental note to investigate the boxing classes later. Although he knew it wasn't going to happen. Harriet wouldn't like it. Not if it meant she'd have to change her schedule to fit in with him. Her work was too important.

CHAPTER TWO

He tapped his fingers on the steering wheel as they drove, his eyes darting between the road and the clock on the dash. They could still make the bell as long as the lights were green at the top of Wilson Road. The windscreen wipers squeaked rhythmically as they flew back and forth. They were on the fastest setting and still couldn't keep up with the deluge. Week three of the first term and they had managed zero late notes so far – he didn't want to break the streak. Last year there had been so many partial absences on Farrah's report from each time they ran late that the report had been accompanied by a personal note from the principal: *Perhaps it's time to invest in a new alarm clock?*

It wasn't really anyone's fault – it was just that neither Malek nor Farrah were morning people. Malek had been ... once. When he was reserve grade for the Parramatta Eels and had to get up at 5am so he could fit in training before his day job. He used to practically leap out of bed, desperate to get moving, desperate to have the leathery feel of the football in his hands, desperate to have the crunch of the grass under his boots. But that all changed with his injury.

Keeping up the on-time streak for these few weeks had already been a mammoth effort involving multiple incentives for both Farrah *and* Malek. Cinnamon donuts on Friday after school when they'd completed the first full week. Macca's pancakes on Sunday morning after their triumphant week two. After an entire month it would be a new app for Farrah's iPad and a case of premium beers for Malek, and so on for the rest of the term. The end of term prize was going to be a shared shopping spree for the two of them with a limit negotiated by Farrah that made Malek's eyes water. But he'd decided it was worth it. Mrs Norris, the principal at Apple Hills College, frightened him. He didn't want another personalised note on the next report. In secret, he'd nicknamed her Chuck, as in Chuck Norris. He thought it was clever.

The school run – and really, the bulk of the parenting – had always been Malek's responsibility. But he didn't mind. Harriet was the clear breadwinner in their relationship. And contrary to the thought that had popped unbidden into his mind earlier, he did *not* feel inferior. He loved his role as a stay-at-home dad.

There was a point in their lives when it all could have flipped. When he was at the top of his game and about to sign the contract to be a first-grade NRL player. That was when the real money was going to start coming in. He was on track to pick up a six-figure salary, with the potential to earn more each year. He'd quit his nine-to-five job on the warehouse floor of a large furniture store in anticipation.

He'd hated the look on the coach's face when the club doctor had passed on the results from his scan. It was a mixture of pity and relief. Pity because he knew Malek would never play again. Relief because they hadn't signed the contract yet. They were able to cut Malek loose with no responsibility for his recovery and no obligation to pay out a contract. They would have to find his replacement fast, but there were plenty of other guys in the reserve grade vying for his coveted spot.

And it was all due to a stupid training accident. One of those frustrating moments when the session was almost over and the coach said, 'Let's just run that drill one more time.' A collision with another player that Malek would usually have come out of unscathed. Instead, for some freak reason, he'd landed oddly. Hit the ground and rolled, felt the pop in his knee and known right then that it was going to be bad. These days it'd be different. Medical advancements meant you'd have a chance at a full recovery. But not back then. Back then it was career-ending. He spent nights awake wishing he'd said, 'Nah, mate, I'm done for the day.' Just wishing he'd headed into the change rooms for a shower. Which was ridiculous anyway. You didn't say no to your coach.

After that, Malek had struggled for a long time to find his place in the world. He couldn't go back to his old job because the same injury that had ruined his footy career also stopped him from doing the physical tasks that were required in the warehouse. He tried working in an office, but between the fluoro lights and the trousers digging into his waist and the uncomfortable necktie, he'd felt like he was suffocating.

Over the years, he'd hopped from one job to another, quickly becoming bored or frustrated, but the thing he struggled with the most was losing the strict routine of his old life. He missed having someone tell him where to be and when to be there. He missed the regimented training schedule and the need to be in bed by a certain time so he could wake early the next morning. Suddenly, he had complete freedom – and he hated it.

Meanwhile, Harriet's real estate career was taking off and she assured him she was happy to support them both while he figured out what he wanted to do, but nothing he tried felt right.

Eventually, Harriet made a suggestion. 'Mal, you need to do what you love, you need to do what you're passionate about.'

He'd been confused. How was he meant to do what he loved when there was no chance he could ever play footy again?

She'd smiled at him and pushed a brochure across the table. The brochure was for a local rugby training clinic. 'You can't play, but you can coach.'

'You think I should apply for a job here?'

'No. I think you should set up your own business. Look at their qualifications. None of their trainers have your experience. None of them reached your level, but their prices are at a premium. You can start by undercutting them and poaching their clients, then, when you're established, you can slowly increase your prices.'

Having a ruthless businesswoman on his side was a big advantage. With Harriet's help, Malek had started an elite coaching business with casual hours and a small number of clients. Most days he was happy that he'd found his place back in the world of football. But there were still times where he couldn't quite tell if he loved the idea that he might be coaching the next big talent or if he hated it.

Regardless, he was happy being the lead parent in their family. It was just unfortunate that most people still had antiquated views of gender roles when it came to parenting, which meant he'd had to field countless comments like, 'Dad's on babysitting duty today, is he?' and rubbish like that. Meanwhile Harriet was constantly subjected to the judgemental remarks from people who thought she was an absent mother, which wasn't fair. Harriet was as involved in Farrah's life as most of the working dads he knew. So why didn't anyone pass judgement on them?

Although he supposed it would be handy if Harriet was open to helping with school drop-off once in a while, because then he really could think about doing something like those early morning boxing classes.

They rolled up to the intersection just as the lights turned green. Malek pressed down on the accelerator and they flew through as it changed straight over to amber, sending a wave of water onto the footpath. Those ones never stayed green for long.

'*Dad*,' Farrah said in a warning tone.

'What?'

'Speed. You're about to hit the school zone.'

Malek shifted his foot across to the brake and slowed down. 'I was on top of it.'

'Sure, you were.'

She probably had a fair point, considering the weather.

'Important thing is, we're going to make it. Third week done. Not one single late note.'

'What was the week three reward? Going out for breakfast tomorrow?'

'Can we make it Sunday? I have a feeling I won't be up for doing much tomorrow.'

Farrah pursed her mouth as they pulled up out the front of the school. 'Are you going to get drunk tonight at the party?'

'Never! I'm a responsible parent. An excellent role model. I drink responsibly.'

'So that's a yes. Okay. Sunday then. And it's just the two of us, right? Mum's not coming?'

'Nope. It's a you and me thing.'

'Good,' Farrah said, pulling at a thread on the edge of her school shirt. 'I mean, not that I would mind, but it's just that it's *our* thing, that's all.'

'It's okay, I knew what you meant.'

'Is she still pretending that tonight's going to be a surprise?'

Malek snorted. 'Sort of. And yet she somehow keeps controlling the plans for this so-called surprise party.'

'Like the weird birthday cake idea?'

'Exactly. Have to give her credit, though, she knows how to get her way – seems like all the guests are onboard with having to BYO one cupcake each. Got your umbrella?'

'Yep,' said Farrah, picking it up from the floor. She climbed out of the car, tugging her pleated maroon skirt down as she stood and then leaned back in. 'Don't forget Tallulah's coming over before the party to help set up tonight.'

Malek gave his daughter a salute. 'Roger that, kid.'

He watched her hurry away under her umbrella towards the school gate and then pulled away from the kerb. Tallulah had only become Farrah's close friend near the end of last year, so it was still quite a new friendship, but they'd become tight fast. Harriet wasn't a fan of their relationship. She thought Tallulah was too overbearing for Farrah, that she wasn't the right fit for their daughter, but Malek had brushed her concerns off. He could tell that Tallulah had one of those *big* personalities that might come across as domineering, but that didn't make her a bad kid.

He wasn't worried.

CHAPTER THREE

Still the heavy rain continued to fall. Malek was sitting at the lights with his left-hand indicator on, mentally running through his tasks for the day. Foamy water rushed along the gutter to his left and swirled at the grate where sticks and leaves had piled up, blocking the drain. He watched an empty Coke bottle tumble by, caught in the flow of the water, and found himself feeling more and more irritated by the size of his to-do list.

God, he was sick of this weather. Sick of everything feeling damp and dreary. Sick of stepping in puddles that soaked through his shoes and made his socks soggy and gross. All he wanted to do right now was get out of the relentless rain and sit down with a warm coffee at his favourite café. But he had far too much to do today.

Screw it.

He whacked the indicator down and the arrow on his dash changed from left to right. Why not just drop by the café first? A double espresso would see him through everything he had to get done today to make sure tonight's party went smoothly.

And maybe one of Colleen's custard tarts? His hand left the steering wheel to rest on his rounded gut. Maybe he should skip the custard tart.

He'd had everything organised for this party weeks ago and really should have been able to relax today, but Harriet had complicated things by throwing out last-minute requests and haphazardly adding new guests to the invite list. He'd had to cancel on an important coaching client this morning so that he could rush around Sydney, searching for two hundred dark-red macarons ('Actually, try to find crimson ones please, Mal') and then he was supposed to find enough time to head out to the airport to pick up Harriet's cousin, Brad, who was flying in from Perth. He hadn't even known that Brad was coming to the party until two days ago.

'Hang on,' he'd said when Harriet casually mentioned Brad's flight time. 'When did you invite your cousin?'

'Ages ago, you knew he was coming,' Harriet had said.

'I can guarantee you I did not.'

'Oh,' said Harriet. 'Sorry. But you get why I wanted to ask him, don't you?'

Malek did get it. Harriet had a terrible relationship with her immediate family. Farrah had never even met her grandparents on Harriet's side. They'd moved to the States with Harriet's older brother when Harriet was still finishing her HSC, leaving her behind to be billeted by another family until she went to university and moved into on-campus accommodation. Malek would never understand how Harriet's parents could have moved away to another country entirely and left their seventeen-year-old daughter behind.

All because her brother, Eddie, had a chance at a promising golfing career.

Brad was the only relative Harriet really got along with. It was in stark contrast to Malek's close relationship with his family, and he knew that, over the years, Harriet had often felt bitter about her lack of family ties in comparison to his, even if she tried to pretend it didn't hurt. So, it did make sense that she'd want there to be at least one representative of her family at her fortieth birthday party. It would have been nice, though, to have known Brad was coming and that Malek was expected to pick him up. Why couldn't Brad make his own way out from the airport? He could easily afford an Uber.

Malek had attempted to surprise Harriet by inviting her parents, but as always, they'd declined, citing the standard excuse that they'd been using for the past almost twenty years: 'We're sorry Malek, but we can't leave Eddie right now.'

Adding to Malek's irritation about today's tasks was that, originally, he was certain that Harriet had wanted the 'theme' of the party to be 'silver and gold bling'. Malek had spent a lot of time sourcing sparkling decorations and garishly bejewelled photo booth props as well as pre-ordering two hundred silver macarons, only for Harriet to suddenly start talking about her 'red velvet'–themed party as though that had been the plan all along. That was when he'd learned the term 'gaslighting'.

'Seriously, I feel like I'm losing it. I'm positive you specifically asked for a "bling" theme,' Malek had said at the time. 'When did it suddenly become "red velvet"?'

'Mal, I always wanted the theme to be red velvet. I've been dropping hints about that since the first day I suggested this party.' And as usual, Harriet had fluttered her eyelashes at him and he acquiesced.

Later that night though, Farrah had nudged him and whispered, 'Textbook gaslighting, Dad,' and tapped her nose like he was meant to know what she was on about. Malek had done his best to give her a knowing look in return, but as soon as he was alone, he'd googled the term. Once he'd finished reading about it, he'd experienced a strange, almost out-of-body experience as he came to the realisation that this was something Harriet did to him quite often. He'd simply never known there was a word for it. Almost immediately, he dismissed it. Just because Harriet sometimes changed plans on him didn't mean she was *intentionally* gaslighting him. He'd set about sending updated information to the party guests, asking them to please wear something with 'a splash of red' instead of 'a sparkle of bling' as the original invite had said.

Next he called the bakery that had the original order for two hundred silver macarons to ask if they could somehow dye the macarons with red food colouring, but he'd left the request too late and the woman on the phone just smacked her gum and reminded him that there were no refunds.

But the main reason all of this was frustrating Malek was that he hated letting his clients down. This morning's session with Sammy was meant to be a chance for him to go over her angled 40/20 kicks before her game this Sunday in the Tarsha Gale Cup. This was her best chance to get her first contract;

they'd been tipped off that a scout from the Dragons was coming by to watch her. Not that the money would be as life changing as it would have been all those years ago for Malek when he'd been so close to that coveted contract; the pay in women's football was atrocious in comparison to men. Malek knew of a friend's daughter who'd been called up to play in the State of Origin for NSW. She'd been paid five grand – an absolute joke when the minimum pay for the men in the State of Origin was thirty thousand per game. Sammy would have to hang on to her part-time job to support her footy career but at least she'd be doing something she loved. And he'd heard that things were slowly starting to change. There was talk of bringing in minimum wages for women's footballers – it was a start at least.

Farrah used to play a bit when she was younger. She wasn't half-bad either, fast down the wing and great at feinting her way around defenders. But she'd lost interest when she'd started high school. Malek still held a secret hope that she might come back to it one day.

He turned into the carpark of a small set of shops and parked right in front of the café, but even the short dash from his car to the café door was enough to get his shirt wet.

Colleen winked at him as he entered and shook the water off himself like he was a large, shaggy dog. She picked up a small espresso cup and waved it at him. 'Usual?'

'Yes, please. You're an angel.'

'If I'm an angel then where are my wings?' She wriggled her shoulders as though to demonstrate the lack of wings on her back and it drew Malek's attention to the fact that her arms were looking particularly toned. He opened his mouth to ask her if she'd lost weight but then thought better of it. Women didn't necessarily appreciate having their bodies commented on, even if you meant it to be a compliment.

Instead, he said, 'Trust me, just because you can't see them, doesn't mean they're not there.'

Colleen turned away to the coffee machine to start on his double espresso and Malek could tell from the slight flush in her cheeks that she was pleased. He silently congratulated himself. It always felt like an achievement when he made Colleen happy. He'd been coming to this same tiny café for several years now and at first Colleen had been curt with him – always polite, but never friendly. With her dark hair pulled back into a tight bun on the top of her head and her clipped voice, she seemed like a severe school matron. But he'd noticed she was much warmer with the regulars, and her face softened when she smiled, with deep dimples appearing on both cheeks. Usually that kind of behaviour would irritate him but for some reason with Colleen, it made him want to be a part of the in-crowd. And the coffee was amazing. So Malek had continued to visit, and he'd slowly worn her down with small talk that eventually turned to banter and now it was like they were best mates.

He supposed they were a bit flirtatious with one another on occasion as well, but it was all very tame. These days, if he saw a new person come in to order something and Colleen switched off the charm to serve them, he felt a mix of sympathy for the newbie and of pride at being one of the regulars who got to see her warmer side.

He took a seat at one of the tall stools in front of the counter and looked out the window at the relentless rain, running his hand through his short, thick hair and most likely ruining the job he'd done combing it neatly after his shower. That had always been a habit of his when he was feeling nervous or frustrated. Why couldn't this rain have cleared up in time for the party? It would have made things so much easier if they could have spread out into the backyard tonight.

'Released without charge,' said a voice to his left. 'Apparently they had the wrong guy.'

'Wrong guy? Or not enough evidence?'

'Good point.'

Malek glanced sideways at the two tradies in hi-vis orange vests. Regulars at the café. He was unable to stop the curious expression from crossing his face before one of them caught his eye and shook his head gravely.

'We're talking about the school girl down in Melbourne – found murdered a couple of weeks back. Cops just released their only suspect.'

Malek's face twisted. He didn't want to admit that he didn't really follow the news much and knew very little about the case. Only that the girl was frighteningly close in age to Farrah.

He settled for a response of, 'That doesn't sound too good,' and then turned his gaze back to the rain outside as he tried to shift his focus to the party planning.

Find macarons.

Airport pick-up.

Blow up balloons.

'Where are you today? You're a million miles away.'

Malek looked up to see Colleen holding his coffee across the counter, her brown eyes searching. 'Shit, sorry. I don't even know where my mind was.' He took the coffee from her and sipped it, unable to hide the pleasure on his face as the hot drink hit his tastebuds.

'All good. I was only asking about your plans for the day.'

'Right, right. Sorry. Busy day,' he said, wrinkling his nose. 'That's probably where my mind was. Trying to keep track of everything I have to do. It's Harriet's surprise fortieth party tonight.'

'Ah, yes, the big surprise that's not a surprise. Hilarious. If it was me, I'd throw my hands up and say, if you want the party, you plan the party.' She grinned and her two dimples deepened.

'If you knew Harriet, you'd know there's no way I'd get away with that. Trust me.'

'You know this party is all anyone is talking about, right? The amount of school mums I've overheard in here, going on about it like it's the event of the year. You two must put on a hell of a shindig.'

Malek tugged at the neck of his T-shirt. 'Seriously? Like who? Uh … what exactly are they expecting from this party?'

Colleen shrugged. 'I don't know who! I haven't bothered to learn any of their names. You know I don't really like that lululemon leggings crowd. Always asking for half-strength almond milk piccolos or turmeric lattes. Taking up two of my tables for hours at a time but never ordering a single thing to eat. They waste my time.'

One of the tradies chuckled as the two of them headed out with their takeaway coffees. 'You should charge them rent for your tables, Col,' he said.

'Not a bad idea,' she replied.

Malek waited until they were gone and then leaned forward. 'Okay, but what have these women been saying?'

'Oh, I don't know really, just going on about what they'll wear, what gift they'll buy that will be impressive enough for Harriet ... and how Harriet always hosts the most amazing parties, and this is meant to be the best one yet.'

'Right,' said Malek, feeling a drop of sweat trickle down his back. 'But don't they realise that Harriet isn't the one hosting? I mean, it's a surprise party *for* Harriet. Or at least it's meant to be. I'm putting on a decent spread, plenty of drinks, great DJ – but it's not going to be Elton John's fucking Christmas party.'

Colleen burst out laughing. 'I love that Elton John's Christmas party is your benchmark for a killer event.' She wiped the corner of her eye and then fixed Malek with an earnest look. 'Honey, I don't know exactly what these women are expecting, but I guess everyone knows that it's not really a surprise party because apparently Harriet keeps inviting people herself.'

Malek quirked an eyebrow. 'Considering you say you don't really like to get involved with that crowd, you seem to know quite a bit of what they've been talking about.'

Colleen glared at him, but with a hint of playfulness in her eyes. 'Shut up. I hear things, that's all.'

Malek took another sip of his coffee. 'Jesus, Harry's really put me in it. I knew she'd added a few extras to the invite list, but I have a feeling there's going to be a lot more that I don't know about. Particularly annoying considering I wasn't allowed to invite most of *my* relos to keep numbers down. Maybe I'll warn the caterers … Just another thing to put on my to-do list.'

'Wait, isn't your family Egyptian?'

'Part Egyptian, part Lebanese. Why?'

'Because you and I both know that any and every aunty, uncle, cousin and second cousin won't accept being left out of a family event. Have you got a death wish?'

Malek groaned. 'You think I don't know that? But Harry was adamant.'

'Your funeral,' Colleen said with a shrug. 'No coaching clients today, then?'

'Nah, Harriet has me driving all over Sydney trying to track down two hundred bloody macarons. I had to cancel the one session I had booked in for this morning.'

Colleen leaned back on the counter behind her and folded her arms. 'Two hundred macarons? Isn't that something you should have pre-ordered?'

'Of course – and I did, I'm picking them up from Mildred's Bakery down the road. But now they're the wrong colour because Harriet keeps coming up with these random last-minute changes to the party. They have to be red instead of silver because the theme is "red velvet" now, not "bling."'

'So, you've already ordered two hundred macarons, but the problem is they're silver,' Colleen clarified.

'Yep.'

He watched as two different expressions swept over Colleen's face: amusement chased quickly away by concern.

'Hang on, weren't you meant to have the last coaching session with Sammy today, before the scout comes to the game this weekend?'

'I was. Had to cancel.'

'Alright,' said Colleen. 'I have an idea. Forget about driving all over the place trying to find a whole heap of red macarons. Let me have Nicky run down the road and collect the silver ones from Mildred's for you and then I'll fix them up.'

'Fix them up? How?'

'I have a few tricks up my sleeve. Trust me. I can make them work into your red velvet theme. That way you can still make your session with Sammy.'

'But ... you've got a café to run, you don't have time to magically fix two hundred macarons.'

'Yes, you're right, I don't have time for this, but that doesn't mean I can't make it happen. That's why it's lucky you're my favourite customer.'

'I am?' Malek couldn't help feeling an inner glow of pleasure.

'Well, look, I'm quite fond of you, but if I'm entirely honest, Sammy's a great kid and I really want to see her do well. What do you think?'

Malek considered the proposal. Could he manage the training session if Colleen took this task off his plate? But what about Brad? He was still meant to head out to the airport to pick him up.

Screw it, he'd call Harriet and tell her that Brad would need to get an Uber like he should have done in the first place. And why should he start stressing about trying to make sure this party was the social event of the year? It wasn't his fault that Harriet kept inviting more and more extras or setting these ridiculous expectations. The party was going to be what it was going to be now. Colleen was right, this session with Sammy was important.

'Colleen, that sounds amazing, you've literally saved my life.'

'You don't know the meaning of the word literal, do you? And don't get too excited, I'm gonna charge you through the teeth for this.'

Malek rubbed his chin. 'Is it through the teeth? I thought it was through the nose.'

'Teeth,' said Colleen, and she bared her teeth and tapped one finger against them. 'The dentist charges through the roof, no? Point is, you might regret letting me do this.'

'No way, really, you've saved me.'

'Alright, alright, here.' Colleen slid a pen and notepad across the counter. 'Write down your address and the time the party starts. I'll drop off the macarons about an hour before that.'

'I did say you were an angel.'

CHAPTER FOUR

Malek pulled into the carpark at Graysmith Park and saw that he had his pick of spots – no one else was out training on a day like today. Thankfully, Graysmith had a synthetic field that he could use even when most of the grass fields were closed due to the heavy rain. It wasn't perfect for replicating game conditions and his preference would be to train Sammy on the grass, but this was better than no training at all.

Sammy should be arriving in about ten minutes. When he'd texted her as he left Colleen's café to let her know he could squeeze in a training session after all, she'd sent back a string of fist bump emojis and smiley faces before adding, *I can be there by 10am. See you shortly, coach.*

He parked his car and picked up his phone to call Harriet. As he dialled, his stomach churned. Why was he feeling nervous about telling his wife that he didn't want to collect her cousin from the airport? She was the one who'd added Brad to the invite list and promised him a bloody personal chauffeur back to their place without asking Malek first. She was the one who kept changing plans for this party and making him run all over the place trying to meet her demands. And she was the one who'd spent the night at Victoria's place last night – *again*. Why the hell should he feel bad?

The ringing on the other end of the phone flicked over to Harriet's voice asking him to leave a message and for just a moment, an ember of rage flared in Malek's chest at the sound of his wife's cool tone.

Farrrk. What was *up* with him today? He hung up without leaving a voicemail and took a moment to calm his breathing. It would be stupid to start a fight with Harriet on the day of her fortieth birthday party. And pointless. It wasn't like Harriet was going to change. Would he want her to, anyway? Sure, she could be ostentatious and aggressively ambitious and, at times, maybe came across as a bit too self-absorbed, but it was these same qualities that made her so successful and often got them exactly what they needed. Like when she demanded that Farrah was moved to a different class in sixth grade because the teacher was an absolute bitch and Farrah was coming home in tears every day. Or when she negotiated with the guys that built their swimming pool to throw in several extra features for free because of delays throughout the build.

But was it any wonder she'd learned to be so dogmatic and self-serving considering the way her family had abandoned her as a teen?

Besides, he'd known who she was when he married her and for all her flaws, deep down, she *was* a good person. She'd supported him through so many things: his career-ending injury; his ongoing panic attacks; and his mother's death. She'd even seen the old VHS recording of his violent outburst at the Jersey Flegg game; one of his ex-teammates had shown it to her at a barbecue several years back. Malek had a feeling the prick had had a thing for Harriet and was hoping it might make her think differently of him. With Harriet's striking good looks, Malek was used to other blokes always vying for her attention. But thankfully, Harriet hadn't judged him for it, she'd simply listened as he'd explained what had set him off that day and had said she understood why he'd cracked.

He took one more calming breath and sent her a text message.

Harry, checking in on your plans for today. I can't pick up Brad, so either you'll have to do it or he'll have to find his own way.

He finished the message then leaned back in the driver's seat to wait. He never put anything more than the bare minimum in his texts. Some people liked to add a string of emojis, like Sammy, or a whole heap of kisses, like Malek's sisters. But that was one thing both he and Harriet were on the same page about: they preferred to get straight to the point.

Despite apparently not having been available to answer his call, his phone vibrated with a reply from Harriet almost straight away.

Hi Mal, full day on the road today. Back-to-back vendors. No problem with Brad, I'll tell the lazy bugger to call a cab.

Malek breathed in deeply through his nose and back out through his mouth, making a whistling sound through his front teeth. He knew he should feel pleased that Harriet wasn't arguing with him about meeting Brad, but why was she being so easy-going about it now, when just the other day she'd acted like it was essential that Malek pick him up?

Maybe he ought to put his foot down like this more often.

A thought occurred to him. Harriet had left her car at home last night – how the hell was she meant to have a full day on the road without a vehicle?

As though she was reading his mind, a second message immediately came through.

Rick's driving me around today 'cause I didn't have time to come home and grab my car this morning.

Which one was Rick again? The photographer or one of her junior agents? Malek couldn't remember, but he supposed she was the boss, so she could get away with getting one of her staff to play chauffeur for the day. Harriet had been working as a real estate agent for a long time now. She was good at her job. Had that real knack for sales. Always charming potential new vendors and buyers. Squeezing every last dollar out of each sale for her clients. She wrote her own ad copy too, and she was good at coming up with new ways to say the same old things. If something was modern, it was fresh, it was contemporary, it was chic. If something was spacious, it was open and airy with abundant storage. And if it was a postage stamp–sized dump, it was 'compact and low maintenance with endless potential to add your own personal touch'.

He tapped out another message: *Okay. Sounds good. What time will you make it home this afternoon?*

I already have my outfit for tonight with me, so I'll get ready at Vic's and arrive at the party at about 8. That works for the surprise, right?

Malek gritted his teeth. Of course she was getting ready at Victoria's place. Of course, she was going to show up with Victoria. Of course this surprise party was an absolute farce because there was literally nothing about it that was a surprise anymore. Why had he ever agreed to this? Why hadn't he told her it should just be a normal birthday party with no 'surprise'?

When she'd first come to him and floated the idea of wanting a surprise party, he'd laughed and said, 'Well, it won't be much of a surprise now that you've asked for it, will it?'

But she'd winked and said, 'Asked for what?' So he'd taken the hint and set to work organising the party, assuming Harriet wouldn't mention it again and that he would pretend nothing was being arranged.

Instead, Harriet had continued to drop more and more clues about what she wanted at this party.

'I was telling Amanda the other day that silver and gold bling would make a great theme for a milestone birthday.'

'Don't you think Carrington Caterers put on an excellent spread at the fundraiser last year?'

'Check out this DJ, he's got great reviews on Facebook.'

Eventually, she'd abandoned all pretences that her comments were off-hand chatter and instead had started giving him outright directions on exactly what she expected. In fact, she'd even mentioned that she was planning her own surprise announcement for tonight. Malek had no clue what it could be, but knowing Harry, it wasn't going to be anything minor.

He sighed and sent back a reply. *Okay, fine. But I have to say, I thought you would be home this afternoon after work. I could have used your help with the final set-up.*

Sorry, but I'm sure you and Farrah will have it all in hand. And doesn't make sense for me to be there when it's a surprise party.

Yet again Malek drew in a sharp breath. He wanted to shout back at her, *Of course it doesn't make any sense! But it also doesn't make any sense that you're controlling every bloody detail of this thing!*

Instead, he put the phone down on the passenger seat and looked out the window just in time to see Sammy walking towards his car from her own little yellow hatchback that her dad had bought as a gift for her eighteenth last year. She had a sports bag slung over her shoulder and her rugby shirt was already spotted with fat rain drops. They were both going to be soaked by the time they finished this training session.

She gave him an over-exaggerated wave, then pointed at one of the benches next to the field to indicate that she was going to go and put her boots on. Malek nodded and pulled his keys out of the ignition. Right, time to focus on footy.

*

'Okay, Sammy, I'm calling it. You've done bloody great today, but there's a point where we have to stop and say you're ready for this game. And I reckon you're as ready as you'll ever be.'

Sammy had the ball tucked under her arm. Her clothes were drenched through, and her short curly hair was plastered to her head. 'Are you sure, though? Because I think those last couple went a little wide. Maybe we should do a few more.' Her eyes pleaded with him.

Malek took the ball from her. 'Sammy, you have to trust me. Your shaping on the ball has been perfect today. The last few did *not* go wide. Listen, I don't say this lightly, but you're the best half-back I've coached in years. You've got this.'

Sammy's face remained uncertain.

'Sammy, I'm serious. I don't blow smoke up someone's arse if they don't deserve it. It only wastes their time and mine. Not only have you been nailing those kicks today, but I also see that same killer instinct in you that my coach used to say I had. You're a force to be reckoned with.'

Sammy suddenly flung her arms around Malek's waist and hugged him tightly. 'Thank you,' she said. 'There's no way I could have done this without you.'

Malek froze. Should he hug her back or was that a bit inappropriate considering their relationship? Then again, soon he likely wouldn't be coaching her anymore. She was a sure thing to get this contract, and then she wouldn't have time to train with him on top of her sessions with the club. There was probably no harm in one hug. He squeezed her back and then pulled away.

'Yeah, you could have. Any decent coach would see your talent. Come on, let's pack up and get out of this rain.'

Sammy didn't move, though. She was staring straight at Malek and then she said, 'No, I'm serious. You've been amazing, I've *loved* having you as a coach.'

Was there a flirtatious tone in Sammy's voice or was Malek imagining it? Harriet had once said she thought Sammy might have a bit of a crush on him, but Malek had brushed it off at the time. The girl had only just turned nineteen, why would she have any interest in a forty-two-year-old bloke?

He broke eye contact to start collecting cones.

'Well, it's been really great coaching you,' he said, trying to keep his voice light. 'Why don't you get going, I can finish packing up.'

'I'm happy to help,' Sammy said, picking up the equipment bag and holding it open for him.

As Malek dropped a stack of cones into the bag, his hand brushed against Sammy's, making him jump back. Sammy gave him a strange look. If there was anything going on here, he needed to shut it down fast.

'Listen, Sammy, sorry, I didn't mean to give you the wrong idea when I hugged you just now … I shouldn't have —'

'What do you mean?' Sammy cut him off. She stuck her tongue out halfway and held it between her teeth, confusion in her eyes, which quickly shifted to realisation. 'Oh my God, no! No, no, no … I wasn't … that wasn't … no! Ew, you're old enough to be my dad!'

Malek's face warmed. Shit, why had he said anything? He'd misinterpreted. He tried to cover it up. 'Yeah, no, of course, *I* didn't think that – I was just making sure *you* didn't think —'

But now Sammy was cackling. 'Can you imagine?' she said. 'Going for the older coach – such a cliché!'

Malek felt like a complete idiot for even thinking it. Bloody Harriet! Why did he always let her get in his head like that?

*

On the drive home, the seat was damp and Malek's wet clothes stuck to him uncomfortably. A roiling blend of frustration and embarrassment filled his stomach. God, he hoped Sammy didn't tell anyone about his misunderstanding. His distraction wasn't helped by the steamed-up windows, and he almost didn't see the two boys fly out across the road in front of him on their scooters. He slammed on the brakes and the car started to aquaplane on the wet asphalt, before the ABS kicked in. He came to a stop just in time.

The two young boys stood frozen in the middle of the road and Malek felt all the rage about the party and the embarrassment about Sammy and the frustration with Harriet simmer over. He opened the door and unfolded his formidable frame from the car. The kids' eyes widened.

'Oi! What the hell were you two thinking? I could have killed you!' he roared at them.

The boys looked at one another and then started backing away from Malek, their faces masks of fear. 'Sorry,' stuttered one. 'We ... We didn't see you.'

The fear in their faces only made Malek angrier. Why should he feel bad for yelling at these boys and giving them a fright? He was trying to teach them a lesson – a lesson that they bloody needed to know. Awlad kasr albilad. They should have been in school.

'Well next time, you two need to *stop and check* before crossing. Got it? Or if not, I'm happy to show you what a good blow to the head feels like.'

He knew immediately that he'd gone too far. The smaller boy burst into tears and then the two of them took off, terrified.

Fark. Why had he added that last part? He'd basically threatened to punch a couple of kids in the head. Usually, he was way better at keeping his cool in this kind of situation.

He got back into his car and punched the dash. *Pull yourself together, Malek. You're losing it.*

He set off again towards home and concentrated on the counting technique that his coach had suggested to him years ago after the Jersey Flegg incident. *Breathe in, count to ten, breathe out, count down from fifteen …*

To be fair, Ollie Cook had deserved to be held accountable for what he'd done that day. Nate had only just been selected to play in the Jersey Flegg Cup after being one of the stand-out players in the S.G. Ball Cup. He was a kid at the start of his career with a heap of promise. Malek was about to age out of Jersey Flegg and was on track to move into the reserve grade. As one of the more senior Jersey Flegg players, he felt a sense of responsibility to look after the newer boys. But at the same time, the way Malek had held Ollie accountable had been wrong, he knew that.

Ollie had been completely reckless and downright dangerous when he'd gone into that intentionally late tackle. A shoulder-barge to an opponent's head when they've already passed the ball and they're still looking the other way was the on-field equivalent of a coward's punch. And Malek had been perfectly positioned to see Ollie's elbow make contact with Nate's skull. He'd heard the crack. Seen Nate go down. Malek knew full well that Ollie could have ended Nate's career and Ollie would have known it too. For crying out loud, a hit like that could have killed the kid.

Malek could still remember the moment the blind-hot fury had swept over his entire body. The rushing that filled his ears. The way time seemed to stop. He'd launched himself at Ollie with pure rage. Hadn't even realised how many punches he'd thrown before his teammates pulled him away.

He'd felt sick when he'd first seen Ollie's face – a bloody, pulverised mess. Even more so when he watched the grainy footage of his attack afterwards. He'd been suspended for four games, a punishment that he'd accepted without complaint. He was just grateful that they were still going to take him into the reserve grade. In fact, back then, the coaches and managers didn't see much of an issue with that level of aggression: 'Listen, we have to suspend you because the refs reviewed the recording and it's plain as day that you went in throwing punches. But looking at that tackle, we get why you lost it.'

Meanwhile, Ollie had two fractured cheekbones and a ruptured eye socket.

Okay, so why was he starting to feel that blind rage again lately? Today it was because everything seemed to keep going wrong. The embarrassment of the mix-up with Sammy, all because Harriet had made him think the girl had a crush on him. The frustration of Harriet making so many late changes to the party, putting this pressure on him. The anger that Harriet had spent the night at Victoria's place, that she was going to get ready for the party tonight there, that she was always with Victoria, that Victoria was such a big part of their lives.

All of it came back to Harriet.

For the millionth time, Malek found himself wondering where it had all gone wrong. How their marriage had seamlessly merged into something else altogether. And somehow, he'd allowed it to happen.

He'd agreed that Harriet could have everything she ever wanted. The supportive family at home. The nice house. The great career. And the icing on the top – a bit of extra fun on the side. The unspoken agreement that she could have her cake and eat it too, if the cake was Victoria.

*

Sophie

Apple Hills College

Word had spread that there was a fight going on under the walkway near the art classrooms. Sophie was grateful for the distraction; Evan had been kissing her from the moment lunch time began and her jaw was starting to ache. Besides, she hadn't even had her sausage roll or chocolate Oak yet.

She was surprised to see that it was two girls fighting in the centre of the tightly formed circle. One was tall with long blonde hair in a plait down her back, like Elsa from *Frozen*. The blonde had hold of the smaller brunette girl's ponytail and was using it to shove her head down and keep her bent double. The brunette was trying to twist out of her grip, hands scrabbling and fingernails scratching at open air.

'What the fuck?' said Evan, delighted. 'Girl fight. Epic!'

'Evan!' Sophie looked around, wondering how long it would take for a teacher to appear and break up the girls.

Why was it that when something like this happened, kids all over the school were instantly drawn to the drama, but the teachers never seemed to catch on fast enough? It was like there was a charge to the air, a fizzing tension that brought everyone running.

The brunette managed to slam her elbow into the stomach of the blonde and was finally able to pull her hair free and stand up. 'Just give it back!' she shouted, breathing heavily.

'No! You're acting like a fucking idiot.'

'It's not your choice!' The smaller girl lunged at the taller one; Sophie saw an iPhone fly out of her hand and clatter to the concrete, the screen shattering.

'Ooohhh,' chorused the crowd, impressed.

'Fucking hell, Tallulah! Now it's broken,' shouted the brunette.

The girl let out a growl of frustration and launched herself at blonde Tallulah, slamming her into the wall behind her. Then the air changed again. The unmistakable voice of an adult cut through the noise of the crowd and kids quickly pulled back, ready to distance themselves from trouble.

Thank God, thought Sophie, as Mr Boyd pulled the two girls apart, while Evan let out a disappointed sigh.

'Just as it was about to get good,' he said.

CHAPTER FIVE

Malek pulled into the driveway and pressed the remote for the garage door. He eased the car into the space beside Harriet's and headed inside, kicking off his trainers on his way down the hall. The house was quiet, apart from the constant patter of rain on the roof. He was keen to get out of his wet clothes and into a hot shower.

In the bathroom, as Malek peeled off his soggy shirt and shorts, he thought again about his seething frame of mind. It felt ... dangerous, being this on edge. Being this skittish and fuming. And why now? Why today? When Harriet had been involving Victoria in their marriage for years.

Time after time, Malek tried to work his way back to figure out exactly how they'd shifted from a monogamous marriage to ... this. But it had happened so insidiously that he couldn't pinpoint the moment. There was the barbecue when Victoria had stayed late after the rest of the guests left. They'd all had one too many and gone for a late-night swim. Malek had left Harriet and Victoria alone in the pool while he'd gone up to check on Farrah, make sure she was asleep. She was only a toddler back then. He'd come back to find Harriet and Victoria kissing in the pool. He could still remember the rush of confusing feelings when he saw them together. The sharp dig of jealousy in his gut at seeing his wife kiss someone else combined with an instant hard-on at seeing the girl-on-girl action. And then Harriet had pulled her lips away from Victoria's and made eye contact with him. 'Join us,' she'd said, beckoning him over.

It wasn't that the sting of jealousy completely melted away, rather that it was overpowered by lust. And somehow, it was almost as though the jealousy itself was a part of the turn-on. A kind of masochistic kink. The fact was, this was something they'd talked about before. In bed together, late at night, Harriet had made suggestions about adding a third. Malek had thought it was all talk, a fantasy to get him revved up. But here was the fantasy, playing out in front of him in technicolour. It helped that he did find Victoria attractive. She wasn't the type of woman he could see himself dating, but she *was* objectively hot, kind of a mix between Trinity from *The Matrix* and Lara Croft. Not nearly as stunning as Harriet – but to be fair, Harriet set the bar pretty damned high.

He supposed if Harriet had jumped at the sight of him, pushed Victoria away and pretended it was nothing, it would have felt like more of a betrayal. His jealousy would have exploded. But because she'd seemed happy to see him, it made him feel like there was no betrayal, like it was always meant to be a bit of fun for the three of them. A one-off because of too many wines.

But over the years there had been more and more occasions like that. And then there were others. Mostly women, but eventually, Harriet started bringing men into their marriage as well. He supposed there had been conversations about it, times where he'd tried to establish just how loose the boundaries were. But it was so hard to wind things back once that freedom had been granted. Besides, the same liberties were being offered to him. The problem was, he wasn't sure he wanted them.

Although he was ashamed to admit it, a part of him had always felt like he was out of Harriet's league. *Everyone* noticed her. Everyone commented on her beauty. So it made sense that she would realise she could have more than just him. Ethically non-monogamous – ENM. That's what Harriet called it. To Malek, that simply seemed like a pretentious way to say she wanted to fuck other people.

At least he never felt neglected when it came to sex. When Harriet was home, the two of them had plenty of sex. She'd always been a very sexually charged person. He just wished he knew at what point he'd essentially agreed to share his wife with someone else. Because as much as Harriet presented this 'ENM marriage' as harmless fun that wasn't meant to be a threat to their relationship, the truth was, Harriet's emotional connection with Victoria extended beyond a casual fling.

However, he couldn't complain because he'd never actually come right out and told her he didn't want their marriage to be completely open. And while he wasn't keen to regularly take advantage of their situation himself, he *had*

had his moments. A night out on the drinks with a bunch of old footy mates had turned into something else altogether when a tall blonde in a tight dress had started hitting on him at the bar. His first instinct had been to hold up his left hand and waggle his ring finger at her, but as the night went on and the drinks kept going down, he'd found himself glancing at where she was sitting and thinking, *What if?*

He didn't approach her until the last of his mates had headed off, which was strange, because plenty of times he'd been witness to the guys both flirting and hooking up with other women despite being married. And yet here he was, perfectly entitled to sleep around according to the parameters of his marriage, but he didn't want his mates to see.

The sex had been ... decent. Not mind blowing, not terrible. But the guilt afterwards had been sickening. It didn't matter that he and Harriet were in an open relationship, it still felt like he'd cheated. He'd gone home and told Harriet immediately, fully expecting her to be enraged with him. Instead, as she'd quizzed him on the details, he realised that she wasn't bothered by it at all – it was turning her on. What followed was one of the best nights of sex they'd ever shared together. He'd been relieved, but he was also a little ... disappointed that she hadn't been jealous. Because if she wasn't jealous, then did that mean she didn't care?

He supposed there would be a lot of men who would think it was great, being able to sleep around as much as they wished. But Malek could honestly take it or leave it. Why bother when he had great sex at home with Harriet and he didn't have to do all that awkward small talk with a complete stranger first?

He stepped into the shower, turned his face up to the gushing water and thought back to another time a couple of years back, when Harriet had flirted with a married couple at a real estate agents' awards night. The husband was your typical luxury home salesman: sharp suit, shiny pointed black shoes, facial hair manicured to within an inch of its life. The wife was a curvy brunette with a gorgeous smile. Malek knew what Harriet was angling for. They had a hotel room upstairs for the night and she wanted to invite the couple back for all four of them to have a bit of fun together.

The bloke was definitely keen. He was all over Harry without a hint of shame. But Malek could tell the woman was only going along with the idea of the four of them sleeping together to please her husband. And the thought of her dutifully fucking him just so that her husband could screw Harriet guilt free made him feel sick.

That was the first time he'd really lost his temper with Harry. He remembered grabbing her by the elbow and steering her out of the function room as soon as the other couple had gone to get more drinks.

'What's up, Mal? Ouch, let go of my arm!'

'*What's up?* Are you kidding me? Harry, surely you can see that his wife is *not* into this.'

'No way! She's already said she's happy to come up to our room later.'

'I'm not talking about what she's said. I'm talking about the look on her face. The tone of her voice. *Fark*, you're a salesperson, aren't you meant to pick up on body language? She's only agreeing to this to make her prick of a husband happy, and I am *not* okay with that.'

'Oh, come on,' Harriet had said, a hint of amusement in her voice, as though Malek was overreacting, as though he was clueless and inferior. As though he was *dumb*. And that was when Malek really lost it. That was when that same white-hot rage had started to envelop him, just like it had on the football field with Ollie Cook. That was when he took one menacing step towards his wife, so that she was backed up against the wall and suddenly, the size disparity between the two of them seemed more palpable than it ever had before.

He couldn't say for sure what would have happened next if Harriet hadn't realised what was developing and switched her tone in an instant.

'Baby, you're absolutely right, I wasn't paying enough attention to her.'

She'd apologised and calmed him down. Guided him to the lift and up to their room, where she'd hugged him tight and stroked his face and told him everything that he needed to hear. She'd told him how much she loved him, that all she ever needed was him, that all she ever wanted was him, that he was enough. And slowly, the rage had subsided and eventually, they'd made love, just the two of them, slow and intense and sweet and tender.

His mistake was thinking that it meant things were about to change. That that was the end of the 'ethically non-monogamous' stage of their marriage. Especially the next day, when she cancelled the movies with Victoria. But gradually, things returned to the way they were.

Now, as Malek felt the hot water stream over him, he wondered if he was going to be able to shake this mood by the party tonight. What if he ditched the entire thing? What if he and Farrah took off up the coast for the evening? Left a note on the front door for the caterers and the DJ and the guests and Harriet: *Gone Fishin'.*

What if he and Farrah would actually be better off alone?

CHAPTER SIX

Malek's stomach churned with guilt as he drove through the pouring rain to the bulk supplies party shop in the industrial shopping district. He couldn't believe he'd thought about ditching Harriet's party tonight. He couldn't believe he'd thought about *leaving* Harriet. That wasn't like him. None of it was. He usually had way more patience than this.

At the same time though, the scales kept tipping and he would slide away from guilt and back towards fury. Because maybe if Harriet hadn't put so much pressure on him – to create the perfect party, by adding more and more people to the invite list, by continually pushing the boundaries of their marriage – then maybe he wouldn't be feeling like he was a rubber band pulled so taut that it was ready to snap.

He shouldn't have needed any more crap from the party shop. The decorations had all been ordered weeks ago, same as the macarons – and then they'd had to be returned and re-ordered in new colours. But of all the things Harriet could have wanted, yesterday she'd suddenly requested a piñata. A piñata! Like this was a children's birthday party. Something red to fit in with the new theme. He'd searched the internet late last night and found a large red heart piñata that was available at Twilight Party supplies. Probably intended for Valentine's Day – maybe groups who hated V-day liked to smash the shit out of a giant heart on the fourteenth of February. But it would do for Harriet's red velvet fortieth.

He really didn't think it was wise to mix alcohol with blind-folded adults swinging wildly at a papier-mâché heart with a baseball bat. But as always, Harriet was insistent. Apparently, it was charming for adults to include little retro throwbacks to children's birthday parties.

*

He was at the counter about to pay for the oversized heart piñata when his phone starting ringing. The loud old-school *brrrrring-brrrring* ringtone made him jump as it always did. He didn't turn it down, though, because otherwise he would miss his calls. 'Sorry,' he said to the woman behind the counter as he pulled it out to answer.

'Mr Osman?' said the voice on the phone. 'This is Angela from Apple Hills College.'

The rain outside sounded like thunder on the sheet metal roof of the warehouse shop. Malek pressed his hand against his other ear so he could hear better.

'We have Farrah here in the office and I'm afraid we're going to need you to come in. I've been trying to call Mrs Osman for the last twenty minutes or so, but I've been unable to reach her, so we thought we'd give Dad a go.'

Malek felt a flicker of annoyance that they hadn't called him first. He'd told them before that he should be the main contact but for some reason they just couldn't seem to accept the fact that Dad was the first point of call instead of Mum. He didn't like to think of Farrah sitting there for twenty minutes waiting if she wasn't very well while they wasted time trying to reach Harriet.

'Not a problem,' said Malek. 'Is she feeling sick? I can come and get her.'

'Sorry, Mr Osman, you misunderstand. We're going to need you to come into the office for a chat. Unfortunately, there's been an incident.'

Malek felt a jolt in the pit of his stomach. 'Is she okay?'

'Farrah's fine. A little rattled, but she's okay. The incident is regarding her behaviour.'

Malek couldn't have heard right. In all her years of schooling, Farrah had never had a single issue in terms of behaviour. Meanwhile, the short, stout woman behind the counter was starting to make loud tutting noises as she waited for him to get off the phone and finish up with the sale.

'Ah, right, okay … understood. I'll be there soon.'

Malek hung up and gave the woman an apologetic look. 'School,' he said, waving the phone at her. 'There's always something with kids.'

Her irritated features softened marginally.

*

As he walked away from the car, he thought he recognised the woman heading for the school gate from the other side of the street – Tallulah's mum. Did that mean Tallulah was involved in the same incident? The woman didn't have an umbrella and was speed walking, her head down. Her dark blonde shoulder-length hair was pulled into a low, sleek ponytail at the nape of her neck, and she was wearing a grey knee-length business skirt with a short-sleeve white silk blouse and high heels. If Malek was going to guess what she did for a living, he would have thought she'd just come out of court or something, but hadn't Farrah mentioned something about Tallulah's mum running her own cleaning business?

Malek had a huge bright red and white golf umbrella, so he jogged towards her and gestured for her to join him under the shelter. 'Tallulah's mum, right?' he asked as she hesitated before accepting his offer. As she recognised him, he saw a wary expression cross her face. Then she pasted on a polite smile.

'Yes, Karen. You're Malek.'

It was fact rather than question and he was impressed that she knew his name. They'd barely met. That seemed to be the case as Farrah grew older: she made new friends and it was no longer about playdates organised by parents. Instead, it was connecting through social media and planning their own catch-ups. Since Farrah had only become friends with Tallulah late last year, there hadn't really been an opportunity for him to get to know her parents apart from a friendly wave from the car.

Up close, he noticed that she had striking green eyes and softer features than he'd first thought.

'I'm so sorry,' said Karen as they continued through the gate together, shoulders bumping as they tried to keep their limbs out of the rain.

'What for?'

'For whatever Tallulah's done to get Farrah into trouble.'

Malek turned his bottom lip outward and frowned. He wasn't used to a parent who didn't immediately take the side of their own child. And as much as he wanted Karen to be correct, to believe that Farrah might be blameless in whatever this so-called incident was, it made him uncomfortable to see Tallulah's mum throwing her daughter under the bus before they'd even heard the full story.

He wasn't sure what to say in return, but settled for, 'Let's wait and see what they have to say. I'm sure there's no need for you to apologise.'

'All ready for the party tonight?' Karen asked as they made their way through the school to the office.

'Pretty much,' said Malek. 'Just a few final touches left now.'

'Harriet was impossible to buy for,' Karen continued. 'As soon as she extended the invite to Robert and myself, I asked Tallulah to ask Farrah for me, but of course she kept forgetting. I wondered about a bottle of Frangelico because I noticed she was drinking that when we were out together last month, but then it didn't seem special enough for a fortieth. And then I thought a nice pair of earrings, because who doesn't like jewellery? But I couldn't for the life of me remember if Harriet's ears were pierced. In the end, I settled on a ...'

Malek didn't catch what Karen had settled on. He was too distracted by his frustration that Harriet had added yet another two people to the guest list without mentioning it to him.

Karen appeared to be on a similar wavelength. 'It was quite unusual to be invited to a surprise party by the person who was meant to be on the receiving end of the surprise,' she said. 'And also, fairly ... unexpected.'

They reached the door of the office and Malek closed the umbrella, giving it a shake before pulling open the door and standing back for Karen to go through first. It was only then that he registered the tone of voice she had used when she'd said, 'And also fairly unexpected.' A tone that he recognised.

Harriet had done something.

Of course she had. Harriet always does something.

It wasn't that Harriet constantly intended to cause trouble, but often she just ... did. It was that same forthright personality that made her so confident and successful. She'd even managed to stir up drama with Malek's side of the family at their wedding. Everyone knew that Malek's sister Lina had what they liked to call 'selective' gluten intolerances. It was one of those running family jokes that they chuckled about behind Lina's back, but no one would ever challenge her on it to her face. *No one* picked a fight with Lina. The problem came when it was time for dessert. A waitress had just placed a decadent piece of – clearly gluten-filled – mud cake in front of Lina when Harriet swooped in and picked it straight back up again.

'All good, Lina,' Harriet had said. 'I'll get someone else to eat this slice. I've asked for a fruit salad for you.'

Lina had reached out for the plate. 'No, no, I don't want to cause you any trouble.'

But Harriet held the cake away from her. 'Don't be silly! We don't want you ending up with an upset stomach on account of our wedding.'

'Yes, well, I find at times I can handle gluten in moderation if I'm careful, so …' Lina held out her hands expectantly. She was used to people giving in rather than risking her wrath – it was just the way it was. As the eldest sister in the family and with a spitfire personality, Lina had always been untouchable.

But instead of handing the cake back, Harriet lifted it even further, as though Lina was a small child demanding a treat and Harriet was her mother putting her foot down. 'Absolutely not,' said Harriet. 'You're my sister now too and I'm not letting you risk your health for my wedding. Look, here's your gluten-free fruit salad.'

Lina's face, as the plate of sliced melon was slid in front of her, was thunderous. And it didn't help that Malek's dad, Hassim, had elbowed Lina and said, 'We finally have someone brave enough to call you on your bullshit, uh?' before winking at Harriet and adding, 'I'll take the cake off your hands, love.'

To be fair, they'd all fantasised about standing up to Lina over the years, but at the same time, Malek hadn't thought that was the best way for Harriet to kick things off with her new in-laws. Lina would have it in for her for good now. She wasn't used to losing and she'd already struggled to warm to Harriet. Their personalities clashed.

He was right. Over the years since the wedding, Lina and Harriet had remained civil enough, but there were plenty more times when they butted heads, especially when his mother announced her diagnosis. But that wasn't something Malek really wanted to think about just now.

So, what exactly had Harriet done to make Karen sound so apprehensive? Could she have said something about Tallulah perhaps? Karen had mentioned just now that she'd been out for drinks with Harriet last month. This was news to Malek. He hadn't known anything about Harriet going out socially with Karen. Despite Malek being the lead parent when it came to school drop-off and pick-up and volunteering in the classroom or the canteen when Farrah was younger, Harriet had still managed to set herself up an impressive clique of school-mum friends by getting involved in after-hours school fundraisers and arranging mums' nights out. But she'd never mentioned Karen's name in relation to one of those nights. Which was even more ominous, because did that mean she had purposely avoided telling him?

CHAPTER SEVEN

Malek and Karen sat side by side outside the principal's office. Fluorescent lighting flickered above them, and the muted tones of the walls were broken up by pops of colour from framed student artworks. A bucket sat in the corner catching a slow leak from a sodden ceiling panel. Malek supposed even expensive private schools weren't infallible when it came to weeks of continuous rain.

Waiting patiently like this, Malek felt as though they were naughty school kids about to be reprimanded for kicking a ball through a class window or throwing toilet paper around the bathrooms. Those were the kinds of things Malek used to get in trouble for. Although he highly doubted Karen would have ever got up to those antics.

As if she was listening in on his thoughts, Karen leaned sideways and whispered, 'Reminds you of being sent to the principal when you were a kid, hey?'

Malek shifted in his chair. He was surprised that she sounded so relaxed considering they were just about to find out how much trouble their kids were in.

'Does a bit,' he said. 'Are you worried? About what Chuck's going to say to us? You don't think the kids will be suspended, do you?'

'Sorry ... Chuck?' Karen arched an eyebrow.

'Oh, shit ... I didn't mean to say that. It's just what I started calling her over the years to myself. As in Chuck Norris.'

Karen gave him a look of bemusement, then said, 'Yep, that suits her. And don't stress, I've been called in plenty of times over the years for Tallulah. I've learned to judge how serious it is by the tone of Angela's voice when she calls me. I'd say the girls are in for an afternoon detention at the most.'

Malek nodded, relieved. 'Okay, thanks. Not used to this. Do you think they'll keep us waiting much longer?' He was still on track for tonight, but not if he was held up here for too long. He started to run his hand through his hair, caught himself and stopped. *Leave your hair alone or you'll end up pulling it all out, mate.*

'Depends on Chuck's mood,' Karen said with a wink. 'So, what did you used to get in trouble for when you were a kid? For me, it was drawing on my jeans with biro instead of doing my work.'

'You were allowed to wear jeans to school?'

'No, not really. But there was a group of us who always did it anyway. We pretended it was a protest against sexism cause we didn't want to wear pleated skirts when the boys were allowed shorts. But then the boys started wearing jeans too, so it lost its impact. I mean, *they* didn't have to wear a skirt. But if I'm honest, we weren't really that woke, we just wanted to wear jeans for the fun of it.'

'I wouldn't have pegged you for a troublemaker.'

Karen smiled. 'Looks can be deceiving, Malek.'

They were interrupted then as the office door swung open and they both snapped their mouths shut as though they'd been caught doing something naughty – talking when they were meant to be waiting in silence. Malek felt his shoulders drop and he realised it was because he didn't want to wind up his conversation with Karen just yet. Her personality wasn't what he'd been expecting and he wanted to chat a little more.

They were ushered into the office together and as Karen walked ahead of him, he had a strange sense that her face was familiar for another reason, that maybe he'd once seen or met her somewhere else, outside of the context of school. It was almost like vertigo, as though he was falling back through time into an old memory, but then before he could grasp what it was, he was jolted out of it as his eyes fell on a thick silver scar that ran almost the entire length of her arm.

The feeling of familiarity vanished. Perhaps it was just that she reminded him of someone he'd once known.

Inside the office, Malek turned to see Farrah and Tallulah sitting next to one another. Farrah's hands were twisting in her lap, her gaze fixed on the floor. Next to her, Tallulah looked like she'd been through a tumble dryer: her blouse had a tear along the seam of her shoulder and dirt down the front, and her long plait was loose and lopsided.

Mrs Norris sat behind her desk and motioned for Malek and Karen to sit opposite her. In the middle of the desk was an iPhone with a cracked screen. 'Right,' she said, lacing her fingers together and eyeballing Malek and Karen from over the top of her glasses, 'since we called both of you, things have taken a turn. We contacted you because your daughters have been involved in a bit of a … scuffle and property was damaged. Several students who witnessed the incident told us that Farrah was the instigator and that she pushed Tallulah quite hard, which led to the tussle and Farrah's phone being knocked to the ground and broken.'

Malek opened his mouth to speak but Mrs Norris silenced him with a simple raise of her palm. It was a baller Chuck move. Malek wasn't even sure what he'd been about to say. He was torn between apologising for Farrah's behaviour and defending her, because it seemed so out of character.

'However,' Mrs Norris continued, 'while you were on your way in, Tallulah has given me a different story. She has taken full responsibility for the fight and for the damage to the phone. And despite the state of her uniform, she's adamant that Farrah did absolutely nothing to retaliate.'

'Oh,' said Malek, 'well, the two of them *are* good friends, so it doesn't really make sense that they'd fight. So … maybe this is a misunderstanding?'

'Well, I don't know about that. As admirable as it is that Tallulah has taken responsibility for what happened, she has offered no alternative explanation as to how her uniform was ripped or why several students might spontaneously make up the exact same story about Farrah being the one to instigate the fight.'

'I'm telling the truth!' said Tallulah. 'Those other kids don't even know what they're on about.'

'Thank you, Tallulah,' said Mrs Norris, 'I've heard your version.'

'It's not my *version*,' said Tallulah, pure disdain dripping from her words. '*It's. What. Happened.*'

'Tallulah!' said Karen. 'Watch your tone!'

'She should watch *her* tone,' Tallulah mumbled in response, quiet enough that she could pretend she didn't mean for Mrs Norris to hear it, but clear enough for Malek to catch her words. He suppressed an urge to snort at how brazen she was.

'Here's what I think,' said Mrs Norris, 'thus far, Farrah's remained tight-lipped and has neither refuted nor corroborated Tallulah's story. However, several of the witnesses to the altercation say they heard the girls arguing over something on Farrah's phone. And as Farrah won't tell us her side, I thought perhaps you might like to compel her to talk to us, maybe even check her phone yourself?'

Malek frowned. He didn't like Mrs Norris's malicious tone or the way she was eyeing Farrah smugly, as though she believed she'd trumped her. Malek had always told Farrah that she was allowed to keep her phone private – if there was anything worrying him, he would ask her permission to look at it. Out of the corner of his eye, he saw Farrah's head jerk up in alarm and then she nudged Tallulah with her elbow.

'You don't need to check her phone!' Tallulah blurted out. 'That's a complete invasion of privacy. And anyway, I can explain all of it. I was angry because Farrah wouldn't let me use her phone to make a TikTok. After *I* pushed Farrah, I tripped, and my shirt caught on the handrail. That's how it got ripped. Just *tell them*, Farrah.'

They all turned to look at Farrah, who lifted her head and stared back at them, wide eyed and nervous. She cleared her throat. 'Um, yeah. What Tallulah said is true.' Then her gaze dropped again and she chewed hard at her fingernails.

Malek hesitated. He could tell his daughter was lying, but he really didn't have the time to nut this whole thing out. He was better off chatting to her alone, maybe over the weekend, when everything had died down. Was he a bad parent if he let it go for the time being? Maybe, but he was going to be a bad husband if he didn't get on with the party prep.

'Looks like the girls are back on the same side, so either way, whatever happened between them has been sorted out,' he said, clapping his hands and forcing himself to sound confident. Then his resolve faltered as he saw that Karen was still planted in her chair. 'I mean, as long as you agree everything is okay?' he asked her.

'Oh,' said Karen, and Malek noticed that she was looking totally bewildered by the events that had taken place. 'Um, yes, I guess you're right.'

Mrs Norris sighed. 'I must say, I really don't think we should be leaving it at that. The girls will have to attend detention on Monday afternoon and I strongly suggest you both chat further with your daughters this evening about this.'

*

On the way out of the school, Farrah and Tallulah walked together, heads leaning in, talking quietly to one another underneath Farrah's umbrella as Malek and Karen followed, sharing Malek's umbrella once again.

'Sorry,' said Karen, 'I was a bit useless in there, wasn't I? I was totally flummoxed. T is always getting into trouble but to hear her taking the fall for her friend ... I was just gobsmacked. She usually only looks out for herself. It's been a long time since she's had a friendship that she valued enough to do something like that.'

Malek smiled. He wasn't going to tell Karen, but he'd actually liked seeing her a little disarmed. He'd initially assumed that she was going to be one of those women who would steamroll over the top of you – just something about the way Farrah had described Tallulah's mum as so organised, so capable, so involved in her daughter's school life. Not to mention the sharp business attire. He'd figured she was probably a bit of a ball breaker. But instead, her sweet face had seemed so surprised and unsure in that meeting. It was endearing – the way she openly admitted how disconcerted she'd felt. Harriet never let her guard down like that.

He knew it was sexist of him to think it, but it was nice that for once he got to play the role of the masculine guy who took care of things. He hardly knew this woman, but the way she'd allowed her vulnerabilities to show through brought out an innate desire to protect.

'All good,' said Malek. 'And I hope you didn't mind that it seemed like I was brushing this under the carpet with Chuck. I mean, I know they obviously did get into it with one another, but I figured if they'd sorted it all out, then it was better not to push them right now. I will chat to Farrah about it tomorrow, though; see what I can find out. But honestly, I got into plenty of schoolyard fights as a kid, and we were always mates again once we'd thrown a few punches and had it all out.'

Karen's eyes widened. 'You think they literally punched each other? I thought it was more of a scuffle. Oh God, I'm being completely naïve, aren't I?'

'Oh, right! Sorry ... Look, I'm sure if there were any punches thrown, none of them really landed. I didn't see any bleeding noses or black eyes. I reckon we're all good.'

'Alright, I suppose you might be right. I'm more than happy to pay for Farrah's damaged phone.'

'No way. We both know that Tallulah was doing her friend a solid when she took the blame for starting that fight. All the kids who witnessed it said it was Farrah who pushed first, which I am apologetic about, by the way. That's not like her at all. So it'll be a good lesson for her to fork out the money from her own savings to pay for it. Don't worry, we'll get to the bottom of it.'

'From the way the girls are huddled together under that umbrella, it does seem like they've got past whatever today was.'

They stopped at the school gate. 'Right, guess I'll see you tonight then,' said Malek.

'Can't wait,' Karen replied, but Malek couldn't help noticing that slight edge had returned to her voice. And once again, that desire to protect stirred inside, and he found himself wishing that she really meant it when she said she couldn't wait to see him tonight.

CHAPTER EIGHT

'Right,' said Malek after they'd driven for a few minutes in complete silence, save for the sound of the constant rain on the roof of the car, all while Farrah chewed at her fingernails like she was a chipmunk, 'your mate covered for you today, did she?'

Farrah dropped her hands into her lap. 'Why do you think that?'

'Come on. It was clear that she made up that story to save your butt. Listen, I'm not worried, you never get into any trouble, so I say you have a bit of a free pass. And it looks like you and Tallulah sorted out whatever the issue was, but I'm not too happy to hear about you starting a fight with your good mate – so just tell me, is there anything I need to know? Anything you want to talk about?'

Farrah shook her head as they pulled up at a red light.

'You sure?'

'Mmm hmm,' she said quietly.

Right, that will have to do for now. Malek would still try and bring it up again over the weekend, but at the moment, it was better to leave it at that. The intensity of the rain increased and Malek changed the setting on the windscreen wipers.

'Nice weather for Mum's party,' Farrah said.

'I know, the backyard's going to be a mud pit.'

Malek's phone started ringing through the car stereo and he jabbed at the button on the screen as Lina's name flashed up.

'Hey, before you say anything, you're on the air with your niece as well, okay?'

Lina started laughing. 'You're using Farrah for protection now, are you? You know if I wanted to swear at you, I could just do it in Arabic, and she wouldn't understand a word I'm saying.'

'I'd understand some,' Farrah said. 'I know ayreh feek.'

Lina laughed again as Malek flicked Farrah's arm. 'Oi! Language!' he said.

'You need to take lessons, habibti,' said Lina. 'Your pronunciation isn't too bad, but if you're going to say "fuck you" to someone, you have to sound like you mean it. Anyway Malek, don't stress, I'm not calling to yell. I'm checking if you need any help tonight.'

'Oh. Really? You're okay about ...' He glanced sideways at Farrah and saw her brow furrow with curiosity.

Lina's voice cut in. 'Yes. It's fine. Nadia calmed me down.'

Malek let out a breath of relief. Thank God for their baby sister, she was always having to play the peacemaker in their family.

'Okay, well, I've got things mostly under control for tonight. Main thing you can do for me is run interference with Dad. I know he's still going to try to bring food even though I've told him it's fully catered.'

'Ha, you really think I can stop him?'

'If anyone can, you can.'

'Okay, I'll do my best. See you tonight.'

They hung up and Malek only had to wait two seconds for the inevitable question from Farrah.

'Why would Lina be mad with you?'

Malek considered his response. It was hard to explain. The latest clash with his sister had all started with Harriet trying to do something that looked like a sweet gesture from the outside, but Malek knew it was more complicated than that. And while Harriet often appeared to be doing things for altruistic reasons, he was aware that sometimes there was an ulterior motive involved – even if it was only at a subconscious level.

'It was nothing,' he said. 'Stupid argument between siblings.'

'Yeah, but what was it about?'

'What was your fight with Tallulah about?' Malek shot back.

'Fine. Question retracted,' said Farrah, rolling her eyes.

Malek smiled. 'It's a bit of a miscommunication with that fun run your mum signed up to for Teta's anniversary. I'll tell you about it properly when we go out this weekend.'

When Harriet had sent out the message to the family group chat the other week to announce that she would be participating in the charity fun run later this year to line up with the anniversary of Malek's mother's death, Nadia had phoned him almost right away.

'Mal,' she'd said, 'she's doing it again.'

At first, he'd feigned innocence. 'Who? What?'

'Come on, you know what I'm talking about. Your wife. She's *fundraising* again.'

'Nads, it's not the same, it's just a fun run.'

'You know Lina is going to get defensive. And you know Dad is going to get upset and confused about people being asked to donate money.'

It was ridiculous, but Nadia was right. It all stemmed back to the year Malek had lost his mother. Maryam had told the family about her diagnosis six months after Malek and Harriet's wedding. Cervical cancer. Stage four. No treatment options that would extend life, only ones that would keep her comfortable until she passed. The family fell apart – they'd never been good with tragedy. Nor with being told that there was nothing they could do. It didn't compute. But that was when Harriet had stepped up. She researched clinical trials and campaigned for new drugs to be put on the PBS. She fundraised for the department of the hospital where Maryam was being treated and set up a GoFundMe for the family to help them pay the medical costs that weren't covered by Medicare. She was formidable in her doggedness to do *something* to help and Malek loved her for it.

But it just wasn't the way his family did things. Financial issues were a private matter. Malek's dad was adamant that he didn't want the donations from the GoFundMe page. 'No, no, we take care of our own, tell them there is no need,' he'd said, and Malek couldn't make him understand that the money had already been given.

Meanwhile, Lina and Nadia had started to feel like their own roles as daughters were being usurped by their new sister-in-law. 'Of course we would investigate clinical trials,' they said, 'if that was what Mum actually wanted! Of course we would campaign for a new miracle drug, if the doctors believed there was something out there that would work.'

Lina was especially affronted. As the eldest in the family, she felt it was her job to take charge, her job to fix things. But her way was different. Her way involved steady prayers and bedside vigils. And the more that Harriet worked to try to save Maryam from an impossible situation, the more Lina grew frustrated.

'This isn't right, Malek. Now is the time for us to come together as a family, not go running off after non-existent miracle cures that unfairly give Dad false hopes.'

Malek was stuck between his wife and his sister: a rock and a hard place. He could hardly tell Harriet to knock it off when she was literally trying to save his mother's life. But Lina only saw an outsider who was getting involved in private family matters. She thought that Harriet was pulling the focus away from her mother and making it all about herself. She believed Harriet got involved in fundraising just to look a certain way to the world. And while Malek knew there were occasions when Harriet did think about optics, he also knew that she genuinely wanted to help.

This time around, Harriet had signed up for a fun run to raise money for cervical cancer research. Her fundraising page was filled with photos of Maryam and a spiel about how she was doing this in honour of her much-loved late mother-in-law.

Lina had been blunt when she'd phoned Malek a week ago: 'Tell me something, baby brother. Your wife, does she realise that our mother was not her mother? Does she realise that this anniversary is about our family, and not about her?'

It was harsh, but he had to admit, Harriet did always seem to somehow make herself the centre of attention – even if it wasn't intentional. She really should have known by now that his family didn't like over-the-top gestures like this, that they wanted to keep things within the family. And even though Harriet was doing something admirable to honour his mother, it frustrated him that she didn't stop to think about how his sisters might react. Sometimes he did wonder if a small part of Harriet did these kinds of things on purpose, knowing it would push Lina's buttons.

But maybe that wasn't fair. Harriet did love Maryam.

CHAPTER NINE

Malek stood at the sliding glass door that led out to their elevated back deck and stared at the driving rain. The pool was overflowing. The backyard had puddles dotted throughout and the grass was muddy. Every now and then the wind would blow the rain sideways and even the covered deck would become slick. Despite the humidity, he shivered. So much for the summer party he'd originally imagined for tonight. How the hell was everyone going to fit? Even if he'd arranged a temporary tarpaulin for the backyard, it wouldn't have helped, not with rain this heavy. Maybe he could at least put some sort of plastic covering up on one side of the deck so that people could stand out there with a bit of extra protection from the rain. That would give them more floor space to work with.

It happened without warning. One second, he was staring out at the deck, thinking about party guests gathering out there, thinking about them laughing, sipping drinks, smoking cigarettes, huddling from the rain – the next he was falling. His stomach was plummeting and the breath was knocked out of him. He scrabbled at the glass door with his hands.

And then the feeling was gone just as quickly as it arrived, and he looked down to see that he hadn't fallen at all. He was still standing completely upright on the carpeted floor. But his legs felt like jelly and his palms had left sweaty prints on the glass door.

What an idiot. How could he even consider guests gathering out on the deck? That would be far too dangerous with the number of people coming tonight. He knew how easily a celebration could turn into a tragedy.

It was New Year's Eve seventeen years ago when the accident had happened.

Malek and Harriet had only been dating for a couple of months. They hadn't even had *the* conversation yet – the one where they figured out exactly where they both stood in the relationship. And while Malek didn't know if they were meant to be exclusive, he wasn't risking things by seeing anyone else. Not only was Harriet the most gorgeous woman he had ever laid eyes on – let alone dated – she was also *incredible* in bed and, for now, that was more than enough to keep Malek infatuated.

She'd been keen when he'd told her about the New Year's party at a friend's place. It was a small, outdated town house, but it was in a great location on the north side of the harbour. They would have uninterrupted views of the fireworks over the bridge from the second storey balcony.

Malek arrived first. Harriet was going to meet him there at nine, after dropping by a get-together with some of her own friends. He could still remember the exact way it felt, being at that party. The way everyone seemed so free, relaxed. The way their faces were animated with pure, carefree joy. And the sounds: laughter, chatter, music, the pop of champagne bottles.

In the end, Harriet missed the 9pm fireworks and Malek remembered a friend nudging him and pointing out an attractive blonde woman across the room. 'Oi, you sure your new girlfriend is going to show tonight? 'Cause that chick has been eyeballing you for the past half an hour.'

Malek had glanced over. He had to admit, the woman was definitely checking him out. But to be fair, women were often paying him more attention these days. He was playing reserve grade for the Parramatta Eels, he was in the best shape of his life and the tight-fitting V-neck T-shirt he was wearing was one size too small on purpose – he liked the way it strained around his biceps. The woman was cute and on another occasion, he might have made a move. But tonight, Malek wasn't interested. His mind was filled with thoughts of Harriet.

Another hour passed and a few more friends tried to coax him into going over and chatting to the good-looking woman in the ripped jeans. 'It wouldn't hurt to just talk to her! I think she's a friend of Johno's maybe? Or Simon? Mate, seriously, what if Harriet's already ditched you?'

But Malek was resolute. And he knew why. It was because he was falling for her. He realised it the moment she arrived. He spotted her from the balcony, climbing out of the cab and walking across the street to the townhouse. She was wearing a blue top with a scooped neck and buttons down the front, and black pants that hugged her bum – she really did have a great arse. Her long dark hair was clipped back on one side and fell over her other shoulder. He felt an unexpected flip in his gut that made him squeeze the balcony railing a little tighter. And while he knew a part of that reaction was straight-out lust, he also knew there was something more. *I think it might be time we had that conversation.*

When she came inside, she threw her arms around his neck and peppered his face with kisses. 'I'm *so* sorry I'm late. The girls were making me feel bad about ditching them on New Year's Eve for some random guy. I told them there is *no way* this is just some random guy. But it still took forever to get out of there.'

Malek didn't mind, he was just relieved she'd made it. And there was still plenty of time to see the midnight show. Plenty of time to make sure they were together for a traditional New Year's Eve kiss.

Ten minutes later, they were out on the balcony with everyone else when Harriet started whispering things in his ear. *Hot* things. Fuck, that woman knew how to get him going. When she suggested that they sneak out of the party so that she could have him all to herself, he hadn't hesitated to ditch his mates for her.

They took a taxi back to his place and all thoughts of missing out on the party or the fireworks quickly left his mind when they walked through the front door and she unbuttoned her top to reveal a black lacy bra before pulling him into the bedroom.

He wasn't sure how soon after their taxi disappeared up the street the accident had happened, but Malek didn't hear about it until two hours later, when the text message came through. Bad news always travels fast, but this was back in the day when messages were often delayed on New Year's Eve.

Today, that text message from his mate Simon was long gone, but Malek could still recite it word for word. He could still remember the plunging feeling he'd experienced in his gut when he read it. The way his skin turned cold and the wave of nausea that overcame him.

The balcony collapsed. Too many of us out there. We don't know yet how many didn't make it. Come back if you can, we need all the help we can get.

Malek wanted it to be a stupid prank, but somehow, he knew instantly that it wasn't. And that one line that played over and over in his mind: *We don't know yet how many didn't make it.*

Harriet was fast asleep next to him as he sat up in bed, his hand clutching the phone, his body frozen. Usually, he wouldn't have even heard the message, he would have been passed out in post-coital bliss. But too many drinks, not enough water and the summer heat had meant he'd been unable to get comfortable. He'd been lying there thinking he should get up for a glass of water when he'd heard the ding of the message come through.

After several more seconds of sitting there, taking in the shocking news, he realised he needed to do something, he needed to move. His friends were asking for help, and he should be there for them. He was about to reach across and wake Harriet, to let her know what was going on, when it hit him. If Harriet hadn't suggested they leave the party so they could be alone, they would have been out on the balcony themselves when it collapsed. Was this divine intervention? Had Harriet just saved his life?

That was the first time he'd felt the strange tingle on the bottom of his feet. The whoosh of vertigo.

When the sensation had passed, he'd woken Harriet gently, explained that there'd been an accident and that he had to go. He didn't give her all the details, only promised he'd tell her everything later.

There wasn't much he could do to help. Simon probably knew that when he messaged, knew that they would have to leave it to the professionals. But maybe he just wanted a familiar face among all the paramedics, police and firefighters. When Malek arrived back at the townhouse in the middle of the night, Simon had grabbed him and hugged him in a way they'd never hugged before. 'I went back into the kitchen to grab another drink,' he said, 'next thing I heard this noise, this cracking sound and then screaming. All hell broke loose. I think … I think at first some people were even laughing … like they didn't think it was serious, didn't realise how bad it was going to be. But it only took seconds for the whole thing to collapse. I've never seen anything like it. The wreckage and the dust in the air and the bod— the, the people.'

'So, what do we do? How do we help?' Malek had asked.

'Nothing,' said Simon. 'I'm sorry, when I sent you that message, the fireys hadn't got here yet and I thought we needed more help to search for people, but … about ten minutes ago they accounted for the last person.' He'd paused, looked down at his feet. 'Malek, five people died. I just … I just can't believe it.'

Malek and Simon had sat out on the kerb together until sunrise. There were moments when they sat in silence, there were countless minutes when they cried, and there were awkward chats where they tried to talk about something, anything, else. But mostly, Simon wanted to recount the story of the balcony collapsing, over and over again, as though he needed to talk it through in order to believe it had really happened.

'I guess we're the lucky ones,' he had said eventually, as they'd watched the sky turn pale yellow with the first rays of the sun over the horizon. 'Me, because I wanted another fucking beer. You, because your new girlfriend talked you into flaking.'

But neither of them felt especially lucky. A heavy blanket of guilt settled around Malek's shoulders. *But why not me? What did I do to deserve to be saved?* Once again he felt the sharp tingle through the bottom of his feet and it was as though the bitumen of the road was falling away from him. He swayed to the side and almost vomited.

Simon grabbed his arm to steady him. 'You're wrecked, mate,' he said. 'Same as me.'

And that had only added to the guilt. Because why should he be wrecked when he hadn't even been here as it happened? When he hadn't had to hear those horrific screams like Simon had? When he hadn't had to look down at the rubble and see the tangle of bodies in the debris?

In fact, Simon was a hero. He'd raced into the chaos and started pulling people free, while neighbours and other party-goers spilled out of homes and called triple zero and rushed over to help. Some people escaped with only minor cuts and bruises and concussions. Others had more serious injuries – skull fractures and broken bones and punctured lungs. At least two people had been rushed away in ambulances in a critical condition. There was every chance the death toll might grow.

And while all of this had been happening, Malek had been having sex with his new girlfriend.

Looking back, he supposed it could have gone one of two ways. He could have resented Harriet for taking him away from his friends at the one time they needed him the most. What if he'd somehow noticed something? Heard something? Realised what was about to happen and shouted for people to get off the balcony in time? He knew that scenario was unlikely, to say the least, but he couldn't get over the feeling that he had no right to escape this tragedy while so many of his friends suffered. But it didn't go that way. It went the second way. Instead of resenting Harriet for convincing him to leave, he felt indebted to her. He felt grateful for this second chance. And he felt like somehow fate or destiny had intervened. He took it as a sign that Harriet was meant to be in his life, and he promised himself he wasn't going to screw this up.

Over the next couple of years, he grew further and further apart from Simon and his old circle of friends until, eventually, he'd shut them out completely. He hadn't meant to do it, it wasn't a conscious, deliberate decision. It was more that every time he saw Irina using her walking stick because her left knee was never going to be the same or Jason wincing with pain whenever he lifted his arm higher than his shoulder, he'd feel that same stab of guilt: *It should have been me.* He knew that he was supposed to want to talk about the friends they'd lost. In the end it was six; one more succumbed to their injuries in hospital on the second of January. But he couldn't do it. Talking about them hurt too much, which was selfish, he knew that, incredibly selfish. They deserved to be remembered, but he was weak. And ultimately, the easiest way to shut it all out was to shut out his old friends and move on altogether.

The first time he skipped the annual memorial for their six lost friends, Simon had sent him a simple four-word message: *We missed you, mate.*

Malek never wrote back.

CHAPTER TEN

Malek stepped back from the glass door and wondered if he should make a sign: DECK OFF LIMITS. But what would people think? Those that knew about his history would assume he was being paranoid, overreacting. Maybe he could just keep an eye on it tonight. If he saw too many people out there, he could shepherd them back inside.

A therapist had once told him that the key to dealing with his panic attacks lay in reconnecting with his old circle of friends. Facing them. Seeing their injuries and realising that wasn't what defined them. Talking with them about the people they all still desperately missed. Accepting that, somehow, he'd been lucky that night, but that it wasn't his fault and that it wasn't divine intervention. It wasn't about who did or didn't 'deserve' it. No one deserved to be caught up in a tragedy of that magnitude. And no one blamed him for not being there. But Malek had been adamant that reuniting with the old group was impossible.

Even if I wanted to see them, they wouldn't want to see me. Not when I abandoned them.

He'd stopped seeing that therapist. There was no point when he was never going to take her advice on board.

Harriet didn't start telling the story of the balcony until many, many years later. When that horrific accident had first happened, Malek could never have imagined that one day they'd be meeting new friends at dinner parties and she'd be gossiping about the fact that she had once saved his life. As though his old mates were nothing more than extras in their own personal Hollywood romcom.

No, that wasn't fair, Harriet didn't see it that way. And besides, she'd stopped sharing the story when she realised it was affecting him.

*

'Right, can you get on to filling the balloons with the helium? And I'll start moving some furniture out of the way.'

'How about I just sit on Snapchat while you do all that stuff?'

'Farrah!'

'Kidding, kidding. I'll start on the balloons. Tallulah's coming round soon so she can help with the furniture if it can wait.'

'Yeah, good call ... you two won't start punching on again though, will you?' Malek winked and Farrah huffed.

'I told you! It was nothing, everything is fine. Hey, did you sort out those cockroaches that Mum mentioned?'

'Shit. I completely forgot about that. I'll go deal with them.'

Harriet had been on at him about getting rid of the cockroaches in the granny flat under the house before the party. He was pretty sure he'd only seen one, but Harriet had been adamant: where there's one, there's more. She'd been renovating it recently to turn it into a self-contained unit with a bed, couch, ensuite and tiny kitchenette. If Malek had it his way, he would have preferred to turn the space into a mancave. It could be the perfect place to play a game of darts, drink a beer. He'd quite like to open it up a bit more as well. Maybe add a large sliding glass door so you could sit on a couch in there and look out at the swimming pool.

The problem was, Harriet had some secret special reason for wanting to set it up as a small apartment. He'd tried a few times to convince her to tell him what the secret was – did she want to rent it out for some extra money? Had their finances taken a hit that he wasn't aware of? But she wouldn't say.

Downstairs in the granny flat, Malek assessed the updates Harriet had made. He supposed working as a real estate agent meant she had a good grasp of simple ways to upgrade the room for minimal costs. She'd picked up plenty of presentation tips from stylists she'd worked with over the years. White venetian blinds that almost looked as good at wooden shutters but for half the price. Simple but modern light fittings. Malek dubiously eyed her 'feature piece' in the centre of the room. It was a sculpture that she'd created herself using driftwood collected from the beach, then tied to hooks in the ceiling via fishing wire. In his opinion, it was far too overbearing for the small space, but Harriet wouldn't be told.

The result of all of this was that the room had strong beachy vibes, which made no sense for a house in Western Sydney. But he supposed the fresh, bright colours did enhance the appearance.

He placed insect bombs around the room, set them off and left them to do their job.

*

Back upstairs, Malek set about helping Farrah with the balloons, but the two soon found themselves laughing as they took it in turns sucking in the helium and quoting chunks of dialogue from *Family Guy* in high-pitched voices. If they kept mucking about like this, then he might not have the place looking as perfect as he'd planned for the party. But he was having too much fun to care. He loved that even though his daughter was a teenager now – and *everyone* had told him she would change, she would be embarrassed by him, she wouldn't want to hang around with him – so far it felt like things were still exactly the same.

Sure, she had an attitude once in a while, and admittedly it freaked him out to see bras in the washing and sanitary pads in the bathroom that didn't belong to Harriet, but apart from that, he felt like their relationship hadn't really changed that much. They still joked around with each other. She wanted them to go shopping *together* when they reached their goal of no late notes at the end of the term, not for him to hand over his credit card and leave her to it. He knew people had been exaggerating when they said everything would be different from the moment she turned thirteen. She was almost fifteen now and he still hadn't seen the supposed change from happy, carefree ten-year-old to moody, door-slamming teen.

As if on cue, Farrah twisted the end of one of the balloons between her fingers and said in a tell-tale voice, 'Um, Daaaad?'

'What is it?' he asked, knowing that she was either about to confess to something or ask for something.

'So tonight … there'll be a lot of alcohol, right? And I know that some of my friends' parents have already let them —'

'No way. I'm not letting you drink. I don't care what other parents have done.'

'You didn't let me finish. I'm talking literally, like, one glass of wine. I'm about to turn fifteen. Heaps of people I know are allowed to have just one and —'

'Dammit,' said Malek, cutting her off again.

Farrah looked up in surprise. 'Fine, forget about it, then.'

'No, no, that wasn't at you. Sorry, I just realised that I meant to duck back out and pick up some extra cases of beer for tonight.'

'Seriously? Don't you already have heaps?'

'Yes, I do. And I thought it was plenty, but today I started to worry that your mum might have added even more extras to the guest list than I first thought.'

Farrah rolled her eyes. 'Oh, yeah, for sure, there are even kids at school that I've never met before who were walking past me today saying their parents will be at the party tonight. I was like, okay, whatever.'

Malek felt that same swell of frustration build in his gut. For crying out loud, had Harry invited the entire bloody suburb?

He saw Farrah watching him and quickly adjusted the expression on his face. He shouldn't let her see how much Harriet was getting to him. That wasn't fair to Farrah.

'Looks like it's going to be a full house tonight,' he said, forcing himself to sound undaunted. 'And sorry, kid, but my answer is still no. I'll reconsider maybe one glass when you're sixteen. But not yet, okay?'

'*Fine.*'

Farrah turned away and Malek hesitated for a moment, staring at the back of her head. Her voice had been sulkier than usual, or maybe even a bit … defiant? Determined? Was she planning on disobeying him tonight and sneaking a drink anyway?

Or … wait. He knew what he recognised in her tone of voice.

She had sounded just like her mother.

*

Fen

Caddie's Park

Fen knew she should keep her eyes on the road, especially in all this rain, but she couldn't help noticing the couple standing out in the rain and having one hell of an argument at the entrance to the small park. The woman was holding a parcel of bright yellow flowers and Fen wondered if the flowers were meant to be a peace offering from the man – if so, it had very much failed.

She eased off the accelerator so she could slow down and get a better view. As she watched, the man turned sideways and she realised that she recognised him. He was a dad from the school. Who was with him? His wife?

But no, because now as she looked again, she recognised the woman as well. They weren't a couple at all. What on earth could the two of them be arguing so passionately about?

She turned her attention back to the road and realised she was holding up traffic. She pushed down on the accelerator.

Forget about it. Whatever it was, it was nothing to do with her. Although it was going to make for an interesting little titbit of gossip at the party tonight.

CHAPTER ELEVEN

Malek speed-walked as he pushed the trolley around the aisles of the bottle shop, rushing to grab extra bottles of wine and champagne. How many more cases of beer did he need? Two? Three? The caterers had advised him on the recommended amount of alcohol based on the original guest list, but how much more should he add when he really had no idea just how big the guest list had grown?

He went back down the same aisle, mentally trying to calculate the numbers. All the mothers that Colleen had overheard in the café. The parents that Farrah had mentioned hearing about today. Brad flying in from interstate and the group from Harriet's spin class and Karen plus her husband. How many had they started with?

He stopped when he got to the end yet again and realised his chest was feeling constricted. His hands gripped the trolley and his knuckles turned white. For a second, he wanted to swing around and smash the trolley into the display of red wine at the end of the aisle.

God, there it was again. That swell of rage and aggression. That desire to hit something, to break something, to see the glass exploding and the liquid bursting out, creating a red river of wine that would spread across the floor.

Why was he *so* angry today?

There was a guy he used to play footy with who was caught out for taking steroids. As much as they were encouraged to use their aggression in the game, this guy was something else altogether. It was the exploding temper that gave him away. The way he could go from zero to a hundred at the drop of a hat. Malek remembered him describing what it had felt like being on them: *Mate, you don't understand how much rage there was, and it was always there, just under the surface, waiting to explode. It felt like I was constantly ready to snap.*

Well, Malek sure as hell hadn't been taking any steroids, but that was exactly the way he'd been feeling today. He needed to find a way to shake it off, otherwise he might end up doing something he was going to regret.

Harriet. It all came back to Harriet. He needed to remember why he loved her. Why he was doing all this running around, trying to make this party perfect. Why she truly *did* deserve to have the best night.

A memory flashed unbidden through his mind. Him on his hands and knees on a bathroom floor, Harriet rubbing his back, making soothing, hushing sounds, rhythmically, over and over again.

Shhhhh.

Shhhhh.

Shhhhh.

And her hand circling, around and around, perfectly in time with the sounds.

Outside the bathroom door, the muffled noise of the New Year's party continued. High-pitched laugher, low rumbling music, glass breaking as someone dropped their wine.

'I'm sorry,' he said, 'I'm sorry, I'm sorry. You should go back out. I'm ruining your night.'

'Shhhhh. I'm not going anywhere.'

Then a rapping as someone banged on the bathroom door. 'Oi, you almost done in there? I need the loo!'

Harriet's swift response. 'Fuck off. You can go and piss in the backyard for all I care.'

The panic attack had hit out of nowhere. He'd been having a good night. It was fancy dress and they'd arranged a sitter for Farrah and gone to the party as Bonnie and Clyde. Maybe it was because he'd had a few too many drinks, or maybe it was because the sounds of the party were just too familiar, too similar to the night of the balcony collapse. Whatever it was, one minute he was pouring himself another drink, the next, his chest had tightened and his breathing had constricted and he'd started swaying on the spot. Harriet had grabbed him by the arm and led him straight to the bathroom, closing the door and shutting out the sounds.

'Hey, hey, you're okay,' she'd said. 'Just breathe, you're okay. I've got you.'

He was so grateful to her for the way she'd cared for him that night. Too many people only ever saw Harriet as this aloof person who took care of herself. But the truth was, if you were one of Harriet's people, she was powerfully protective of you.

He loved that about her.

*

'Hey, bud, you all good? You need a hand with something?'

Malek's head snapped up and he realised he was blocking the middle of the aisle with his trolley. He had no idea how long he'd been standing there, frozen in place as he relived that New Year's Eve party. The young staff member was watching him with a mixture of concern and apprehension. Malek guessed he was probably trying to assess whether he was going to cause trouble.

Forcing himself to smile, Malek rolled the trolley to the side and apologised. 'Don't know where I drifted off to there,' he said. 'In another world, apparently.'

The staff member appeared relieved. 'All good. Something I can help you with?'

'Yeah, that'd be great actually. I can't seem to find the Pepperjack shiraz.'

The young guy gave Malek a funny look and coughed uncomfortably. 'Right there, my man. Directly in front of you.'

*

Farrah and Tallulah held one end of the couch while he held the other.

'Nope,' he grunted, 'left ... left – I mean *my* left!'

Farrah had put on her own mix of pre-party music while they moved the furniture around and the pounding of the heavy bass was making it difficult for them to communicate. He indicated the correct direction with a jerk of his head and Farrah called out, 'Oh, *left*!' and they all shuffled sideways.

As they struggled with the oversized couch, he noticed Tallulah whispering something to Farrah. He was about to suggest they save the chat for later when he felt the couch tipping in his arms. 'Hold it, hold it …' he wheezed, straining to keep it under control, but too late – the furniture crashed to the floor, all three of them springing back as it landed so as not to catch their feet underneath it.

'Shit,' said Malek. 'I feel like that was bad … did we dent the floor?'

Farrah glanced back at him guiltily. 'Sorry, Dad, I got distracted.'

He saw her shoot a look of irritation at Tallulah and decided not to ask. Evidently, whatever had gone on between them at school today wasn't quite as done and dusted as he'd first thought.

'Nah, it's all good. I was only kidding. I'm sure the floor is fine. But I'm not picking that bloody thing up again. I say we try to slide it and if it scratches the tiles, that's too bad.'

'Maybe we could put some sheets down under it or something, Mr Osman,' said Tallulah sweetly, 'to protect the floor.'

She beamed at him and Malek felt a strange prickling sensation on the back of his neck. Tallulah hadn't spent a lot of time at their house, so Malek still didn't feel like her knew her that well. There was something too sickly sweet and fake about the way she spoke to him. Like she knew that's how you were meant to talk to adults in order to win them over, but the moment the parents were out of earshot, she was more likely to be calling him a wanker and lighting up a cigarette. Or actually, not a cigarette. Kids didn't smoke these days, they vaped – weird-flavoured shit like cherry or blueberry. He didn't get the appeal. Was it wrong that secretly he would prefer to catch Farrah with a pack of Horizons than a vaping pipe?

He wondered what it was that Tallulah had whispered to Farrah just before they dropped the couch.

Maybe he was being paranoid because of the girls' fight today. Maybe there was nothing more to it than Tallulah just being polite because that was what she'd been taught.

*

'These macarons are gorgeous, Mr Osman! Wow!'

Farrah, Tallulah and Malek were all standing around the island bench, admiring the beautifully presented tray of macarons that Colleen had just placed in front of them. Each of the two hundred silver biscuits had been hand-painted with intricate designs in deep red and were arranged among red rose petals. Caterers bustled past, carrying wrapped trays of food.

'Colleen totally rescued me on this one.'

'It was no trouble,' said Colleen. Then she paused and said, 'Well, no, that's bullshit. It was lots of trouble, but I enjoyed it. Haven't been able to flex my creative muscles like this for a while. And I'm going to enjoy the handful of cash you're giving me for it even more.'

'Message received. Grabbing my wallet,' said Malek.

Colleen glanced through to the living room. 'Place looks amazing. You do all this yourself?'

'Mostly, with some help from the girls,' said Malek, nodding at Farrah and Tallulah.

'You've nailed the red velvet theme. Love the fairy lights woven around the red drapes.'

'Do you need us anymore, Dad?' Farrah asked. 'Can we go up to my room and get changed for tonight?'

'Go for it, kid, I'm all good.'

The girls disappeared upstairs and Malek followed Colleen as she headed through to the living room and continued examining all his hard work.

'Reckon you could have a career in party planning,' said Colleen. 'Anything you can't do?'

'Plenty,' said Malek. 'And that would be my worst nightmare.'

'Well, I guess I'd better get out of your way.'

The doorbell rang.

'Hang on, I haven't given you your money yet. Just give me one sec,' said Malek, hurrying away to see who it was. All the caterers were already here, and it was too early for any guests.

He opened the door to see Harriet's cousin, Brad, standing under an umbrella and holding a huge suitcase on wheels. He'd forgotten all about him flying in.

'G'day, mate,' said Brad, letting go of his case so he could shake Malek's hand. 'Long time, no see.' Brad was his typical laid-back self in khaki shorts, a Mambo T-shirt and a pair of thongs. His sandy blond hair was somehow always perfectly dishevelled, as though he'd just walked in off the beach.

'Good to see you, come on in out of the rain.'

Brad closed his umbrella, shook it off and left it leaning by the door while Malek stood back to give him some room.

He raised his eyebrows as Brad struggled to pull the suitcase across the threshold. 'Ah, you planning on staying long?'

'Ha, no, no. You know what Harry's like: impossible to buy for,' Brad said, kicking off his wet thongs and wiping his feet on the old towel Malek had placed inside the door. 'Remembered she once mentioned an artist that she loved, so I tracked down one of his paintings and got it framed. Had to use this case just to fit it in.'

'Jeez, that's generous. None of my cousins would ever buy me a gift as expensive as that.'

Brad shrugged. 'Yeah, but you know how it is. I mean, we're not *cousin* cousins.'

Malek made a face as they headed down the hall to the staircase. 'What? What are *cousin* cousins? What other kinds of cousins are there?'

'No, I just mean … you know, we call each other cousins cause our families grew up together, but we're not actually related.' Brad stopped at the foot of the stairs and looked back at Malek with a grin. 'Otherwise, that would make what we did in Year Ten pretty weird.'

Malek stared back at him. 'Brad, I seriously have no idea what you're talking about. Harry's always told me that you're Iris's son. Her aunt on her dad's side.'

Brad's face scrunched up in confusion and he said slowly, 'Yeah, my mum's name is Iris, but not the Iris you're talking about!'

Malek suddenly registered what Brad had said about Year Ten. 'Hang on, what do you mean what you two did when you were younger ... you guys never actually ...'

'Yeah, obviously! I mean, we were each other's firsts. You knew that!' Brad gave a half-hearted laugh, but it was clear he was starting to realise this conversation wasn't going quite the way he'd expected.

'No. I most definitely did not know that.'

'Balls,' said Brad, letting go of his bag and scratching distractedly at his arm. 'Sorry, bud. I genuinely thought you knew. I mean, I always thought you were hella easy-going with the two of us being so close, considering our history, but I figured that's just 'cause of the ... ah, the flexible nature of your relationship.'

'Right,' said Malek, rubbing his hand on the back of his neck. 'Well, this is all news to me. I can't believe Harry lied to me about you being her cousin.'

'No, no, I'm sure it's not like that,' Brad said, waving his hands in front of him. 'This sounds more like a misunderstanding.'

Malek was about to tell Brad that this was clearly more than just a misunderstanding when Colleen appeared next to them.

'You know what?' said Brad, relief evident on his face now that Colleen had saved him from their conversation. 'I'm going to get out of your way. I'm sure you're busy trying to get on with everything. Spare room upstairs on the left, yeah?' He turned away quickly, dragging his huge case up the stairs with one thump after another.

'Look, I didn't mean to eavesdrop —'

'Bullshit,' said Malek. 'Of course you did, it's your favourite thing to do.'

Colleen grinned at him. 'Point taken.' Then her face softened. 'Are you okay? That conversation sounded kind of … well, shit.'

Malek couldn't help snorting. Trust Colleen to be so blunt. 'Yeah,' he said. 'It was a bit.'

'You want to have a quick chat before I get out of your way? I can make you a coffee?'

'You don't have to make me a coffee in my own house! I should be offering you one. Actually, you want a proper drink? I could use a pre-party beer right about now.'

'Sure, why not?'

Malek grabbed two beers from the kitchen and they sat in the living room away from the bustling caterers.

'So, that was Harriet's "cousin", was it?' Collen said, using her fingers to make air quotes.

Malek gave another small laugh. 'You heard the whole thing?'

'Yep. For what it's worth, I do know a lot of people who grow up with close family friends and call them cousins or aunts and uncles. It *is* possible that this was a genuine misunderstanding. Especially if his mum happened to have the same name as Harriet's aunt.'

'Yeah, I know. That one just really blindsided me. I could have sworn Harriet told me her boyfriend in university was her first.'

'Maybe she regretted sleeping with a close friend, so she tried to forget about it. Or maybe he was particularly forgettable in bed,' Colleen said, with a sly grin.

'Maybe.'

'I have to ask, what did he mean about your "flexible" relationship?'

Malek fiddled with the bottle in his hands. 'Oh, right. I guess we're sort of in an open marriage. It's not really a secret or anything, I just find I don't tell many people about it, whereas Harriet's happy to share our personal matters with the world. Although I draw the line with my family. I know they wouldn't understand – and thankfully she knows to tone it down in front of them.'

'Okay, but what do you mean by "sort of" in an open marriage? Surely either you are or you aren't.'

'Fair point. Okay, we are, it's just that it's a bit one-sided, that's all.'

'This is seriously blowing my mind. I never would have pegged you as the type.'

Malek laughed dryly. 'Neither would I, to be honest.' He took a swig of his drink and realised that Colleen was staring at him, a funny look on her face.

'What?' he asked.

'I'm just processing what this means.'

Her eyes sparkled and Malek blinked back at her. Was she being ... suggestive? But then, he'd already made this mistake once today with Sammy and completely humiliated himself. On the other hand, his relationship with Colleen was vastly different from his relationship with Sammy, and they'd definitely had their flirtatious moments in the past.

Screw it. He was sick of Harriet getting to have all the fun. Why not push things a bit further with Colleen?

'Hey, listen, why don't you stay for the party?'

He could see her considering the offer.

'What's the crowd going to be like? Apart from the lululemon group?'

'It'll be a bit of a mixed bunch. Lots of parents from the school like you said, but also Harriet's workmates, some old friends, some family. My sisters are coming, you've met them before – they've been in your café for lunch with me a few times.'

'Oh, yeah. Macchiato and piccolo right?'

Malek chuckled. He liked the way she remembered people by their coffees. 'That's them – although they usually go by Lina and Nadia. Nadia was the one who pestered you for your baklava recipe.'

'You know, she was very persistent. I almost gave in to her. But I can't go giving away family secrets to anyone.' Colleen tapped her finger on the top of her bottle. 'Hmm, I liked your sisters, they were easy to chat to. Maybe I will stay?' She glanced down at herself and patted one hand on her black jeans. 'Or maybe I won't. I'm not really dressed for it.'

'Are you kidding me?' Malek ran his gaze over Collen. She had changed into a different top from the one she'd been wearing in the shop that morning. It was a sleeveless white linen blouse with buttons down the front. 'That shirt is perfect. And people won't be that dressed up anyway. Actually, I wanted to say earlier … your arms are amazing … have you been —?'

'Have I been working out?' she asked, grinning. 'Hell of a cliché, Malek.'

'I knew that was going to sound stupid, sorry.'

'No, not at all. I appreciate it. Who wants to do a bunch of triceps dips and not at least get a compliment out of it?'

'Good. Because you really do look great. Here's the only thing though – the dress code includes a splash of red because of the theme. Wait here one second.'

He hurried out of the room and returned a few minutes later holding a red scarf with white polka dots. 'Farrah said you can wear this if you like. What do you think?'

Colleen swallowed the last mouthful of her beer and put the bottle on the table. 'Alright,' she said, standing up and taking the scarf out of his hands. 'Let's give it a go.' She stood in front of the mirror that was hanging above the sideboard, then pulled her hair out of the tight bun she always wore. She ran her fingers through her hair a few times, then said to Malek, 'Do me a favour, hold this up for me.'

He stood behind her and gathered up her hair, while Colleen expertly wound the scarf around her head and then tied it at the nape of her neck. Malek let her hair fall back down.

'How is that?' she asked.

'Stunning.'

*

Malek leaned against the doorframe with his arms folded and watched Brad as he unzipped his suitcase on the spare bed. He'd left Colleen downstairs chatting with the caterers while she had another beer.

Brad glanced up at him and then jumped back. 'Bloody hell, mate, you scared me. I didn't hear you come in.'

'Sorry,' said Malek, not moving.

'Jeez, sometimes I forget what a big unit you are. I still reckon you should have been a bouncer after the footy career didn't pan out.'

Malek was pleased. He hadn't meant to be intentionally intimidating, standing there in the doorway, but then again, it didn't hurt for Brad to be reminded of his size and strength. He still couldn't get his head around the fact that not only had Harriet and Brad slept together, they'd actually been each other's *firsts*. And Harriet had kept it from him. Was this that gaslighting thing again that Farrah had told him about? Or not quite the same? He still didn't entirely understand it.

Brad nodded in the direction of Farrah's bedroom. 'What does she think of Harry's plans?'

Malek's eyes narrowed. 'What plans?'

'You know, her big announcement tonight.'

'She told you about that?'

'Yeah, big step, hey? Having Victoria move in downstairs. I know you're super chill, I mean, you'd have to be to have an open marriage … but was Farrah okay with it? I guess younger kids these days are used to all sorts of …'

Reeling from what Brad had just said, Malek stopped listening. Surely that couldn't be right.

'Wait,' he said, going into the room and closing the door behind him. 'Are you saying that's what her announcement is all about? That's why she's been doing up the granny flat? She wants Victoria to *live* with us?'

Colour slowly drained from Brad's face. 'No,' he said. 'Don't tell me I've put my foot in it again. She told me it was a surprise, but I didn't think she meant she was surprising *you*. I assumed you knew.'

'No, Brad. I didn't know. I didn't know that the two of you are not actual cousins and I didn't know that my wife was planning on moving her girlfriend into our house and I didn't know that she was going to announce it in front of everyone tonight, including my bloody dad and my sisters, when she *knows* that I prefer my family not know about that side of our marriage. This is beyond a fucking joke.'

Malek hadn't even realised that he'd been slowly advancing on Brad as he was talking, not until he saw that Brad was backing away from him, holding his hands up, shrinking in size.

'Okay, take a breath. Maybe I've got my wires crossed or something.'

Malek wasn't sure how much more he could take. Time after time, he kept trying to give Harriet the benefit of the doubt, but she just kept *pushing* him. That feeling of teetering on the edge was back, and right now, all he wanted to do was punch something. His body was wound so tightly he felt like he might explode.

Brad's annoyingly pitying face seemed like a bloody good target right about now, so he spun around, looking for something, anything, else that he could hit or smash or break.

Farrrrk.

He took two quick strides and slammed his fist into the bedroom door. His hand went straight through the fibreboard, leaving his arm stuck in a jagged, gaping hole as splinters of wood fell to the carpet.

He heard footsteps and then Farrah's voice in the hallway outside.

'Uh, Dad, why is your arm sticking out of that door?'

Harriet

Did you push him too far?

You're not a cheat, let's make that clear. Cheating would indicate lies and secrets. Deception. That's not what it was like with Vic. Or with any of the others. You and Malek have an agreement. An ethically non-monogamous marriage where he knows exactly what's going on. Besides, he has the option to explore too.

But what if he changed his mind? You're not naïve. You know Malek didn't want this open marriage as much as you. Yes, you were the driving force ... but he did agree to it. And you did believe he was happy.

Unless ... Could you have gotten that wrong?

Stay on task. Think about this logically. A sudden blow to the back of the head like that is violent. It's vicious. It's ... passionate. It's a moment of pure rage and complete hatred. Think about the force of it, the way it knocked the breath out of you, made your teeth rattle in your mouth, the sensation of falling, the floor rushing up to meet you, and then ... nothing, darkness.

Can you picture Malek with a weapon in his hands? A crow bar. A baseball bat. Some sort of wrench or spanner or a great big length of pipe. You can't – he's your husband. But isn't that what most people say when someone snaps? They say they never saw it coming. They say he was a normal man, a loving husband and father … until he wasn't.

You've seen the photos on the news. Photos of ordinary smiling families. Which photo would they choose for your family? The shot of the three of you standing in front of the Big Banana when you visited Coffs Harbour last summer? Malek's arm around your shoulders. Farrah's head dipping, her cheeks pink with teenage embarrassment. Would people study that photo? Search for signs that Malek was a monster? Clues to reassure themselves that their own spouse was different? Would someone leak to the press that footage of him beating the shit out of Ollie Cook in that game all those years ago? Would everyone salivate over it, judging his bloodlust and speculating about his state of mind?

Well, they'd be wrong. Malek might have a temper, but he's not a monster. He explained that incident to you. And when he'd described Ollie's injuries, there were tears in his eyes. He was crushed under the weight of the self-loathing and regret. He hated that feeling of losing control. But the fact is he did lose control, didn't he?

Look, if it was Malek, you need to find the turning point. The thing that made him snap. Come on, work it out. Did something happen today, something that set him off? If you work your way back, retrace your steps, then maybe you can find more clues. What can you feel? What can you see?

There's something in your mouth. Crumbs, under your tongue. What are they from? Were you eating something when you were hit from behind? What kind of food?

It tastes … sweet. What flavour is that? Chocolate?

Think back. Start at the beginning of the day. Picture the moment you woke up this morning. What did you see when you opened your eyes, what did you hear?

It hits you. This morning, you woke up next to Victoria. You stayed at her place last night. That couldn't be it, could it? You really have been staying there a bit more often recently. Was it one too many times?

But is that motive?

Come on, babe, think. Is there anything *else?*

Yes, actually. There is. What if he found out about your special announcement? You were going to tell him yourself – tonight! At the party, that was always your intention. It was going to be on your terms. If he found out first, before you got the chance to explain, could it have set him off?

God, this is impossible. You've never felt this helpless before. This isn't you. You always get what you want. But not this time, because even if you do figure it out, it's not going to matter, is it? Because you're still going to be dead.

You'll never get to see your daughter grow up. You won't get to see her graduate high school or get married or have children of her own. You won't know what career she ends up choosing or if she travels or studies or takes after her dad and starts playing footy again.

And it's all because there is someone out there who hates you enough to want to end your life. To risk losing their own life to a jail sentence. Or maybe they won't end up in jail. Maybe they're going to get away with it.

Well, fuck that. You are *going to figure it out. You must. You have to hold on. Yes, you're getting weaker, but you can't let go yet. Just hold on long enough to work it out and then you can tell someone* who it was. When they finally find you, your last act will be ensuring that your killer is caught.

You need to move on. You've exhausted all of the possible motives for Malek and you still haven't come to a solid conclusion. You don't have enough time to stay on the one person forever – you must progress with the list.

SUSPECT TWO

the school mum

CHAPTER TWELVE

Karen

Friday, early morning

Carob. Carousel. Karma. Karaoke.

Karen Kingsworth placed her palms together so that her hands were only touching lightly and then stretched her arms up towards the ceiling while gently twisting her body at the waist so that she was facing out the window to her left. She could see the sycamore tree that needed trimming and the never-ending downpour and the Thompsons' overflowing gutters. They would be around to complain soon.

This wasn't working. None of it was working. Not the sunrise yoga. Not the view that only reminded her of jobs that needed to be done. And not the 'positive word play'.

It was another Karen who had suggested the word association task. She probably shouldn't have joined that group in the first place. Online support for Karens: *A place for us to take back our beautiful name! Practical ways to deal with internet trolls. Non-combative ways to explain to people that using the name Karen as a slur is unnecessarily offensive to women named Karen!*

An old friend had added her to the group – Karen Wood from university. She'd accepted the invite with what she thought was a sort of ironic attitude. Like, she was okay with making fun of herself! She didn't really care about the fact that people had started using the name Karen as an insult. That Karens supposedly had a specific look involving blonde bobs with chunky streaks. Her intention was to have a bit of a laugh and then leave the group. But she'd hung around longer than she'd meant to.

Blonde, curly-haired, hippy Karen had suggested the word-play strategy as a way to associate their names with pleasant things again. *Think of positive words with a similar sound,* she said in her post. They could rhyme or they could start with a K or even a hard C. *Chant them to yourself like a mantra.* 'Carrot, kale, cabbage' had been her initial suggestions. Apparently, she was into juicing. Karen had been confident she could come up with something better. But it appeared she'd been wrong.

Carob had seemed like a nice word at first. Something about the round smooth sound of it. With an *almost* satisfying finish. Almost like toffee and almost as sweet and chewy. But then it just made her irritable when she realised what it represented: a cheap imitation of chocolate. Carousel seemed like a quaint, pretty, delightful word. But all that spinning in circles made her queasy. Karma ... well, that one could be a word full of satisfaction, but it all depended on whether you were on the giving end or the receiving end. And karaoke. A word full of promise. Promise of fun, rowdy nights making new friendships and sharing delicious secrets and a voice like a nightingale. But that wasn't what happened, was it?

Instead, it was a night full of seediness and sticky floors and plummeting stomachs when the wrong secret was hissed across the table and friendships were broken before they'd even begun.

Stop it, don't think about that.

She had been told that the secret wasn't even true; it was nothing more than a cruel joke. So why couldn't she let it go? Probably because there was too much evidence to support it. The fact was, her husband, Robert, had been behaving strangely recently. He'd been vanishing at odd times and pulling away from her and *something wasn't right.*

It just seemed so unexpected that things could have taken a turn between the two of them. The smart thing to do would have been to just *ask him,* but she couldn't even bring herself to form the words. Besides, their relationship had always been solid. For God's sake, the man had even taken her surname when they married. Admittedly, she knew a big part of that decision had come from him always having hated his own surname: Cumming. He'd been bullied mercilessly throughout his school years for it and the moment he'd learned Karen's surname, he'd said how much he would have loved to have grown up with the name Kingsworth. Annoyingly, a lot of people reacted weirdly to the news that her husband had taken her name. Sometimes – and she hated to admit this – she could tell that their opinion of him changed, that they somehow found him less manly.

The other problem with Robert taking her surname was that it meant she felt like she then had to give in to him on other things. Like when they were coming up with a name for their first child. When Robert had said that he wanted to name their daughter after the great-aunt he'd adored, Karen had thought it was going to be something beautiful like Ruby or Audrey or Lillian. She'd almost laughed out loud when he'd told her his great-aunt's name was Tallulah. It's not that there was anything particularly wrong with the name, it was just that the only time she'd ever heard it before was when her high school had chosen *Bugsy Malone* for the school play in Year Twelve, and her best friend had played the female lead: Tallulah. So all she could think of when she heard the name Tallulah was 1920s gangsters with Tommy guns and flappers with fur shawls and cloche hats. But the name had grown on her over the years and at least 'Tallulah' wasn't synonymous with entitled middle-aged women like 'Karen' was.

She transitioned into her final pose, held it for thirty seconds and then rolled up her yoga mat. Time to get on with her day. There was the usual morning rigmarole of getting the kids out the door to school and then she had several product deliveries to make, two demonstrations *and* she had to make a batch of cupcakes. She also needed to find a spare moment to buy a birthday gift for Harriet. Usually, she would never leave it this late to buy a present but over the last few weeks, every time she'd thought about trying to choose something for Harriet, a bad taste had crept up the back of her throat and she'd put it off, done something – anything – else. Maybe she could ask Robert to pick something up on his way home from work. But no, that was ridiculous. There was no way he'd choose the right thing. The gift needed to be perfect. Not because Karen wanted to impress Harriet.

Not because she liked Harriet. But for precisely the opposite reason. Because she bloody well hated Harriet.

As she put her yoga mat away and headed into the ensuite to shower, Karen considered how absurd it was that she felt the need to buy the perfect gift for someone she hated. She knew it didn't make any sense, that instead she should be buying the woman a cheap bottle of wine or a pair of ugly socks. But for some reason, shopping for someone she didn't like almost became competitive, as though she needed to prove something by choosing the ideal present. As though she needed to win. She just didn't know what she was winning.

Obviously, she should have turned down the invite to the party. That would have been the right thing to do. The safer option. Especially knowing that she was more than capable of evening the score when it came to dealing with your typical mean girls. And a fortieth birthday party was not the place to be evening the score.

But Karen couldn't help herself. It didn't matter that Harriet had apologised for what had happened. Or that this invite had only been extended as a peace offering. Karen had to take this opportunity, the same way she'd pounced almost thirty years ago when the chance to exact revenge on her younger sister's school bullies had presented itself to her at the local bowling alley. Ariella had never forgiven her for that. Yes, Karen had taken things a little too far, but those girls had deserved it after the way they treated Ariella. They were your typical bunch of queen bees, thinking they were above everyone else. And Ariella had always been the type to fight cruelty with kindness.

These days, Ariella had a whole easy-going, bohemian vibe that was far from Karen's lifestyle. Maybe that was because their parents had given her the beautiful, floaty name of Ariella rather than the hard, choppy name of Karen. At least their older brother, Doug, had drawn the short straw on names like she had. She knew for a fact Doug never liked his name either. But she didn't get to see Doug as much since he'd moved up to Brisbane and joined the Queensland Police Service.

She stripped off and stepped into the shower, squeezed body wash onto the loofah and started scrubbing at her body. As always, the fingers of her right hand felt along the raised bump of the scar down her left arm. For some reason, over the years, it had become a habit to always run the tips of her fingers down the full length of the scar when she was in the shower. Sometimes it was an absent-minded action and she thought nothing more of it; other times, touching it took her mind straight back to the night that it happened. Today, though, she didn't have time to relive past trauma. She had other things to think about.

Things like revenge.

*

Karen tutted as the small sports car zipped around from behind her four-wheel drive and slotted into the spot two cars ahead. You weren't supposed to do that. You were meant to wait your turn. Safety first around a school. Especially in all this rain. But there were always people who thought their time was more important than everyone else's. It didn't matter how many times they printed the rules for the Kiss and Drop zone in the school newsletter; each and every morning, there were several parents who ignored the rules and messed up the system. Ruined the perfect flow. Of course there was no way she could complain. No way she could comment on the school's Facebook page or try to signal the driver, not unless she wanted to be labelled as a whinger who was living up to her name.

She glanced into the rear-view mirror at her two children. Tallulah caught her eye from the back seat. Her daughter gave her a fake, sickly smile.

'Tallulah, don't do that,' Karen said, her voice even.

'Don't do what?' Tallulah asked, eyes round and innocent.

'You know what.'

'What did she do?' Ralph leaned forward, straining against his seatbelt. 'Mum, what's she in trouble for?'

'She's not. It's fine, she didn't do anything.'

Ralph slumped back against his seat and the car crept forward as the line moved. The windscreen wipers squeaked each time they swept from left to right. Probably needed new wiper blades. At some point she was going to need to have a chat with Ralph, explain what was going on with Tallulah. He knew that something had changed, that there had been a shift within their family dynamic, and it was clear that it was worrying him. But Karen didn't really know where to begin. *You see, Ralph, when some kids hit the teenage years, they turn into demonic monsters almost as though it's a rite of passage. Any chance you could skip that stage when you get older?*

The car in front pulled away and Karen took the spot at the head of the queue. 'Right,' she said, twisting around in her seat, 'got your umbrella, Ralphy? Bag? Sports gear?' Ralph always seemed to leave something behind.

'Got it all,' he said, lifting up his bag to show her.

'Good boy.' She turned her attention to Tallulah, who had the back door open and one foot out, letting the rain drip into the car. 'Have a really lovely day, sweetie,' Karen said, aware that her voice didn't sound quite right.

'Okay, *sweetie*,' Tallulah replied.

Ralph looked between them, his face concerned, confused. But then Tallulah was out of the car and Ralph was following her, hauling his bag onto his small frame and leaving his umbrella on the seat.

'Ralph! Umbrella!'

He reached back in and snatched it up. 'Thanks, Mum, bye!'

Karen kept her face composed until she was three streets away. Then she pulled over and cried. She still couldn't get her head around it. The notion that her family seemed to be falling apart. That her marriage wasn't what it used to be. That she couldn't even ask her husband one simple question. That Tallulah had turned out this way. That somehow, she'd raised a delinquent. And she had no idea if her tactic for dealing with Tallulah was pure genius or completely reckless.

God, Karen missed the days when she and her daughter would chat over milkshakes and donuts and Tallulah would share everything that was going on in her life with abandon.

Tallulah had always been a strong-willed, stubborn kid – but she'd been *Karen's* strong-willed, stubborn kid! When had that changed? She knew that it was all a part of growing up, of becoming a teenager and gaining independence and wanting your freedom, but she still couldn't understand why Tallulah suddenly seemed to view Karen as the enemy. Why every single thing that Karen said or did was somehow wrong. If she tried to show Tallulah a funny meme, Tallulah said Karen was 'cringe'. If she suggested a family movie, it was 'childish'. If she laughed, it was too loud and if she was upset, she was dramatic. There was no winning. And the constant phone calls from the school. It seemed like Tallulah was in trouble every second day.

Karen had hoped Tallulah's friendship with Farrah might have been a turning point. Farrah seemed like she could be a good influence on Tallulah, but so far, Karen was more worried that the opposite was happening. That was why she'd taken the drastic measure of setting up the secret account. A move that she still wasn't sure was the right choice, but it had felt as though she didn't have another option. If Tallulah wasn't going to talk to her, how else was she going to protect her?

Sometimes she wondered if everything would have been better if Tallulah hadn't become friends with Farrah. Because then Harriet wouldn't have become a part of her life.

She never should have agreed to go to that mums' night out that Harriet organised three weeks ago. It had started with an out-of-the-blue call from Harriet, suggesting that they should get to know one another seeing as Tallulah and

Farrah were becoming such good friends. Karen had been taken aback. Despite Farrah's father, Malek, being the more hands-on parent at school, Harriet had somehow formed an expansive clique of school-mum friends. Everyone knew who Harriet was. Not only because she had the kind of ridiculously stunning good looks that made you feel like you were a sludge-covered swamp-troll who was lucky to be bathed in the glow of her beauty when you stood next to her, but also because she was famous for her raucous mums' nights out. But Karen had never known her well enough to get an invite. Even with their daughters becoming friends, she hadn't thought it would ever happen, because the kids were older now and didn't need their parents to sort out their playdates.

That night out had held so much promise for Karen. The promise of new friendships and of cutting loose and experiencing life in a way that she felt she hadn't done in such a long time. There was just something about Harriet. Something that made you feel like you were in for the wildest night of your life. She was the sort of person who knew all the places to go. All the little hole-in-the-wall bars that Karen would have walked straight past, thinking they were nothing more than unassuming grey doors in even more unassuming brick walls. But there was Harriet, twisting the knob, pushing the door and leading the group down a dark, narrow staircase that opened at the bottom to a jazz club with speakeasy vibes or a wine bar with drum and bass thrumming through the walls and leather booths and ten different types of gin or only one signature cocktail.

Although Karen had to admit there had always been something about Harriet that had made her feel uneasy. It felt stupid to say it, but it was as though there was almost something dangerous about her. There were rumours of a previous night out that had ended with one of the women being arrested for trying to skinny dip in Darling Harbour. And another about a time when someone got lost and turned up the next morning in a stranger's bed on the other side of Sydney. Not to mention the mothers she'd heard about who'd been drawn into Harriet's circle then unceremoniously dumped. But was it really Harriet's fault that some people had gotten too carried away? And presumably the women who had been cut out had done something to deserve being ostracised.

Karen hadn't wanted to give in to those warning signs and ruin her night. For God's sake, she was a mum with a teenage daughter, an eleven-year-old son, a work-from-home business that was a hell of a slog, and a husband who was hiding something from her and also … Well, let's just say a husband who lately didn't seem to align with her in terms of their needs, and all she'd wanted was one night where she got to have *fun*. So it was no wonder she'd been willing to crush her instincts in favour of trusting Harriet.

She just really wished she hadn't.

*

Quinton

The Mason property

Quinton leaned against the island kitchen bench while the team did their jobs around him. His boss, Harriet, walked through the door and the junior agent immediately stood up straighter. Harriet somehow always looked sharp and professional but still crazy hot and super sexy at the same time. He could never quite put his finger on what it was. She wore the smart business suits all the agents wore, but she added these tiny touches, like a pair of Chuck Taylors or an extra open button at the top of her shirt or smoky eyes, and it just tipped her into a whole other category.

'Fully wired for smart home capabilities,' Harriet said.

'Yep,' said Quinton, scribbling a note down on his pad. 'I know a few potential buyers who'll love that. And the heated pool too. Reckon this one will go like that,' he added, snapping his fingers.

Harriet smiled at him. 'That's what I like to hear.' She headed off for another room, presumably to check on the floorplan guy.

Rick walked in from the other direction, carrying his tripod and making a clicking noise with the side of his mouth while pointing with his thumb to the doorway. 'You're going to be in my shot, mate.'

'Alright, I'll get out of your way,' said Quinton and picked up his folder. There were a few different photographers on Harriet's books and while Rick took amazing photos, his interpersonal skills were severely lacking. He also somehow always seemed … greasy? Was it too mean to think that? But Quinton didn't know how else to describe him.

'Actually, can you do me a favour?' Rick said. 'Can you shoot me Harriet's address for the party tonight? I think I accidently deleted the email her husband sent through with the deets.'

Quinton frowned. Was that a little odd? Had Rick even been invited to the party? But he could hardly say no.

'Sure thing,' he said. 'I'll send it now.'

CHAPTER THIRTEEN

Karen's face was completely free of any indication that she had been crying in her car by the time she walked in the front door of her home. She never liked to wallow for too long. Sure, it felt like things were falling apart, but she still needed to get on with life. And tonight at the party she'd take back some control.

She startled as she heard a noise from down the hall. The house should be empty. She felt a flutter in her chest and was about to shout out, 'Who's there?' when she heard her husband's voice call, 'That you, Karen?'

She breathed out slowly. 'Yep, it's me. What are you still doing here?' Robert should have gone to work only minutes after she'd left to take the kids to school.

'Working from home today, love.'

Karen's mouth twisted. He hadn't mentioned anything about working from home.

She heard his footsteps heading down the hall and when he appeared in the doorway, she thought she detected a worried look on his face.

'I thought you were heading straight from school drop-off to your first deliveries of the day,' he said, scratching at his beard.

'And I thought you were going into the office,' Karen murmured to herself.

'What's that?'

'Nothing. I had to come home for some supplies. No time this morning to stock up the car before the school run.' She paused and then tried to make her voice sound casual, relaxed. 'How come you're working from home today?'

'Oh, no real reason, just wasn't in the mood for the commute in the rain. Besides, we've got that big party tonight, so I didn't want to get home too late for us to head out.'

Karen forced a smile, but she was agitated. It annoyed her how excited Robert was about this party. Yes, everyone knew Harriet threw amazing events, but considering he *also* knew that they'd only been invited as a peace offering after Harriet had been nasty to Karen, he might have held back his excitement just a little. Although maybe that wasn't fair, seeing as Karen had avoided telling Robert the full details of what happened. But then, he never took the day off work when there was an event that *she* had planned for them. In fact, he'd been half an hour late when she'd organised a family dinner out for her last birthday.

'Fair enough,' said Karen. 'Better let you get back to it then. Oh, wait, quick reminder in case you haven't seen it on the calendar, next weekend I'm going out with the Mosman crowd – dinner and drinks.'

Robert wrinkled his nose. He would never complain about her seeing those friends – he knew they were important to her – but at the same time, he didn't love the fact that she'd met them through an old boyfriend.

'Ah. That came up fast.' He gave her a quick peck on the forehead and then looked her up and down. 'I never understand why you wear such nice clothes for your product parties. Don't you do demos on kitchen sinks and things? Wouldn't it make more sense to wear jeans and sneakers and rubber gloves?'

Karen pinched the bridge of her nose. 'I've told you this before. When I dress this way, people take me more seriously as a businesswoman rather than seeing me as some housewife with a pet project.'

'Right. Sorry, of course. Still, though, you wouldn't want to get bleach on that nice suit jacket.' He headed back down the hall.

Karen stood still for a moment, considering Robert's earlier excuse. *No real reason … wasn't in the mood for the commute …* Had he sounded nervous? Caught off guard? Or was she simply imagining things?

Her phone buzzed in her pocket with a notification and she pulled it out to take a look. A message from Victoria, Harriet's best friend, who Karen had only met three weeks prior at the mums' night out.

Making sure you're still coming tonight! No bailing last minute, right?

Karen smiled as she replied to Victoria. *We'll be there. Even if I was getting cold feet, there's no way Robert would let us miss the event of the year! Feels like half the school is buzzing about her party.*

Despite not knowing one another well, Karen and Victoria had texted back and forth several times over the past few weeks after exchanging numbers at the night out. It had been a long time since she'd made a new friend as swiftly and easily as she had with Victoria.

*

Saturday night, three weeks ago

Karen didn't even learn Victoria's name until the second bar. And at that point, she still thought she was another mum from Apple Hills College. There were about fifteen of them out for the night. But Karen only recognised a few of the faces and none of them were the women she'd gotten to know from volunteering at the canteen or going along to the P&C meetings. These were Harriet's kind of women. And men. That had been a surprise. She'd thought the night out was girls only, but apparently single dads were included in Harriet's mums' nights out: one of the dads Karen had met at the school election barbecue the year before when she and Robert had been helping out, but the other dad was new to the school.

So far, Karen had made it through the night skating over the surface of conversations with the other parents, sometimes joining in to share a murmur of agreement or quick anecdote. But now she and Victoria were in the line together for the loo and had started chatting. Victoria was a good ten centimetres taller than Karen, wearing faded grey jeans, a sleeveless black top and bright pink stilettos. Her dark hair was in a high ponytail that showed off a shaved undercut with lined patterns and a tattoo of a small dragon curled up at the base of her neck. She was makeup free apart from a deep lipstick that made it look as though her lips had been stained from eating blackberries, and she had the most perfectly shaped full eyebrows Karen had ever seen. In short, it was as though Karen was staring up at her polar opposite.

'What year is yours in?' Karen asked as they shuffled towards the front of the line.

''Scuse me?' Victoria replied, her tone friendly.

'Oh, at Apple Hills? Sorry … I assumed that's how you knew Harriet.'

'Ah. No, not me. I don't have any kids. I'm an old friend of Harry's. Known her since university.'

'Really!' Karen's voice was louder than usual. She could feel it happening, but she couldn't control it. This was the first time in years that she'd had more than three drinks. And by her count, she'd just finished her fifth. She hated that she became loud when she got drunk. There was nothing worse than being fully aware of something you were doing but being in no way able to stop it. At least she knew from her younger days that, after two more drinks, while she would continue to be loud, she would no longer care about it.

'That must have been so much fun, going to uni with Harriet!' God, her voice was positively screeching. She felt like such a dork next to tall, relaxed Victoria. Such a frumpy, noisy mum out on the town, such a … *Karen*. She really needed that next drink. They shuffled forward in the line.

Karen thought for a second she caught the quickest flash of something cross Victoria's face, but it vanished so quickly she wasn't sure if she'd imagined it. At the same time, though, she also realised that while Victoria was absolutely stunning, she had faint grey circles under her eyes.

'I suppose. Sure.'

'She just seems like the sort of person who really knows how to …' Karen realised she was about to say, *knows how to party* and stopped short. Good Lord, could she sound any more like a middle-aged housewife? Apparently, she could – because the next thing that popped into her head was even worse.

'I've always loved the name Harriet. My favourite book when I was a kid was called *Harriet's Holiday* and it was all about this hippo called Harriet who goes on safari. I used to read it over and over again.'

Fortunately, she was stopped from babbling any further as they'd reached the front of the line. To her credit, Victoria gave her a warm smile and said, 'Sounds cute,' before heading away to the free stall.

Not only was Victoria gorgeous and effortlessly cool, she was also friendly. It was equally delightful and disgusting. It wasn't fair when there were humans who had all of that. Not when Karen was here looking the way she looked and acting the way she acted. Karen suddenly wished that Ariella were here. Ariella could match Victoria for effortless coolness. Ariella would carry a conversation with her easily, she wouldn't even flinch at Victoria's style. And even though Ariella had entirely different taste and a different way of carrying herself – she was more likely to be wearing a flowing top, long dangly earrings and strappy sandals – she would probably click with Victoria in an instant.

Although, what good would that do for Karen? Having a cool sister didn't magically make her cool too. In fact, it would be ten times worse if Ariella were here. Because then Victoria would be kind and chatty to Ariella and Karen would be left out in the cold, feeling even more frumpy. It would be better if Doug were here, actually, he was sweet and dorky and earnest and would make Karen feel less out of place. Although she was pretty sure she'd heard a couple of the mums giggling with one another about taking pills earlier – so she guessed if Doug were here, he might cause a bit of a downer by arresting her new friends.

Back at the bar, Karen found herself standing next to the new school dad. He pushed a shot across to her. 'It's Karen, right? I'm Cosmo. Here, Harriet ordered these for everyone, you don't want to miss out.'

'Thanks,' said Karen, about to ask what was in it then deciding that she was probably better off not knowing. She threw the shot back without thinking more about it. Besides, maybe she'd look more interesting or spontaneous if she didn't care what was in her glass.

'Okay,' said Cosmo, 'let me give this a go. I hate coriander. I know how to crochet. I love listening to German death metal.'

Karen gaped back at him, bewildered by the three strange statements. 'Um, alright,' she said. 'That's … that's nice.'

Cosmo's face dropped. 'Oh,' he said. 'Am I doing it wrong?'

Harriet appeared behind Karen, draping an arm around each of them.

'Accepting drinks from strange men, are we?' Harriet said.

'What? No! This was … he said it was from you!'

'Relax, I'm only kidding. Besides, Cosmo here is a teddy bear, of course you can accept a drink from him. Did you pick which one was the lie?'

'I'm sorry?'

'Cosmo's two truths and a lie?'

Karen shook her head. 'Harriet, I'm totally lost.'

'Oh, wait! You were in the bathroom when I got this started, weren't you? Sorry! We're playing a game – it's going to last the whole night. Everyone can have as many turns as they like. All you have to do is tell two truths and one lie and everyone else needs to figure out which one is the lie.'

'Right,' said Karen. She was about to ask what the point was when she realised that that would probably make her seem like a spoilsport. 'Okay, I think … I think you don't know how to crochet.'

Cosmo beamed. 'Wrong. My grandmother taught me when I was twelve. I can make a mean pair of socks.'

'It was the coriander!' Harriet said happily. 'Can you believe he loves it? Blergh.'

'Oh,' said Karen. 'Well I mean, I quite like —'

'Did you know Cosmo has a son in the year above our girls? The new boy that all the girls are falling head over heels for.'

'I didn't,' said Karen. 'So, you're new to the school?'

'He's new to the whole state,' said Harriet. 'Karen's gorgeous daughter, Tallulah, is good friends with my Farrah,' she added, turning to Cosmo. 'I wouldn't be surprised if she's got a crush on your son too.'

'Sorry, which one is your son?' Karen asked.

'His name is Serge, he's in Year Ten.'

'Oh, so how do you two know one another? Have you got another kid in Year Nine with ours, Cosmo?'

'No, only Serge. Harriet sort of just …'

'It's okay, you can say it. I totally flirted with you at the supermarket.' Harriet turned to Karen and held her hands up. 'Okay, don't judge me. I swear it was completely harmless; I needed his help reaching the last box of cornflakes on the top shelf. But then we started chatting and I found out his son went to our school and he was new to the area. He didn't know a soul here, so I offered to introduce him to some people.'

Cosmo gestured at the other parents in groups around the bar. 'She was definitely true to her word.'

'Where were you before Sydney?' Karen asked.

'We moved from Brisbane,' said Cosmo.

'Brisbane! That's where I grew up,' said Harriet. 'Which part?' she asked at the same time as Karen said, 'Oh, my brother recently moved up there!'

Cosmo looked between them and then responded to Karen. 'Your brother is lucky,' he said, 'it's a lovely place.'

'What made you move?' Karen asked.

'Work,' he said, with a note of finality to his voice that didn't invite follow-up questions. Harriet seemed to miss the hint – or perhaps she'd caught on but decided to ignore it.

'Don't want to elaborate on that?' she asked with a laugh.

Cosmo gave her a tight smile, 'Oh, sorry, it's just my job … it's all a bit boring,' he said. But Karen noticed a ruddiness creep up his neck and saw him lean back and scratch irritably at it. That was odd.

CHAPTER FOURTEEN

Karen carted the boxes of products through from the living room to the garage to put them in her car boot. She was grateful for the garage with internal access on rainy days like today. Most people had thought there was no way she would make money by joining a multilevel marketing business selling cleaning products, but Karen seemed to have a knack for it, working her way up through the tiers as she sold more and more products and recruited other salespeople beneath her.

She put the last box in the boot and felt her phone vibrate in her jacket pocket yet again. She pulled it out, expecting another message from Victoria, but instead it was a notification from her secret account. Even though there was no one around, she immediately dipped her head and hid her screen. She was about to click through to it, but then changed her mind and locked her phone. If she started looking now, she was likely to end up down a rabbit hole and she needed to get moving. She'd check it later. She slid her phone back into her pocket and closed the boot. Right, first up, two quick client deliveries and then stop by the shops.

That would be the only chance she had to get that bloody gift for Harriet before the rest of her day was taken up with product parties and baking.

She hopped into the driver's seat and reversed out of the garage, wondering what other people would be buying for Harriet. If she'd managed to become better friends with some of the other school mums at that night out, then maybe she could have asked to go in on a group gift. But there was no way that would have worked. Not after what happened at the third bar.

*

Saturday night, three weeks ago

'I like having sex more than my husband does.'

Karen recognised her mistake as soon as the words were out of her mouth. The other three women were all staring at her, their faces a mix of amusement and shock. She was supposed to say all three statements at once, not just shout out one random thing completely out of context. But she'd become nervous after walking over to the small group of school mums she barely knew and had frozen up, immediately forgetting what her other two statements were going to be.

'Um, okay, that's … good to know,' said Kelly.

'No, no,' said Karen, 'That's not — I mean, I was trying to play a round of the game. I didn't actually —'

'You heard they found that girl, didn't you?' Amanda cut over the top of her.

There was an eruption of chirped responses from the other women.

'The one down in Melbourne? Yes, horrible, I can't even imagine.'

'I was really hoping she'd be fine, just another runaway who turned up at a friend's house.'

'I know, I had a feeling, though, the way she went missing. I knew it was going to be bad news.'

'Sorry,' said Amanda, looking sideways at Karen. 'Didn't mean to derail your two truths and a lie.' Her voice was completely disingenuous, but Karen decided to give her the benefit of the doubt.

'Oh, that's fine, I messed it up anyway. I don't think I heard about that girl, what happened?' she asked, hoping her voice was hitting the right level of curious but respectful, considering how drunk she was. She was really regretting joining these women.

'That sixteen-year-old girl, the one that was reported missing just outside of Melbourne. It was all over the news because the family were very active on social media – it went viral,' said Amanda.

'They say it's better to know, don't they?' said one of the other women. Karen thought her name was something like Jean or Jane. 'At least then you don't have that false hope of one day —'

'Sorry,' Karen said, 'but what *did* happen to her?'

'Murdered. They found her body in a creek. Apparently, she'd been out on a date with some new secret boyfriend. Terrifies me to think that our girls are only a year or two younger than her. Doesn't it make you scared? Like, how do we keep them safe? I mean, can we please just wrap them up in cotton wool and keep them home forever?'

Karen felt unexpected tears well up behind her eyes and she blinked rapidly. She couldn't shed a tear in front of women she barely knew for a young girl she'd only just heard about. They would think she was ridiculous. But she couldn't help picturing Tallulah in that same girl's position. Sneaking out for a date, nervous but exhilarated. She could see her accepting the boy's hand, laughing at his jokes, leaning in for a kiss, the boy's hands around her throat. Her face changing, slipping from joy to confusion to fear to terror.

Oh God, the idea was too horrendous. 'We *have* to teach them.' Karen knew her voice was too loud, too sharp. Too … emotional. She could tell by the way all three women turned to look at her, quizzical expressions on their made-up faces.

'Sorry?' asked Jean or Jane.

'Our girls. We have to teach them how to protect themselves. We have to make sure they know that they can't go off with strange boys to strange places, that they —'

'Wait,' Amanda said. 'Are you saying the onus is on the girls? That they're the ones who have to make the change?'

Immediately Karen realised she'd taken a misstep. 'Well, no, I just mean —'

But the other woman kept talking. 'Because that's what it sounds like. And you do realise that's an awful lot like victim blaming, don't you? Next, you'll be saying we should teach them not to wear short skirts, low-cut tops.'

Karen swallowed, her mouth suddenly dry and sticky. Hadn't Amanda just said two minutes ago that she wanted to wrap her daughter in cotton wool and keep her home forever?

'Surely it's the male behaviour that needs to change,' Amanda continued. 'The boys are the ones we need to teach, not the girls.'

'Obviously,' said Harriet, slipping in between Amanda and Karen and placing a hand on Karen's back. 'But Karen does have a point. There is absolutely no harm in *also* arming our daughters with the knowledge they need to look out for themselves until the men of the world stop taking what they want.'

Amanda appeared chastened. 'Oh ... well, I mean, absolutely ... I wasn't saying there was any harm in it ... I just meant, you know, it's important not to victim blame.'

'I highly doubt Karen was victim blaming. I think you've twisted what she said to fit your agenda.' Harriet glanced sideways at Karen and gave her a reassuring nod before facing Amanda again. 'You must be heading off soon. Didn't you say you're on cricket-mum duty tomorrow morning?'

Amanda's face dropped further and she fumbled with her handbag. 'Yes, I was ... I mean, I am.' She checked her watch. 'Oh goodness, you're right, it *is* getting late. And Xavier's game *would* be on at seven am, wouldn't it?' She gave an awkward laugh and scanned the group. 'Anyone want to share a cab?'

The other two women seemed to physically recoil from Amanda. 'No, all good, I think we're going to stay a little longer, aren't we?' said Kelly.

'Yeah, you go ahead,' said Jean-or-Jane, shifting her body away from Amanda and moving closer to Kelly. She touched Harriet's arm across the table. 'My shout for the next round, hun. I was thinking Aperol Spritzes, if that's good with you?' It was clear that everyone loved Harriet, and no one wanted to be on the receiving end of her disapproval.

Karen bit her lip to stop from snorting. She couldn't believe how *high school* these women were behaving. There was a flurry of cheek kisses and then Amanda was gone, but not before she'd shot Karen a look that could have curdled milk.

As much as Karen appreciated Harriet having her back, she couldn't help noting how quick she'd been to dismiss poor Amanda. If Harriet could turn that quickly on someone who'd been part of her inner circle for some time, then Karen needed to be careful. What if she took another misstep and Harriet turned on her?

CHAPTER FIFTEEN

Karen had wandered in and out of about six or seven shops already trawling for a gift for Harriet and she was running out of time. Maybe she needed to accept that it wasn't going to be the perfect present after all. Maybe she should just buy a nice bottle of champagne and leave it at that. She checked the time. She had to be at her first product demo in forty-five minutes. She was trying one more shop, and if she didn't find inspiration there, then she was giving up and buying alcohol. And then she was going to sit down and take ten minutes for herself to have a bloody cappuccino.

The moment she saw it in the next shop, she knew she had to buy it. A small, bejewelled hippopotamus statue that was objectively hideous, yet she simply couldn't look away from the thing. Kind of like the way Harriet had that dangerous allure that was so hard to pull away from. It didn't matter that the hippo was the most ridiculous choice ever because it was just too perfect. It took Karen straight back to the days she'd spent reading about Harriet the Hippo over and over as a kid. Of course, it wasn't going to mean a thing to Harriet, and it would probably end up out of sight in the back of a cupboard somewhere, but Karen didn't care. This gift was going to be her own private joke and Harriet didn't need to know the origins. She wondered if Victoria would remember her mentioning her love of a book about the hippo called Harriet? Probably not, but even if she did, she'd probably think it was amusing too.

Five minutes later, she sat down with her coffee and her tissue-wrapped hippo and opened up the secret social media account on her phone. She tapped through the notifications, looking at the photos and reading the descriptions. She sat and thought, then typed a comment in the appropriate voice before closing it again. Nothing ground-breaking in there today. That was a good thing.

She looked around the café and saw a small child in a *Star Wars* raincoat staring at her. She smiled back at him but then she saw the child tug on his mother's arm before saying loudly, 'Mummy, what's on that lady's arm?'

Karen's hand automatically went to the scar, and she was about to make eye contact with the mother, to reassure her that it was fine, that kids didn't know any better, that she was happy to explain to the little boy what had happened to her arm, but instead the woman gave the child a small smack on the hand before standing up and leaving with the upset boy in tow.

Oh, great, now that kid would associate people with scars with the nasty feeling of getting into trouble from his mother. Honestly, why didn't more parents *talk* to their kids? Explain why a comment could be inappropriate and insensitive so the child could learn? Karen remembered that she'd just been using her secret social media account instead of properly communicating with her own child, and she let out a small scoff at her own actions. She was just as bad.

No, she was worse.

She slumped back and sighed, catching sight of a stool, microphone and guitar set up in the corner. A poster on the wall behind it said: 'Friday and Saturday Open Mic for Talented Musicians'. She felt like walking over there, picking up the guitar and playing it. But that was absurd. She hadn't played her guitar in years. She wasn't even sure if she could still remember how to play anything. Besides, look what had happened the last time she'd tried to sing in public.

*

Saturday night, three weeks ago

'Alright, everyone, put your names down. No one gets out of this.'

Harriet was holding the sign-up sheet for karaoke and tapping it with a pen. The response from the group was a mixture of groans and whoops. Their numbers had dwindled to six now and they were all crammed into a booth together. Karen was squeezed between Victoria and Cosmo, while on the other side, Harriet, the woman Karen had taken to calling Jean-Jane and Kelly sat in a row. On the stage off to the right, two men in business shirts and loosened ties were leaning into one another precariously as they attempted a pitiful rendition of Cold Chisel's 'Khe Sanh'.

Karen had tried not to react when Harriet had announced that they'd all be partaking in karaoke, but she was pleased. She loved singing and was more than capable of carrying a tune. She'd first met Robert at a karaoke bar.

His method of picking her up had been misguided, to say the least. He'd signed up to sing a duet and then when he took the stage, asked for 'the blondish girl in the black top and pink skirt' to please come and join him. Karen had point blank refused to get up there with this complete stranger, but the crowd in the bar had cheered them on and, eventually, she gave in and took one of the microphones.

The reason it was such a misguided plan was that Robert was, in fact, an awful singer. She still remembered asking him afterwards why on earth he thought showing off his terrible off-key voice would endear him to her. But he'd said he didn't care what he sounded like, all he knew was that he'd heard her singing 'Girls Just Want to Have Fun' earlier in the night and desperately wanted to hear her sing again, so he was willing to completely embarrass himself in order to make it happen.

She supposed his method wasn't that misguided, seeing as it worked. Here they were twenty years later, married with two kids. She still remembered him whispering in her ear after they'd finished singing, 'You have the voice of a nightingale.' She knew she should have found that a bit much, a tad too corny. But instead, it had sent shivers of delight up her spine.

Karen found herself feeling nostalgic for those early days, when Robert had seemed so completely infatuated with her. When she had been confident enough to jump up and sing

Cyndi Lauper in front of a roomful of strangers. She knew that after this many years of marriage, things couldn't still feel like they had in the honeymoon stage, a relationship had to grow and change, but God, it would be nice to experience a fluttering stomach or tingling hands or the buzz of a first kiss all over again.

It was obvious that Harriet was known for being a decent singer herself. Karen could tell by the way Jean-Jane and Kelly were gushing as she chose her song and signed herself up. This was perfect. Karen had been enjoying herself tonight for the most part but she'd still felt like a bit of an outsider. Now she was going to have something in common with Harriet. A way for them to connect! Perhaps after they'd each performed a solo number, they could get back up and do a duet together! *Steady on*, she thought, *you're hardly about to become Thelma and Louise.*

'Alright,' said Harriet, leaning into the table and gesturing for everyone else to do the same. 'While we're waiting for our names to be called, let's play a few more rounds of two truths and a lie.'

Kelly clapped her hands together. 'Oh good! I haven't had a turn yet. Okay, let's see ...'

Harriet spoke over the top. 'I don't know how to swim. I wear coloured contacts. I have no sense of smell,' she said, completely ignoring the way Kelly's face dropped.

Cosmo elbowed Karen. 'What do you think?'

'Um ... I guess maybe the sense of smell could be the lie?'

Victoria smirked. 'You should know better than to play this in front of me, Harriet. I know all your secrets and lies.'

150

She glanced around at the others and then locked eyes with Harriet. 'Harriet was a champion backstroker as a teen.'

'Victoria!' Harriet scrunched up a serviette from the table and tossed it at her. 'Don't ruin it!'

'Ah,' said Cosmo. 'Thwarted by the history of friendship. So, you have no sense of smell, Harriet?'

'Yes,' said Harriet, giving Victoria a pointed look. 'None at all. Never had. Once in university I almost caused an explosion because I didn't know there was a gas leak.'

'That's an exaggeration,' said Victoria. 'You asked someone for a lighter for your smoke and they immediately told you about the gas leak. End of story.'

'Vic!' Harriet exclaimed. 'Why are you spoiling everything tonight?'

'Ooh,' interrupted Jean-Jane, 'I think they just called my name for karaoke. Wish me luck!' She slid out of the booth and skipped away to the stage.

Victoria leaned in close to Karen. 'I'll bet you ten bucks she's going to sing Britney Spears.'

Karen snickered. 'I bet it's Whitney Houston.'

'You're on.' Victoria shook her hand under the table.

Harriet shifted forward. 'What are you two conspiring about?'

'Nothing you need to know,' said Victoria.

Harriet slumped back and scowled and Karen sensed that she might be playing a dangerous game by being too friendly with Victoria. But she was getting along really well with her, and Victoria was much easier to chat to than Jean-Jane or Kelly.

In the end, they were both wrong about the song. Kelly had chosen 'I Will Survive' and the entire song was painfully screechy.

The next hour was spent working their way through several rounds of drinks as well as some shared bowls of nachos and wedges that were far too late to help soak up any of the alcohol. And all the while, they continued guessing at each other's truths and lies, and taking their turns to sing. Cosmo performed a passable but far too quiet version of 'Come on Eileen' and Victoria belted out a slightly off-key Spice Girls song.

Meanwhile, they'd found out that Jean – Karen had finally deduced her actual name – had cheated her way through her university degree by paying someone to do all of her assignments and had cut off her friend's ponytail in high school, and Kelly had either never had an orgasm, had eaten soft cheese throughout her pregnancy or had scraped the side of a car in a shopping centre carpark without leaving a note – they still weren't sure which was the lie.

Harriet took her turn and sang Miley Cyrus's 'Party in the USA' with perfect pitch. Karen was impressed. Harriet was good. But – as egotistical as it was to think it – she knew she was going to be better.

She was pretty sure her turn was coming up next.

CHAPTER SIXTEEN

Karen pulled into the driveway of the small single-storey home and peered out at the rain. Would it ease off if she waited a few minutes, so she could carry her boxes to the door without getting wet? It didn't seem likely. And the product demo was due to start in two minutes. She was going to have to dash through the downpour.

Still, she didn't move. Instead, she leaned her head back and thought again about the way Harriet's temperament had changed that night during karaoke. It must have been something to do with what Harriet was looking at on her phone as she returned to the table from the stage. That was the only thing that made sense. Prior to that she'd still been friendly and chatty with Karen. But Karen had noticed her staring intently at her phone screen and had seen her face slowly darken before she'd lowered the phone and slipped it into her pocket.

Karen had racked her brain trying to figure out what Harriet possibly could have seen to make her attitude suddenly backflip, but she couldn't come up with a single thing. All she knew was that from that moment on, it seemed as though Harriet was out to get her.

Karen massaged her fingertips against her temples. There was no point going over all of it again. She might never know what it was that had set Harriet off. Even Victoria hadn't been able to figure it out and she was Harriet's best friend.

She really needed to get out of this car and get moving. At least she knew this sales party would result in some good revenue. It was a group of her mother's friends and they were all very supportive of Karen's business. Her mum's old tennis friend Gail was hosting, and her mum was going to try to drop by too. She suspected they thought her job was just a fun hobby to keep herself busy and they bought her products with the same indulgent smiles that they used to give her when they bought homemade lemonade and cupcakes from her front-yard stall when she was six. But Karen didn't mind, sales were sales. She turned up the volume on the radio as the news came on. May as well hear the latest before she got out – anything to delay running through the rain.

'Melbourne police say they are investigating new lines of inquiry after the release of their only suspect in the case of murdered teen Amber Rhodes …'

Karen turned the volume back down. She didn't feel like hearing about that story just now, apart from the fact that the case being reopened would be devastating for that poor girl's parents. It was also just another reminder of her faux pas at the karaoke night. She climbed out of the car, collected the boxes from the boot and made the dash to the front porch.

Gail opened the door as Karen lifted her hand to knock.

'Come in, come in!' she said. 'My goodness this rain, will it ever end?'

Karen hoisted her box of supplies up on her hip. 'Thanks,' she said as Gail held the door aside for Karen to squeeze through. 'I know what you mean, I feel like I can't even remember what the sky looks like.'

'Now, everyone's set up in the lounge for you. Can I get you a cup of tea, dear?'

'Just a water for now would be great, thanks, Gail.'

Karen headed through to the lounge room, where seven older women were sitting on dining chairs that had been placed in a semicircle in the middle of the room. They all fell quiet and watched her attentively as she walked in, as though she was a school teacher about to tell them off for chatting.

'Hi!' she said brightly. 'Carry on, I'll get set up.'

There was the usual flurry of questions from the women then. 'How are the kids?' 'How's Robert?' 'What about this rain!'

Karen chatted to them as she unpacked her products and set up the display on the coffee table in front of them.

Then a question cut through the chatter and took her by surprise.

'Karen, I heard you had a run-in with some nasty school mums recently? They really can behave like children sometimes, can't they?'

Karen felt her cheeks burn as she looked up. 'Where did you hear that, Irene?' she asked.

'Oh, I can't remember, dear. I suppose it was probably your mother. Is she coming today?'

'She might be, she wasn't sure if bridge club would finish in time. Um, you think she told you about it?' Karen was trying to keep her voice casual. 'I didn't think I mentioned that incident to her.'

What worried her was how on earth her mother even knew about her altercation with Harriet. And if her mother somehow knew about it, exactly how *much* did she know? Because the evening hadn't ended well.

Not well at all.

*

Saturday night, three weeks ago

Karen couldn't understand it. Somehow, her name had disappeared from the karaoke list.

'But I was right there,' she said to the guy who was running the stage. 'I'm sure my name was after Harriet. I was going to sing Adele.'

He shrugged. 'I don't know what to tell you. You're not on there and we're not taking any more now, we'll be finishing up shortly.'

Victoria gave her a sympathetic look. 'If it helps, I'd be relieved if my name dropped off the list. I'm going to buy another drink; can I get you one?'

Back at the table, Harriet cocked her head and examined Karen with wide eyes. 'Did you figure out what happened?' she asked, her voice sweet – *too* sweet. It was something about her eyes that told Karen her concern was not genuine.

'Um, no,' she said. 'It's like I was never on the list.'

'Oh, honey, that's so annoying for you. But never mind, you've probably been saved from totally humiliating yourself up there!'

Karen felt like she'd been slapped in the face. Even Cosmo seemed taken aback by Harriet's harsh comment. Unfortunately, though, the one person who'd be likely to call Harriet out on it was Victoria, and she'd missed it, detouring via the bar on her way back to the table. Karen decided to brush it off. Maybe Harriet thought she was helping.

'Anyway,' Harriet continued, 'we're in the middle of trying to figure out if Kelly lied to us about being arrested or having sex in a Kmart change room. Sit down and help us. We've already decided that she *did* steal a top from Jeanswest when she was a kid.'

Kelly leaned forward and took a large sip of her cocktail through a straw, before sitting back and beaming at them. 'I never said I was a kid when I stole that top.'

'Oh my God,' said Harriet, hitting her playfully. 'Don't tell me you did that just recently, you deviant!'

'I say she's lying about being arrested,' said Jean. 'I can't see it.'

'Really? Even though she admitted to stealing *recently*?'

'Does that mean you can picture me having sex in a Kmart?'

'A bit of public sex is nothing to be ashamed about,' said Harriet. 'Adds to the thrill.'

'If you're tucked away in a change room it's hardly public, though, is it?'

157

Karen listened to the group bickering and giggling and decided that she really couldn't care less which statement was the lie. Victoria arrived back from the bar with their drinks and slid into the booth next to her.

'Thanks,' Karen said as she took her gin and tonic. She nudged Victoria and said quietly, 'I noticed you haven't had a turn of this game yet tonight.'

Victoria grimaced. 'Trust me, it's not a good idea for me to share my secrets. What about you, have you played a round?'

'I tried to earlier, but I stuffed it up and then everyone got sidetracked anyway.'

Their quiet conversation was interrupted when Jean suddenly squealed, 'You *did* have sex in Kmart!'

'Oh, what a shock,' Victoria whispered. 'Honestly, these confessions are all so tame.'

They continued to chat while Jean took another turn. Karen barely even paid attention to her three statements, something about skinny dipping and bullying someone in high school. But eventually Harriet zeroed in on them.

'Hey, you two! Stop having little private conversations. It's your turn, Karen. Maybe you could use your two truths and a lie to tell us how you got that massive scar on your arm.'

One of the other women gasped and Karen swallowed, taking a moment to decide how to respond to Harriet's blunt comment. She felt Victoria stiffen next to her and sensed that she was about to have a go at Harriet, so she brushed her hand against Victoria's thigh under the table. She didn't want her to step in. She wanted to deal with this on her own.

'If you want to know about the scar on my arm, you should just ask me,' Karen said calmly.

Once again there was that dangerous look in Harriet's eyes. Like she was ready to pounce on her prey. 'Yes, but it's so much more fun if it's part of the game.'

For a moment, Karen considered obliging Harriet and including the incident from so many years ago in her two truths and a lie. But immediately she realised it wasn't the type of thing that should be cheapened by being talked about in a silly game. Fuck this. She could come up with something good on her own terms. Something more shocking and interesting than anything that had been said so far. She didn't care if it resulted in Harriet or the other mums thinking badly of her. For whatever reason, Harriet seemed to have already turned on her anyway. She took a deep breath.

'I'm currently catfishing someone on the internet. When I was a teenager, there was a girl who I didn't like very much. I broke two of her fingers so badly she needed surgery. I once lit a bushfire that destroyed hundreds of hectares of land and three houses.' She tried to keep her voice even and steady as she spoke, not wanting her tone or pitch to give her away.

Harriet's eyes widened. 'Well, aren't you trying to kick things up a notch?' She leaned forward and rested her chin on her hands, her eyes boring into Karen.

Karen felt the hairs on her arms stand up and wondered if she'd just made a terrible mistake.

'Tell me something,' said Harriet, 'did you follow the brief correctly? Only one of these is a lie, right? 'Cause I'm having a hard time believing that any of those statements are true for you, let alone two of them.'

Karen tried not to take offence. 'I did it right,' she said coolly.

'She's hard to read, isn't she?' Cosmo said cheerfully, seemingly unaware of the tension between the two women. 'But I think the lie is the catfishing one. It's too weird.'

'I ... I don't ... know,' said Kelly. 'Surely she didn't light a bushfire. Who would admit to that?'

Jean took Kelly's lead and jumped in. 'Okay, but if that's the lie then she physically assaulted someone. Breaking someone's fingers is hardly minor. Maybe she *did* start the fire, but it was an accident and she already owned up to it and paid the price?'

'Doesn't breaking someone's fingers sound a bit too ... mobster?' said Cosmo.

Karen was watching Harriet's face as the others tried to nut it out. She realised that this wasn't going to plan for Harriet. *Ah, she doesn't like that the attention is on me, does she?*

'Alright, whatever,' Harriet snapped, 'I think we might be debating this a bit too seriously.'

Bingo.

'Besides,' continued Harriet, 'I still don't think she followed the rules correctly.'

'Come on, Harriet!' said Victoria, apparently done with remaining quiet. 'If she said she did it right, then I'm sure she did.'

Karen was about to defend herself again but Harriet turned to Cosmo.

'Okay, you're up,' she said.

Even though Karen had been able to tell that Harriet was getting jealous, she still felt stung. With everyone else who'd had a turn, they'd stayed focused on that person until the others had worked out which one was the lie. But evidently the same consideration didn't apply for Karen. She felt silly and embarrassed for trying to take Harriet on. Victoria squeezed her hand under the table.

'No, no,' said Cosmo, looking uncomfortable as he seemed to catch on that the game had taken a nasty turn. 'I already did one earlier,' he said. 'Shouldn't we keep trying to work out Karen's?'

'Yes, but yours were all super innocent, Cosmo,' Harriet said, her voice becoming light again. 'I want to hear a *real* secret from you.'

Cosmo glanced worriedly at Karen, but she gave him a reassuring smile. 'Go for it,' she said, trying hard not to let Harriet know that she'd upset her.

Cosmo cleared his throat. 'Uh, okay. So, two truths and one lie, right? Let's see. One: I have a third nipple. Two: I get my eyebrows waxed. Three: One day I will make the person who is responsible for my brother's death pay for what they did.'

'Shit!' said Harriet. 'You really understood the assignment!'

Cosmo nodded. 'You said you wanted something good.'

'Okay,' said Harriet. 'First question, how did your brother die?'

Cosmo shook his head firmly. 'I cannot answer that because then you will know if that one is the truth or a lie.'

'Someone pull up his shirt,' said Jean, 'then we can just see if he has a third nipple.'

'No, no, there's no need!' said Kelly. 'I'm a beauty therapist, I can tell those eyebrows are totally all natural. That one is the lie.'

Karen chewed on the inside of her cheek. If Cosmo really had lost his brother, they were all being a bit too flippant about it. But she supposed he was the one who'd chosen to include it in a game.

As though she'd had the exact same thought, Harriet suddenly touched Cosmo's hand. 'Hey, sorry, we shouldn't be joking around like this when you've just shared that your brother passed. My brother is gone, too. Eddie. It's been years, but it never really gets easier, does it?'

Karen felt Victoria stiffen up again. She glanced sideways, trying to see if Victoria was okay. Maybe she'd been close to Harriet's brother?

'Thank you,' said Cosmo. 'It's nice to talk to someone who knows how I feel. I do miss him very much.'

'I totally get it,' said Harriet. 'My brother was like my best friend.'

Victoria tensed up even more and Karen realised she was shooting daggers at Harriet with her eyes.

Harriet seemed to become aware of Victoria's expression and, for a moment, her confident façade wavered, but then she composed herself. 'Let's move on,' she said, 'I'm bringing the mood down.' She smiled brightly at Victoria. 'Your turn, Vic!'

Victoria glared back at her. 'Nope. I'm not taking a turn.'

Harriet pouted. 'But everyone has to have a go!'

'Harriet, do you really think it would be a good idea for me to take a turn?' she said, raising her eyebrows.

Harriet's face changed and yet again that uncharacteristic look of uncertainty flashed across her features for just a moment. 'Actually, yeah … okay, never mind.' She picked up her drink and took a large sip, then put it down and zeroed in on Karen. 'You know what?' she said. 'I think I'll take another turn instead. Here goes.'

She took a beat. 'My eyes are blue. My hair is blonde and I recently slept with the husband of one of the women here tonight.'

CHAPTER SEVENTEEN

'Hello darling.'

Karen turned around to see her mother coming through the living room door. She was brushing water droplets off her coat and her mascara was running from the rain.

'Mum, I didn't think you'd get here.'

'Nell!' said Irene. 'We were just wondering if you were going to make it. How was bridge?'

'It was fine. Bethany and Toni bickered as always and then they each took turns complaining to me about the other.'

'See!' said Irene, turning back to Karen. 'Some women simply never stop behaving like school children! Arguing and gossiping about one another, it never ends.' She nodded her head at Nell. 'I was commiserating with Karen about those horrible women who gave her a hard time.'

'Oh, yes, that was terrible, wasn't it?' said Nell. She glanced at Karen and Karen noticed an inscrutable expression cross her face, but then it was gone, and she couldn't tell what it meant.

'How did you know about that, Mum?'

'Your sister told me.'

Now Karen was really confused. 'Ariella? But how did *she* know?'

The only person Karen had spoken to about the incident was Robert. And even then, she'd left out plenty of details. But she had a good reason to. Robert had been sympathetic but hadn't really asked a lot of follow-up questions, which had been a little hurtful.

Nell shrugged. 'I presumed you told her.'

'No. I didn't. What exactly did she say happened?'

'I can't remember exactly, just that there was some sort of silly game at one of those mums' nights out, and some of the women got carried away and were a bit nasty. Honestly, I don't know why you all insist on having those get-togethers just because your children go to school together. We didn't have to all go out *drinking* together to deal with motherhood when you were young.'

Karen gritted her teeth as she tried not to bite back.

'Alright, well,' Nell continued, 'I guess you'd better get this show on the road.'

Karen finished with her set up, then as Gail came through from the kitchen with cups of tea, she launched into her usual spiel.

'Ladies, I know most of you are already well aware of the incredible power of Tuffer Cleaning products, so I don't have to convince you about how worthwhile these products are, instead, I'm going to show you some of our newest items that are absolute household must-haves.'

She started passing products around, rattling off statistics and ingredients. Tuffer Cleaning was unique in that they had zero interest in competing against the all-natural, environmentally friendly products that were carving out a spot in the market these days, and instead touted their products as strong, old-fashioned chemicals that got the job done. And as much as Karen was all for taking care of the environment, she just couldn't go past how well these things actually cleaned. Sometimes you needed bleach and elbow grease instead of watered-down, jojoba-scented organic crap that could barely wipe away dust let alone lift mould or grease. The company line was to avoid all mention of environmental impact and to steer the conversation in a different direction if potential customers started asking about things like organic ingredients, to simply embrace the fact that these products were bloody potent – that's why they worked.

One of Karen's favourite jokes was to say, 'If you ever get fed up with your husband, Tuffer Cleaning products are the only ones I'd trust to truly clean up the crime scene!' It went over well with most of her audience members, who would laugh good naturedly about it. Karen found that a surprising percentage of women had fantasised about offing their partner at least once in their life after one too many toilet seats were left up or garbage bins weren't taken out. But she did sometimes get the odd look from people who thought the comment was a bit too dark.

After chatting about the various new products, the group all obediently followed Karen into Gail's bathroom for a demonstration on the tapware and then the tile grouting in the shower. They chorused the obligatory oohs and ahhs as she polished up the chrome taps and showed how the grouting changed from a murky brown to a bright white.

When the product demo was over, as expected, each of the ladies ordered one or two products to 'support Karen's little hobby'. They weren't amazing sales, but they were enough to make the time worthwhile. The only one who didn't purchase anything was her mother.

'You know how I hate those harsh chemicals; I'll only ever use Sylvie cleaning products,' Nell stage-whispered to Karen as she wrinkled her nose at the Tuffer bottles.

'I know, Mum, you don't have to tell me every time.'

'Well, it's just that the fumes from Tuffer could knock out a hippo!'

'Mum! It's okay, I get it. I really don't know why you worry about coming to these demonstrations, you don't have to.'

'Because I want to support my daughter, of course!'

Karen didn't bother pointing out the irony of her mother stating in front of her customers that she only used Tuffer's biggest competitor's product, while claiming she was there to support her business. There was no point.

Nell hung back while Karen packed up her display and Gail showed the other women out.

'Are you sure Ariella didn't tell you how she heard about my night out?' Karen asked as she stacked spray bottles and tubs back into her box.

'No. You must have told her about it.'

Karen huffed. 'Mum, I would know if I'd told her. Besides, Ariella and I don't really chat that often.'

'Well, how else would she know about it?'

'That's what I'm trying to figure out!'

'I don't understand why the two of you don't really chat. I talk on the phone with my sister almost every day.'

'We've always been different, Mum! We have different friends, we have different interests – you know this!'

'Being different doesn't mean you can't enjoy one another's company!'

Karen groaned. 'You know we don't click! I've always been closer to Doug than Ariella. Why are you suddenly pretending things have magically changed?'

Nell sniffed. 'Well excuse me for imagining my daughters might have finally grown up and started behaving like sisters for once.'

Karen thought back to that night again. What if Ariella had somehow been there? Maybe out with her own circle of friends? If she'd overheard the stupid game and watched as Harriet had turned on Karen. But if Ariella was there, why wouldn't she have come up and said something? Just because they weren't close, it didn't mean they would ignore one another if they happened to end up at the same bar on a Saturday night.

She pictured the karaoke bar, the groups at the other tables. But it was three weeks ago, she'd been drunk and it was dark. They were nothing but faceless figures.

*

Saturday night, three weeks ago

'Harriet!' shouted Kelly. 'You're supposed to try and hide the truths from the lie. We can all see that your hair is brown. So that means …' Kelly's eyes sparkled with excitement. 'Oh my God. You've slept with the husband of someone who was here tonight?' Her face changed. 'Wait … please tell me it wasn't my Daniel?'

Victoria interrupted. 'No,' she said, responding to Kelly, but making eye contact with Harriet, 'there is no way that she cheated with your husband. There is no way that she cheated with *anyone's* husband here tonight. She's just attempting to make a terrible joke.'

Harriet shrugged. 'What can I say, I've followed the rules of the game perfectly. So, if you guys have deduced which ones are the truth then …'

'Harriet, stop it,' said Victoria. 'This is going too far.'

'Well, good luck to you if you coaxed my husband to get it up for you,' said Jean, 'he's been having …' She paused and held up fingers to make air quotes, '"problems" in the bedroom. But the man refuses to try Viagra. Honestly, I don't understand why men get so sensitive about this kind of thing. He's in his fifties, it's perfectly reasonable that he might need a bit of extra help to get things working the way they used to.'

Cosmo coughed uncomfortably.

'Well, then it has to be one of the mums who left earlier,' said Kelly. 'There's no way she'd say it if they were still here.'

'Harriet, seriously, tell them you're making this up,' said Victoria.

Harriet stretched her arms out in front of her, lacing her fingers together. 'Here's the thing,' she said. 'I'm in an ENM marriage, so when I sleep with people apart from my husband, I'm not doing anything wrong. However, if that other person happens to be attached, then that's their responsibility. And maybe that person's wife would appreciate knowing the truth about their husband. Maybe I'm doing them a favour by giving them the chance to find out.'

'Right. And you didn't think about how *I* might feel hearing you say this?'

Harriet's smug demeanour wobbled. 'Vic, come on. You know what my life is like.'

'Yes. And you know how I feel about you.'

Perplexed looks were being exchanged around the table, but Karen was catching on. She'd felt all night like there was something more between Harriet and Victoria, and now it was making sense that Harriet was becoming jealous about Karen chatting so much with Victoria.

'Vic, do you really want to have this conversation here? In front of everyone?' Harriet said, a touch of desperation to her voice.

Victoria sat back and folded her arms. 'You're kidding, right? Considering your two truths and a lie game and all the secrets you're spilling. Now you're worried about airing our dirty laundry?'

'No! I just meant I didn't think you'd want to talk about it like this!'

'Sorry,' said Jean, leaning in. 'Are you two … more than just friends?'

Harriet's voice was nonchalant as she responded. 'Like I said, Malek and I are in an open relationship. Vic's my girlfriend.'

'No, I'm not,' Victoria snapped. 'Just because we sleep together on occasion doesn't mean you get to call me your girlfriend.'

'Come on, you know we're more than just fuck buddies.'

'You know what, screw it. I am going to have a turn of your stupid game.' Victoria picked up the drink in front of her and downed it in one.

Suddenly Harriet's face paled. 'Vic, wait, are you sure you want —?'

Victoria held up a finger. 'The third thing I'm going to say is true.' She held up a second finger. 'The first thing I said is a lie.' She paused, staring hard at Harriet and then she unfurled a third finger. 'I once got away with murder.'

CHAPTER EIGHTEEN

Saturday night, three weeks ago

Victoria was breathing hard and everyone else at the table had fallen silent. As Karen watched, Victoria's face was slowly sliding from rage to shock, as though she was just now realising the magnitude of what she'd said and was wishing she could pick the words up like Scrabble tiles and swallow them. Meanwhile, it was the first time Karen had seen Harriet completely lost for words.

It was Kelly who broke the silence. 'It's like one of those riddles,' she said. 'You know, like where there are two statues at a secret entrance and they say, "One of us always lies, the other always tells the truth" and you have to figure out what's the right question to ask them to figure out who is who.'

'Oh, yes,' said Cosmo, clearly attempting to match Kelly's upbeat tone. 'We have to work it out.'

'Except this isn't some riddle,' Jean retorted, her voice a little shrill. 'She's just said she killed someone. Shouldn't we ... do something?'

'Do something like what?' Kelly shot back. 'You want to perform a citizen's arrest? Come on,' she added, half-laughing, 'she clearly hasn't killed anyone! It's a trick with the two truths and a lie, she said the first thing she said was a lie. And the first thing she said was that the third thing was true. Which means she didn't kill anyone.'

Jean seemed relieved.

'Hang on …' Kelly said, and Karen could see her brain ticking over. 'But then, which two statements were true? What if the second thing she said was the lie?'

'Oh my God, this is hurting my head,' said Jean. 'I can't work it out.'

Victoria stood up, swayed a little, and then said, 'I'm sorry, guys. Just forget it. I wasn't being serious. I was only trying to top Harriet's stupid statements,' as she walked away from the table unsteadily.

Karen wasn't sure what to do. Should she go after Victoria, try to talk to her? Or would she prefer to be alone?

'So, she was only joking, right?' Cosmo said, looking concerned.

'Of course she was,' said Harriet, quick to compose herself. 'She's fine. She just needs a minute.'

Cosmo still appeared unsure, but then he leaned towards Karen. 'Uh, what does ENM mean?' he asked.

Harriet jumped in before she could answer. 'Ethically non-monogamous,' she said. 'Have you heard of polyamorous couples?'

Karen stood up. 'Bathroom break,' she mumbled. 'Be right back.'

She found Victoria at the other end of the bar, ordering herself another drink. Karen slipped in beside her. 'Are you okay?'

Victoria kept her eyes straight ahead. 'That was a complete clusterfuck, wasn't it?'

'A little,' said Karen. 'But to be fair, I think this entire night has been heading that way.'

'I can't believe she thinks it's okay to call me her girlfriend. She knows I don't agree with that. Being ENM is *not* the same as being poly – and even if it was, I've never wanted to be in a full relationship with someone who's also married.'

Victoria dipped her head and turned to face Karen. 'You're probably wondering what's the difference? Why am I okay to sleep with a married woman but draw the line at her calling me her girlfriend?'

'Um, no … I think I get it,' Karen said carefully. 'Maybe, if you keep it more casual like this, you feel like you can stop at any time? Like there's an escape exit.'

Victoria lifted her chin thoughtfully. 'Huh. That's actually not a bad way to explain it.' She turned back to accept her drink and tap her phone to pay. 'Sorry, I should have checked if you wanted one.'

'All good. I think I've had more than enough tonight.'

'You know, I don't even know why I'm upset. It's always been this way and she's never going to change. I knew what I was getting myself into, so why am I blaming her?'

Karen hesitated. She didn't really feel equipped to help Victoria with this, but she wanted to try.

'Maybe it's just reached the point where you're fed up?' she asked, trying hard to keep her voice gentle and even despite how incredibly drunk she was feeling.

'I guess,' said Victoria. 'Malek does know that there's something more between us than just sleeping together, by the way. I don't know if that makes it better or worse to be honest. Because the thing is, knowing isn't the same as being okay with it. It's more like he's just … accepted it because he knows he can't change her.'

Victoria took a large gulp of her drink and then looked at Karen. 'Do you think I'm an absolute arsehole? They have a kid, for God's sake. What the hell is wrong with me?'

'Nothing is wrong with you,' Karen said. 'You're just in a difficult, messy situation. But she's the one who's married, not you.'

'I have tried to end it. A few times. But Harriet is so … persuasive. She always gets what she wants. Every single time we get together, I think it'll be the last, but it's like … It's like I'm addicted to her.'

'Yeah, she doesn't come across as someone who takes no for an answer. Can I ask … how did it start?'

'It used to just be a casual thing in our university days. I think I always knew deep down she wasn't actually gay, that she was only having fun. But I convinced myself that one day she might come around. I mean, she's definitely bi, so I didn't see why she might not fall for me eventually. And we did come close to a relationship in our early twenties, that's why I get so angry with her for using the term "girlfriend" in such a thoughtless way now. Because I still remember the first time

I heard her say it back then – and it meant so much to me. But then something happened and things changed and … now I'm rambling. Please, you have to know, she hasn't always been this way, you know?'

Karen angled her head to the side. 'What do you mean?'

'I mean she didn't used to have this … this nasty streak, where she suddenly turns on someone. I swear most of the time, she's kind and caring and she looks out for other people. The funny thing is, when I first met her, I thought she needed to be a bit more selfish! Her family was pretty messed up. You heard her mention her brother, Eddie, earlier? Well, he's not dead.'

'Wait, what? She lied about her brother dying?'

Victoria twisted on her seat and crossed her legs, leaning on the bar with a sigh. 'I know, I know. It's awful. But did you notice the clever way she worded it? "My brother is gone too." She didn't say outright that he died.'

'Still, the implication was clear!'

'Exactly. And I know why she said it. Eddie had a drug overdose in the US, the same year Harriet got married while his parents were here for her wedding. And prior to that there was already this weird dynamic in their family where Harriet could never live up to the same standard as Eddie, nothing she did ever seemed to be good enough for her parents. He was on track to be a pro golfer, which is why the three of them moved to America, chasing his career. So, Harriet was this massive people-pleaser, always trying to get approval from others. But then when Eddie had his overdose, it got even worse. Her parents refused to leave his side.'

'Wow, okay, that does sound rough. But I can't get my head around Harriet being a people-pleaser. She's so sure of herself, so confident.'

'Yeah, well, she didn't used to be. I think there were a few different catalysts that made her change. There was her twenty-first birthday. She'd been dating this guy for about six months and he talked her out of organising any kind of celebration. She convinced herself that this meant he was planning a surprise party for her. She didn't let on that that's what she thought was happening until it was too late for me to do anything about it – otherwise I would have tried to save the situation by organising it myself.'

'Oh no,' said Karen, 'that's horrible.'

'Yep. It turned out the dude just didn't want her to plan something on the weekend of her birthday because he wanted to go down to Melbourne for the Grand Prix. I mean, I don't know why he didn't just tell her that and we could have arranged something for the following weekend. But I think he was just a bit of an arsehole. On top of that, she'd assumed her parents were going to turn up for her twenty-first too. This was before Eddie had the overdose. But they thought a golf tournament he was competing in was more important than her milestone birthday.

'Then after her wedding, it became clear her parents resented her for taking them away from their precious Eddie – I mean, the guy was an adult, he was the one who chose to take those drugs. I'm still furious with them for blaming the wrong child. Probably the final straw was that they wouldn't visit again a year later for Farrah's birth. I understand that they didn't want to leave Eddie, but his condition wasn't changing. He's never fully recovered. They should have been there for her. Harriet's been over to visit them and Eddie, but she's never taken Farrah with her. I think she really thought they would give in eventually and want to come and meet their granddaughter, but they're so single-minded, I don't know that they ever will.'

'Why didn't they all just move back here to Australia after Eddie had the overdose?'

'First they stayed because his sponsors were footing the bill for his medical treatment, thinking he would get better and be able to play again. Then later, I don't know, I guess they'd settled over there. Or maybe they were afraid to move him. Honestly, I don't know what goes through their minds. I think they're just awful parents who treated Harriet like crap.'

Karen shook her head. 'I can't imagine treating my son and my daughter differently to one another.'

But Victoria seemed to be lost in her own world. 'Sometimes I don't know why I haven't been strong enough to change things. But, you have to understand, the way she's acting tonight, that's not the real her. She can be loyal and protective and the way she's stood up for me over the years … I can't really explain it, but she saved me. I kind of owe her.'

Karen was about to ask what she meant by that, but Victoria charged on. 'To be honest, when she married Malek, I thought that was going to be the push I needed to let her go. To move on. I mean, she was still my best friend, but knowing that she'd chosen someone else to spend the rest of her life with meant I knew I had to shut down those feelings. Get back out there, meet someone else. Somehow, though, she drew me back in. Or maybe that's not true. Maybe I drew myself back in.' Victoria sniffed and turned away for a moment. 'I guess we better go back. I think it's probably about time we called it a night, really. I didn't even realise it's two in the morning.'

'Is it?'

Karen followed Victoria back to the group and as they threaded through the tables it occurred to her that they'd never even broached the subject of Victoria's two truths and a lie.

When they arrived at the table, everyone fell quiet. At first Karen assumed it was because they were uncomfortable after Victoria's earlier outburst, but it only took a moment to notice all eyes were on her. She looked from one face to the next. Cosmo's eyes were full of sympathy, Kelly was bright red, and Jean was fiddling nervously with the straw in her drink. Karen turned to Harriet last. There was a strange expression on her face. Somehow it was both a mix of satisfaction and regret all at once.

'What?' said Victoria. 'What's happened?'

Jean and Kelly glanced at one another. 'It's nothing,' said Kelly.

'Don't worry about it,' said Harriet. 'The girls just decided to play detective on my earlier two truths and a lie while you were gone. That's all.'

Victoria sat down, but Karen remained standing. 'Okay, but why is everyone staring at me?'

Cosmo glanced away while Jean shot a furtive look around the table and then said, 'Listen, Karen, maybe one of us should go for a walk with you … talk privately?'

Karen's mind was whirling. What on earth were they on about? Go and talk privately about what? But Victoria seemed to grasp what was going on faster.

She grabbed Karen's arm. 'Hang on,' she said. 'Just wait a second.'

'Look, I'm sorry,' Harriet said. 'Can we all please stop tiptoeing around this? We're adults and she deserves to know.' She eyed Karen. 'The girls asked me a few questions and they figured whose husband I slept with.'

Karen felt her heart begin to beat faster. She zoned out Harriet's voice, let the words wash over her. This couldn't be happening.

'Fuck, Harriet,' said Victoria, watching Karen nervously. 'You are joking, aren't you? This is a really bad prank, right?'

Harriet shrugged. 'No, it's not.' She faced Karen again. 'Karen, I slept with Robert. I'm sorry, honey, but like I said, isn't it better if you know the truth?'

Karen held very still. She opened her mouth to speak and then closed it again. She felt her stomach swirl and for a moment she thought she was going to throw up right there at the table. She'd had way too much to drink. *Way* too much.

And then she looked back at Harriet and that was it. That was the moment that bitch had the nerve to *smile* at her. Karen didn't even have time to think before she lunged across the table.

CHAPTER NINETEEN

Karen needed to work fast. She only had a small window to get this done before her next appointment. It wasn't ideal that Robert was working from home. She would have preferred a completely empty house. No chance of getting caught. But at the same time, she was confident that he wouldn't come out of the study for the next thirty minutes. She'd heard him start a conference call and they were never short.

When Karen had learned that every guest was required to bring one red velvet cupcake to the party, she'd thought it was the most ridiculous thing she'd ever heard. But now she was pleased because it provided her with an opportunity. She wondered if it mattered at which point she added the extra ingredient. With the butter and sugar at the beginning? With the flour and baking powder at the end? Should she google it to double-check? But she didn't have time for that. She needed to get it into the oven before she had to leave again.

Just before adding the extra ingredient into mixture, she wondered one more time if she really wanted to cross this line, but then she recalled that night again and her resolve hardened. She tipped in the whole bottle.

*

Saturday night, three weeks ago

Karen's chest was heaving. Every person at the table was staring right at her, each with a horrified expression on their face. She looked down at the drinks she'd knocked over when she'd made a grab for Harriet. Different coloured liquids from various cocktails were spreading across the table. There was a bright green stain on Cosmo's shirt and the front of Jean's dress had turned translucent from one of the spills. On the far side of the table, Harriet was completely unscathed.

And then a voice spoke in her head. *What did you just* do, *Karen?*

She scrambled back from the table, her head spinning, blood rushing in her ears. 'I'm ... I'm sorry,' she stammered. She turned and fled.

The moment she reached the bathroom she felt her stomach convulse and she just made it into one of the stalls in time.

A few minutes later she heard footsteps, the door of the stall was pushed open and someone squeezed in behind her, crouched down and started rubbing her back as she clutched the toilet bowl. Tears were streaming down her face and every time she threw up, the taste and smell only made her vomit more.

'You don't ... You don't have to ...' she tried to say in between retches. She glanced down and saw the bright pink stilettos. It was Victoria who'd come to check on her.

'It's fine,' Victoria said. 'I'll stay.'

Eventually, when it felt like she could finally breathe, Karen sat back and wiped her mouth with her sleeve.

'Here,' said Victoria, passing her a glass of water. 'Little sips.'

'Thank you.' Karen rinsed her mouth out and then looked up at Victoria. 'Why ... *how* did you stay in here with me like this?'

'Trust me, I've dealt with much, much worse. I work as a community corrections officer. Sorry, parole officer is probably what you would call it; community corrections is the new title. I've seen everything, babe. And a drunk woman throwing up in a toilet doesn't come close to topping the list.'

'I'm so embarrassed.'

'Why? You're not the one who was being a total jerk. Harriet was. And listen, I really don't think she slept with your husband. I think she's full of shit and she was just trying to cause trouble.'

'But you don't understand. Robert's been acting weird lately. Sneaking off, working late, that sort of thing. And he also hasn't really been that into me recently ... if you know what I mean.'

Victoria started to speak but Karen cut her off.

'I don't even know why I tried to dive across the table like that. I mean, what did I think I was going to do? Punch Harriet in the face? Jesus. I've never punched anyone in my life. I didn't mean to knock over all those drinks. God, they went *every*where.'

'Karen, it's fine. It was a huge shock for you when Harriet said that. No one was judging you for the way you reacted.'

'Yes, they were. I saw the looks on their faces. I must have seemed like a drunk, homicidal, jealous wife.' Karen put her face in her hands and then said quietly through her fingers, 'What if ...? What if I really did want to hurt her?'

'If you did want to hurt her, then that only proves you're human. Everyone has moments where they feel like they're capable of violence. The important part is whether you act on it. Yes, you lunged across the table – but then you came to your senses and you stopped. You pulled back. It was a momentary lapse in sanity because, for a second, you thought your world was falling apart. Trust me, I know the type of person who would actually go through with hurting someone, and it isn't you.'

'But you don't even know me.'

'I know enough. You're not the type.'

'I don't get it. Even if Harriet didn't sleep with Robert, if this was all simply to stir up trouble – why? What for? Who does that?'

'I'm not sure. But Harriet does stupid things sometimes. I'll talk to her. I'll get to the bottom of it.'

'Well, I still don't think it was a lie. I think it all makes sense. It explains Robert's dodgy behaviour lately.'

'Or maybe there's another explanation. We both know she was acting differently towards you just after your karaoke song was cancelled. It was like she suddenly had it in for you. I thought it was because she was jealous that I was chatting to you so much. But did something else happen? Did you guys argue about something?'

'No! I have no idea. Before that we'd been getting along great. She even stuck up for me with her friends when I put my foot in my mouth earlier. But you're absolutely right. Something changed. I did see her looking angry with something on her phone but I have no clue what it could have been.'

'Okay, don't worry, I'll get it out of her. But I still think it's a lie. Harriet has her moments, but that was too far, even for her. Anyway, they've all gone now, so you don't have to face anyone when you come back out. Cosmo was making sure everyone made it into an Uber. The whole lot of them were smashed.'

'I can't talk, I'm the one on the bathroom floor.'

'Yeah, well, who knows how many times the Uber will have to pull over for that lot on the way home.'

They sat in silence for a few minutes as Karen got her breath back.

'I guess we can't stay on the floor forever,' she said eventually.

Victoria patted her leg. 'I'll sit here with you for as long as you like.' She paused, then added, 'Hey … can I ask you something?'

'Yes,' said Karen.

'Who are you catfishing?'

'Oh. You …? You knew that one was a truth?'

'I'm good at reading people. I know you didn't start a bushfire. When you said that one, your eyelid twitched.'

Karen's head dropped. 'This is going to sound bad. Really bad.'

'Try me.'

'It's my daughter, Tallulah.'

Victoria let out a low whistle. 'Okay,' she said slowly. 'Will admit, it doesn't sound great.'

'Let me explain,' said Karen. 'Over the past couple of years, Tallulah's been pulling away from me more and more. We used to talk, but now I know nothing about what's going on with her. She became friends with Harriet's Farrah only late last year and I was really happy. Farrah seems like such a sweet kid. But then I saw something on Tallulah's Instagram. A photo of the two of them with a bong sitting on the table behind them. You could tell they'd both been smoking from the way they seemed in the photo. Look, I'm not completely naïve. I know that teens are going to experiment, and I know that in the scheme of things, pot isn't even that bad – I mean it's legal in most of America. But they're still only fourteen.

'And it worried me that Tallulah might be the one influencing Farrah to try these things – from everything I'd heard about her, Farrah seemed like the kind of kid who never got up to anything, whereas Tallulah was constantly getting into trouble. But when I confronted Tallulah, she denied it, acted like I was seeing things. She'd deleted the photo, so I had no proof. And then she blocked me on all of her social media accounts, so I no longer had any way of monitoring her. I was desperate to find a way to know what was going on in her life.'

'Ah. I see. So who are you pretending to be?'

'Just a young Instagram model. I figured if I set up a fake account with a pretty girl who was a bit older than Tallulah, it would be someone cool that she looked up to, so she'd accept a follow request from the account. I just used pictures from the internet to create her. You think I'm awful, don't you?'

'No, I don't. I think you're a mum who cares about her kid. But I do think you're going about it the wrong way. If your daughter finds out you're deceiving her, it's only going to make things worse.'

'I know. God, I feel so ashamed.'

'Don't. We all do things we regret.'

Karen hesitated. Once again, Victoria's words from earlier flashed through her mind. *I once got away with murder.* Was now the right time to ask her about that?

But then Victoria stood. 'Come on,' she said, 'let's get you home now too. Here, put your number into my phone so I can text you once I get the truth about Robert out of Harriet.'

*

Caramel, carnival, cartwheel.

Nope. It still wasn't working. She sat in the car and examined the house where she was meant to be doing the next product demonstration. Something about it was giving her a bad vibe. It had a kind of pretentious feel to it, but she couldn't put her finger on why. The house was Hamptons style with a cute swing chair on the front porch. But for some reason instead of looking sweet and inviting, the swing chair seemed somehow unnatural or fake, as though no one had ever sat on it and possibly no one would ever be allowed.

She thought about the cupcakes that she'd left baking at home, having given Robert strict instruction to take them out and leave them on the bench to cool as soon as the timer went off. At least it was handy that he could do that for her since he was working from home. But had she taken things too far?

Maybe.

But then she remembered the phone call she'd received from Harriet two days after the karaoke night.

'Karen, listen, I'm calling to apologise. I was totally out of line the other night and you need to know the truth. I lied about sleeping with Robert. I'm so sorry for scaring you like that.'

Karen had experienced a small kernel of hope, but it was quickly squashed. Because how could she possibly trust anything this woman was saying?

'Everyone thought it was easy to pick the lie because I said my hair was blonde,' Harriet had continued, 'but I was trying to be tricky. I'm naturally a blonde, I dye it dark, so that one was the truth. And that means the "sleeping with someone's husband" statement was the lie. You get it?'

Karen had stopped herself from snapping back, 'I don't really give a shit that you think you got clever with your two truths and a lie, because I still don't trust a word you're saying.' Instead, she had said, 'Thank you, Harriet, I appreciate the apology, but I still don't understand why you would say it in the first place.'

'That's a fair question. I've had some concerns recently about Farrah's friendship with Tallulah; I was worried they might not be so well suited. But during the karaoke night, I saw that Tallulah had left a nasty comment on a post Farrah had put up on Instagram. I got upset. That combined with being so drunk … I wasn't thinking straight. I switched into mama-bear protection mode, and I decided to take it out on you. First, it was just cancelling your song – I knew you were looking forward to singing. But then … Obviously, I know it's not an excuse for what I did next.'

Karen still wasn't convinced. 'What was the comment?' she asked. *I never spotted that one.*

'Don't worry about it,' said Harriet. 'I spoke with Farrah the next day and she assured me she'd sorted it out with Tallulah, and everything was fine again. I really am sorry.'

Karen wanted to believe that Harriet was being genuine, that her story was true, but it still all seemed so far-fetched. The conversation had ended with Harriet inviting Karen to her fortieth. 'Your husband is totally welcome too,' she'd said. 'It's fully catered, apart from the cute cake thing we're doing. I'll text you the instructions on that. Have a fun night out on me and let me make up for my bad behaviour.'

For the millionth time, Karen wondered why she hadn't just come right out and asked Robert directly about all of it. But deep down, she knew why: she was afraid of the answer.

She was about to brave the rain and get out of the car when she saw a woman walking up the driveway of the home. Presumably one of the guests for the product party. She was holding a coat over her head, trying to protect herself from the rain. There was something familiar about her ... Karen squinted her eyes, trying to see her through the rain-spattered windscreen. The woman turned as she took the stairs to the front door and Karen bit her lip as her face slid into place in her memory.

Shit. Amanda, the woman who'd decided that Karen was a victim-blamer when she'd become emotional about the news story of the young girl down in Melbourne. Karen had been trying to avoid all school parents since the karaoke night; who knew what rumours were being spread among the mums after everything that had happened? She glanced down the street and saw two more women walking towards the house, huddled together under an umbrella. One was Jean, and the other was a woman she didn't know, but she did recognise her from school.

This was going to be a nightmare. Amanda was probably still furious with her for the way Harriet had taken her side that night. And the rest of them must surely know about the way the night had ended, with Karen knocking all those drinks everywhere like she was some sort of deranged psychopath about to attack Harriet.

How could she possibly stand up in front of these women and deliver a professional presentation? None of them would take her seriously. At least she would have a drink in her hand and Robert by her side when she faced them tonight at the party. Plus, Victoria had assured her she'd have her back.

Her phone rang on the seat next to her, making her jump. She snatched it up.

'Hello, Karen speaking.'

'Mrs Kingsworth, this is Angela from Apple Hills College.

Unfortunately, we need you to come in. There's been an incident with Tallulah.'

Karen didn't even bother to ask what it was about. There was always something with Tallulah. It was as though she was attempting to break some kind of record for after-school detentions.

'Of course, it's not a problem, I'll be there as soon as I can.'

Karen hung up and looked back at the house. She could always call Robert, ask him to go and find out what had happened with Tallulah.

Fuck it.

She found the number of the party's host and tapped out a quick message to her. *Sorry, a family emergency has come up and I have to cancel today.*

Then she turned the engine back on, put the car into drive and took off from the kerb. In the rear-view mirror, she could see more women arriving for a sales presentation that was no longer going to take place.

This wouldn't bode well for future word of mouth.

*

Rick

Birch Avenue

Rick often wondered what it would be like to be married to Harriet. Would it be a turn-on that she was into chicks? Or would you feel emasculated? On the one hand, he'd found it pretty damn sexy when she'd started kissing that cute bartender at their work Christmas drinks, so maybe life with Harriet would be a hell of a lot of fun. But on the other hand, would you wonder if it meant you weren't enough for her?

Rick had tried to make a move on her once but she'd shot him down, which was a bit insulting really. What? He wasn't good enough for her? Apparently, though, he was good enough to chauffeur her around to all their appointments. And now he was stuck waiting for her because she'd gone off between jobs and expected him to then pick her up again before they headed to the last house. But she was nowhere to be seen at their planned meeting place. He'd give it two more minutes and if she didn't show, he was leaving without her.

Maybe the timing was off the first time he hit on her. Maybe he should try things on with her again one of these days. Maybe he needed to be a little more persuasive. She probably liked guys who were a bit more assertive. Yeah, next time he tried, he'd be … not forceful, but more commanding. That kind of thing would turn her on and she wouldn't tell him no with that sneer on her face that made him feel like a dick.

And if she did tell him no, maybe he'd tell her that wasn't the right answer.

CHAPTER TWENTY

Karen was surprised to find that she was feeling relaxed as she sat next to Malek outside the principal's office, waiting for them to be called in. Was it because Tallulah had been in trouble so many times now that Karen no longer felt nervous about seeing the principal. Or was it because she was enjoying chatting to Malek?

He wasn't what she had expected at all. She'd only ever seen him in the distance or said a brief hello in passing. And she'd always thought he had a bit of an intimidating, perhaps even arrogant, air about him. But now she realised that was quite wrong. She'd perceived him to be intimidating because he was tall and broad, and had that assured ex-professional sports player stance about him. Everyone knew he'd almost been a huge rugby star until he'd been injured. That was probably why she'd always felt like he was someone familiar. But now that she was chatting to him up close, she realised he had a calm, gentle vibe about him. He was friendly and chatty and sweetly nervous about facing the principal. Not at all what she imagined of Harriet's husband.

Actually, if she'd never seen Malek around the school before and she was going to guess who Harriet would be married to, she would have described a slick, well-dressed investment banker, barking orders into a phone and clicking his finger at a secretary for a double-shot espresso. For some reason that seemed to fit with her image of Harriet's partner more.

As she sat there, joking about being sent to the principal's office, she thought back to Victoria describing the guilt she felt being the other woman in this man's marriage. Karen had to admit, she was feeling somewhat sad for Malek right now too. Malek didn't deserve this. Even if he was fully aware of what was going on, that didn't make it okay.

She thought again about Harriet's 'prank' admission: that she'd slept with Robert. And how Robert was continuing to behave strangely, heading out at unexpected times or getting home late.

Malek smiled at her and a thought appeared: *How would you feel if I slept with* your *husband, Harriet?*

The moment it crossed her mind, her hands turned clammy. What the hell was she doing? Thinking about sleeping with this lovely man next to her while they were chatting about their daughters getting into trouble. Besides, even if she were willing to do something like that, something drastic to get back at both Harriet and Robert, who the hell was she to assume that Malek would have any interest whatsoever in her?

The door next to them opened and Mrs Norris poked her head out. 'Mr Osman, Mrs Kingsworth, you can both come in now.'

Karen wiped her sweaty palms on her pants. *Pull it together, Karen.*

*

They drove for several minutes in silence before Karen finally spoke.

'What did you do to upset Farrah?'

'How are you even asking me that? She's my *friend*. Didn't you see me standing up for her in there?'

'I saw you lying, yes. And I get that it sounds like she *did* push you first … But what I'm wondering is what it was that *you* did to make her push you.' Karen didn't mean to sound so combative, it was just that Tallulah always managed to bring it out in her. She didn't seem to be able to control her tone when it came to her daughter, even when she was hating the harsh, judgemental, nasally whine to her own voice.

'Congratulations, Mum. Victim blaming again. Bet you feel really good about yourself.'

'What do you mean, *again*?'

'Mara's been telling everyone how her mum came home after your mums' night out and said how sexist you are; how you think it's a girl's responsibility not to get raped instead of the guy's responsibility to, you know, *not rape.*'

They were coming up to a red light and Karen hit the brakes harder than she'd intended. They were both jolted slightly in their seats as they screeched to a stop. Karen gripped the steering wheel tightly. Thank God for decent tyres, especially in this weather.

'Learn how to drive, Mum,' Tallulah muttered under her breath, but Karen barely heard her. She couldn't believe that one of the women had gone home after that night out and told her bloody *family* about their conversation – including her fourteen-year-old daughter. Who does that? And the woman damn well knew that what Karen had said had been taken out of context, that she'd been drunk and emotional and unable to articulate her point.

'Tallulah,' said Karen, trying hard to keep the frustration out of her voice. 'I absolutely did not say that. Mara's mother is mistaken. She's twisted my words.'

'Whatever. Seems to fit with you assuming I did something to get pushed.'

'Come on! You know that Farrah never got into any kind of trouble before the two of you became friends, whereas you constantly did. How can you possibly expect me not to assume that this is about your influence on her?'

'Maybe because you're *my* mum, not Farrah's. And so I kinda thought maybe you'd be on your daughter's side by default.'

Karen let out a groan of frustration. 'Tallulah! This isn't about taking sides. I just want to understand what happened. I appreciate that you tried to do something good for your friend by covering for her, but sometimes the better thing to do is to tell the truth, the whole story, and whatever it is, we can all work it out together.'

'There's nothing to work out! It's sorted. Farrah and I are fine. She wants me to come over early this afternoon to help them set up for the party.'

'After the two of you were in trouble for fighting today? Do you really think that's wise? I was thinking maybe you should skip the party. Maybe I should, too.'

'Mum! No! Farrah's counting on me to be there.' Now Tallulah let out her own groan of frustration. 'Do not ruin this for me!'

'Calm down! It would help your case if you would just tell me what happened.'

'There's nothing to tell.'

They pulled into the driveway and Karen sighed as she checked the time. 'There's no point in me coming in. I'm going to have to turn straight back around and pick up your brother. Dad's inside, he's working from home today.'

'Can't you drive me into the garage? I'm going to get wet running up to the front door.'

'Tallulah! It's literally three steps. I need to go and get Ralph.'

'Okay, fine. But when you get back, I need a lift over to Farrah's.'

Karen clenched her jaw. 'I haven't even said if you can go.'

'Well, if you don't take me, I'll call an Uber. I'm going.'

'Right, and how will you pay for an Uber?'

Tallulah opened the car door and got out, swinging her school bag onto her shoulder. 'With your credit card,' she said as she slammed the car door shut.

Karen felt like screaming as she reversed out of the driveway.

*

Karen had forgotten her bloody umbrella again, but she couldn't wait in the car because traffic had been bad and she'd parked miles away, so Ralph wouldn't know where to find her if she didn't walk up to the school.

Once again, though, it seemed there was a chivalrous man ready to rescue her from the perils of frizzy hair and damp clothes. This time it was Cosmo who motioned for her to join him under his umbrella.

'Thanks,' she said. 'You'd think I'd remember an umbrella by now considering how many days it's been raining.'

'Maybe you're just optimistic,' suggested Cosmo. 'It has to stop eventually, doesn't it?'

'Ha,' said Karen. 'I'm not feeling particularly optimistic lately.'

Cosmo rubbed his chin. 'That's no good.'

'It's fine,' said Karen, 'no big deal.'

Cosmo hesitated, looking like he wasn't sure if he should say what he was thinking. 'Listen,' he said, 'I've been wanting to say to you, I didn't like the way you were treated at that karaoke night. Harriet's been great to me since I moved up here, inviting me out and introducing me to people – but I'm a bit wary of her now after seeing the way she spoke to you. I'm sorry that happened and I'm sorry I didn't speak up at the time.'

Karen shrugged. 'Look, it is what it is, but that's nice of you to say. That reminds me,' she said. 'I hope you were able to get that stain out of your shirt? I did mean to offer to pay for the dry-cleaning but haven't had the chance.'

Cosmo shook his head firmly. 'Do not worry about it at all.'

Karen paused and then said, 'You're right to be wary of her though. Remember how she empathised with you about your brother by saying that her brother was gone too? Later Victoria told me that her brother is still very much alive. I mean, he's unwell, but he's certainly not dead. I just thought you should know, because I don't think it was right of her to lie to you about that.'

Cosmo's face darkened. 'Thank you for telling me,' he said. 'You're right, it's not okay for her to lie about that. In my family, that would be considered extremely disrespectful ... not to mention dangerous. You can't tempt fate like that. I'm not saying I'm particularly superstitious, but there is a line you don't cross.'

'Sorry, I shouldn't have upset you.'

'No, I'm glad you told me. You'll have to excuse me; I can see Serge coming. I promised him I'd give him a hand carrying his woodwork project back to the car.'

*

'The sheep don't have names, but I've called one of the axolotls Jerry and the other one is Bob. Get it? It's from that TikTok. Anyway, when I go online with Benji tonight, we're going to build a new mod for them and then we're going to see if we can ...'

Karen was letting the words wash over her. She always tried hard to listen when Ralph chatted to her about Minecraft, but she never understood half of what he was saying. So, inevitably, her mind would drift off and she would find herself thinking about something else, like the grocery shopping list or the admin she needed to get done or, as was the case this time, Tallulah, and she would nod along and say, 'Mmm, hmm, hmm,' every now and then and hope that she wasn't meant to be answering any specific questions.

As she pulled back into the driveway for the second time and hit the remote for the garage door, the tone of Ralph's voice suddenly changed.

'Mum, she looks *mad*.'

'What? Who?'

'Tallulah,' said Ralph, pointing to the front porch. Karen turned and saw her daughter sitting by the front door, her arms crossed and her face like thunder.

'What the —? Why is she sitting outside?'

By the time Karen had parked in the garage and was getting out to ask Tallulah what had happened, her daughter was already storming past her and into the house, where she hurled her bag across the room.

'Tallulah!' she called out. 'Wait! What happened? Why were you stuck outside?'

Tallulah spun around and went back through to the internal door that connected the entrance way of the house with the garage. 'Oh, I don't know, Mum? Maybe because *you left me locked out and Dad wasn't home.*'

'But ... but he was working here. And even if he went out, why didn't you use your front door key?'

'Argh!' Tallulah screamed. 'Because I forgot my key today!'

She stormed off again and Karen was left standing by the car, wondering why the hell it was her fault that Tallulah had forgotten her own house key.

Ralph climbed out of the car with a nervous look on his face. He stood still for a moment as though trying to think of something to say to help, but then simply said, 'Can I go online with Benji, now?'

Karen shrugged. She couldn't be bothered checking if he had homework to do first. 'Sure,' she said. 'Go for it.'

'Yes! Thanks, Mum, you're the best.'

At least one kid still liked her.

But where the hell was Robert?

Harriet

The two of you could almost have been friends, but you sure put an end to that, didn't you? So, is she capable of murder?

You knew from the start that Tallulah might be a bad influence on Farrah. There were rumours that she was always in trouble, often being summoned to the principal's office. Even so, when you invited Karen out, your intentions were wholly innocent. You just wanted to get to know her. It was important to find out if Tallulah was going through a rebellious phase or if Karen was a bad mother.

You know all about bad mothers, don't you?

Bad mothers who make their daughters feel unloved, who make their daughters feel less than, make them feel like second-class citizens who could never live up to the standard set by their brother.

But everything changed when you saw the comment from Tallulah on Farrah's Instagram post during the karaoke night. A photo of Farrah, her cheeks pink, a huge smile on her face, a mischievous spark in her eyes. The caption read: Okay people, time to vote. I have a crush … so do I tell this guy how I feel? Or keep it to myself? What if he doesn't like me back!!

Below the photo, there was a comment from Tallulah: Farr, no. Don't embarrass yourself. He is way out of your league. *It was followed with several laughing face emojis.*

The comment was bitchy and uncalled for.

You could have spoken to Karen about it. Told her to pull her daughter into line. But what if she didn't think it was that bad? What if she had that attitude some parents have of 'let them sort it out themselves'?

So instead, you wanted to teach Karen a lesson.

You don't mean to turn on people. When you start out nice, friendly, it's genuine. It's real. People often think you're fake – you're not. It's just the impression that you give off. But once they cross you, you can go cold on them in an instant. And yes, sometimes you lose control, sometimes your body kicks into bitch mode and you're thinking, Stop, stop it. You're being too mean, you're going too far.

But at the same time, another voice is in there. This voice is quiet. It's vindictive. It whispers in your ear: Keep going, Harry. They deserve it.

You hate that voice.

You love that voice.

Hey, babe? You're losing focus. You need to get back to the point of all of this, you need to figure it out. Was it Karen?

Concentrate. Think about the moments before the blow to your head.

Chocolate. Earlier … you said you thought you could taste chocolate. Was that real? Or was that your imagination?

You lick your lips and your mouth is dry but … is that a fleck of a cake crumb on your bottom lip? You were right! It is chocolate. Chocolate cake! When were you eating cake?

It comes to you. You see the cupcake in your hand. You see your fingers peeling back one side of the red wrapping, ready to take a bite. But then something happened after you bit into that cupcake, even before you got hit from behind.

Your eyes started to water. There was a scalding sensation at the back of your throat. Your breathing started to constrict. That cupcake, it tasted wrong, didn't it? Like chocolate but also like something else. There was something off about it.

So what does that mean? Was it just a bad cupcake or something more sinister? Was there a special ingredient baked into it? Did someone try to poison you? It sounds ridiculous, but you have to consider every possibility.

The burning. That's the giveaway. The way your throat felt like it was being scorched from the inside out. If the cake was just bad, it would have tasted off and it might have made you gag – but this was different.

Maybe it really was poisoned.

What was the special ingredient? Rat poison? Some kind of household chemical? Crushed up prescription meds? It would have to be a high concentration to elicit such a strong reaction so fast.

Karen has a cleaning business. The cleaning products she sells are decent stuff. Strong. Potent. Is that the kind of stuff you could use to poison someone? Probably. That means Karen has motive and means. Where did the cupcake come from? Did it come from Karen?

Now you have two murder weapons: poison and some kind of blunt instrument. So where does that lead you? Does that mean this murder was somehow both premeditated and a crime of passion? Or did someone really want to make sure they finished the job? Perhaps the plan was to weaken you with the poison first so that you wouldn't see them coming when they hit you from behind? Or maybe the cupcake was just a fail-safe in case they didn't get the opportunity to attack.

God, this is so frustrating. What if you don't work it out in time?

No. You must know. Do not let go until you've figured it out.

Who's next on the list?

Victoria.

Victoria, the best friend you adore. You know full well that she's still in love you, and you keep sleeping with her even though you know it hurts her to feel like she's second best to Malek.

But there's no way Victoria could ever hurt you.

SUSPECT THREE

the best friend

CHAPTER TWENTY-ONE

Victoria

The room was still pitch black thanks to her full-length block-out blinds, but her body clock told her the sun had begun to rise. On a clear day, if Victoria was to roll up the blind and then stand in the left-hand corner of the room on her tiptoes with her neck strained to the side, she could just make out a sliver of the ocean and watch it turning pink and orange as the sun rose above it. But she wouldn't do that right now. She wanted to keep the room still and dark. She didn't want to break the spell that was cast by the sounds of steady breathing from the woman sleeping next to her. Besides, her ocean view would be nothing but a grey smear today. She could still hear the heavy rain falling; it hadn't stopped all night.

She lifted the covers carefully, slid out of bed and touched her feet lightly to the floor. The steady breathing remained the same. She crept from the room, down the hall and into the kitchen. She considered switching on the coffee machine now, staying up, starting her day. She would kill for a long black. But at the same time, she didn't want the night to be over. She just needed a moment to herself and then she would sneak back into bed and pretend to be sleeping.

Sometimes she hated how she let herself feel this way. It was foolish. She knew full well that Harriet was never going to change. That she was never going to choose Victoria over Malek. And would Victoria even want her to? Would she want to break up a family? Some days her desire for Harriet was so strong that she thought, *Yes. Yes, I would break up their family so I can have her all to myself. And would it really be that big of a deal? People got divorced all the time. Farrah was a teenager now, she'd cope with her parents splitting up.*

But other days she questioned if she even still loved Harriet. What if she was mistaking love for something else altogether? Sometimes she wondered if the basis of their relationship was more like Stockholm syndrome than true love. Obviously, not in the literal sense! Harriet had never kidnapped her, but she did have a hold over her – a shared secret from their past that bound them together. Harriet held the power to completely unravel Victoria's life if she wished.

Not that she would. For all of Harriet's flaws, she would never do something to intentionally hurt her. She might occasionally come across as selfish and hard, but Victoria knew that, at heart, Harriet was a good person, that she cared about the people who were important to her. It was just that she was overly protective, and she'd been hurt one too many times in the past. That was why she'd developed a tough exterior. But Victoria had seen her softer side enough times to know that it was there. There was the time when Victoria had had her heart broken by a girlfriend who'd decided to move overseas. Victoria had been devastated. Then one day she'd come home from one of her uni lectures to find her dorm room filled with bright yellow sunflowers. Bunch after bunch had been placed around the room. The note from Harriet said, *Something to brighten your world until you're ready to find your own sunshine again.*

Sunflowers had been Victoria's favourite from that day onwards.

Victoria crept back down the hallway to her bedroom and paused at the doorway to listen. Still nothing but the sound of deep breathing. Harriet was fast asleep. God, Victoria envied how deeply Harriet could sleep. Victoria couldn't remember the last time she'd woken in the morning and felt well rested. Her GP had recently given in and prescribed more powerful sleeping tablets, but while they knocked her out, they didn't leave her feeling refreshed. The sleep she got from sleeping tablets was more like being under anaesthetic and left her feeling groggy and dry-mouthed. The doctor had pushed once again for her to talk to someone – a psychologist or a counsellor – to explore the reasons behind her insomnia. But Victoria gave her the same old story: *My job is pretty high stress. Lots of worries on my mind.* Victoria already knew why she couldn't sleep. She knew exactly what was at the root of it all. But she couldn't tell her doctor that. The Hippocratic Oath didn't protect you if you confessed to murder.

There were days, though, when she thought she might just blurt out the truth to someone. Where the weight of the guilt and fear that someday her past would catch up with her were too much. On those days, it felt like her past was clawing its way up the inside of her throat, desperate to be free. That was probably why she'd lost control of her senses at that karaoke night and risked everything by telling those two truths and a lie.

She went into the room and moved closer to the bed, then stopped once again to watch Harriet. Her hair was across her face, a strand stuck to her bottom lip. With her eyes closed you could really appreciate just how long her lashes were. All natural. Other women had always hated her for that. Asleep like this, you could almost believe Harriet was the person she used to be. The sweet girl Victoria had met in her first year of university. The girl who still thought her parents were going to come through for her, even though they'd already let her down, time and time again. The girl who hadn't yet had her heart broken by the stupid boy who ruined her twenty-first birthday. Or the girl who hadn't yet been forced to take control on the worst night of Victoria's life.

That was the girl Victoria had fallen in love with. She was the one that kept Victoria coming back for more, even though she knew she should put her foot down and say no. That she should say, 'Stop using me. I'm worth more than that. I *deserve* more than that.'

Her eyes travelled down from Harriet's face to her neck. The covers were just below her arms and as she watched the rise and fall of Harriet's chest, for just a moment, a strange sensation came across her. Victoria saw herself yanking the pillow out from underneath Harriet's head then holding it down over her face, pressing and pushing until Harriet fell still and quiet.

Victoria's skin turned cold and she shuddered. Where the fuck had that come from? Why would her mind create such a sickening image? 'Intrusive thoughts' – that's the term she'd learned on TikTok for horrendous things that jumped into your brain unbidden. Things that you would never, ever actually do. Things that you would never seriously consider doing.

But what if it was different for Victoria? Because she'd already killed once before, hadn't she? And maybe once you've taken a life, it's in your blood. Maybe those intrusive thoughts became something much more sinister. Maybe deep down inside, there was a part of her that knew she was capable, that knew that if Harriet was gone, everything could be different. Victoria would finally be able to move forward with her life.

Stop it!

This was ridiculous. One horrendous mistake from her past did not define her. And she could never hurt Harriet. Never.

Victoria stared at her best friend's sleeping form. Harriet was going to be a part of her life forever – whether she wanted it or not.

She felt a tightening in her chest, like someone had wrapped their arms around her and were squeezing and squeezing. Oh God, she was going to be trapped in this toxic cycle forever, wasn't she?

Harriet shifted in her sleep and the tightening around Victoria's chest released. She took in a few deep breaths and then tiptoed back around to her side of the bed, climbed in under the covers and closed her eyes.

*

Victoria felt an arm snake its way around her waist under the sheets and then glide up to cup one of her bare breasts, but she kept her eyes closed. Her lips twitched as she tried not to smile, but she remained motionless, her breathing even as she pretended she was still asleep. The hand massaged her breast and a moment later she felt soft lips on the back of her neck. She couldn't stop the involuntary shudder of pleasure in response.

'I *knew* you were awake.'

Victoria rolled over to face Harriet.

'Yeah, well, as long as I kept my eyes shut and faced the other way, I could pretend you were someone else.'

'*Victoria!*'

'What? You can't blame me for having fantasies. You're the one who's married to someone else. Why should I stay faithful in my imagination?'

'Who were you fantasising about anyway?'

'Sam Kerr.'

'Well, why aren't you in bed with her, then?'

'Jesus, Harriet. You *know* who Sam Kerr is. Captain of the Matildas. *And* plays for Chelsea. Bit difficult for me to be in bed with someone who I've never actually met.'

'Oh … right, sorry. I knew that name was familiar. You know I don't really pay attention when you make me watch the soccer. I much prefer watching *you* watch the soccer. You get so passionate, it's gorgeous. Anyway, I'm glad you don't know her personally, I would have been jealous.'

214

'You can still be jealous. I also have a crush on Yumi my Pilates teacher.'

'No, you don't. If you had a crush on her, you would have asked her out by now.'

'Not true. I haven't asked her out because she's not gay. Also a bit of a barrier.'

'I'm not gay and I sleep with you.'

'You're different. You're in an entire sexuality category all of your own.'

'Ooh, I like that.'

'It wasn't meant to be a compliment.' Victoria sat up and turned away, suddenly irritable. 'We should get moving, we both have work.'

A finger ran down the length of her spine.

'We still have a little time. Why are you cranky? Come back and let me cheer you up.'

Victoria looked back at her friend. 'You know, Harriet, you're not as irresistible as you think you are.' She didn't really mean that, though. Harriet had that classic Hollywood kind of beauty that meant she really could get away with anything, and she knew it.

Harriet lightly traced her fingertips up Victoria's back again, circled around her shoulders, stroked her neck, ran them down one arm and then the other. Victoria shivered with pleasure.

'Yes, I am,' said Harriet. 'You told me so yourself last night. Those were your exact words. You said, "Harriet, you are irresistible."'

Victoria laughed despite herself. 'I did not!'

'Of course you did. I distinctly remember. I mean, it was hard to hear with your thighs against my ears and you were moaning a lot, but trust me, I got the gist. Lie back down, let me show you.'

There was a low rumble of thunder from outside and the sound of the falling rain increased in intensity. Victoria allowed herself to be pulled back into bed.

CHAPTER TWENTY-TWO

'You're not going to flirt with Robert tonight at the party, are you?'

Harriet sipped her coffee and licked her lips. 'Who?'

Victoria rolled her eyes. 'Stop it, you know who I'm talking about. Karen's husband. She's still not completely convinced that your ridiculous prank wasn't true. You really did a number on her.'

Victoria picked up one of the cupcakes in front of her and dipped a spatula in a container of Betty Crocker icing. She was trying to work fast to get this done so she could leave for work, although she couldn't help noticing that Harriet was taking her time with her toast and coffee.

'Is that for tonight? You're not meant to ice it.'

'It's fine, I know what the instructions are. I'm icing the rest of the batch and leaving the one for your party un-iced. What's the deal with the BYO cupcake anyway?' Victoria smoothed the icing across the top of the cake in her hand, placed it into a container and picked up the next one.

'Haven't you seen pull-apart cakes before? You put a heap of cupcakes together into a shape and then ice the whole thing so it looks like one big cake, but then instead of having to cut pieces, people just pull out a cupcake. I'm going to have the caterers arrange them into a giant 40.'

'Why not just have the caterers make the cupcakes?'

'Because this is a nice personal touch, having all the guests contribute. And because I read it in a story about Beyoncé doing it that way for her birthday.'

'You think all her famous guests each baked their own cupcakes? No way. Anyway, don't change the subject on me. You never answered my question about Robert.'

Harriet at least had the good grace to appear chastised. 'Oh, right, him. No, of course I won't flirt with him tonight. I'll be on my best behaviour. Besides, I called Karen and apologised like you wanted me to. I told her it was a joke and I invited them both to the party. I don't know what else to do!'

'I still don't get why you said it in the first place.'

'Come on, we were blind drunk and we *all* said some things we shouldn't have,' said Harriet, giving her a meaningful nudge.

Victoria winced. 'Point taken. God, why did you have to start that game?'

'Because it's usually good for a bit of fun. More importantly, why would you take a risk like that? You could have come up with literally anything else for your two truths and a lie.'

'I don't know! Like you said, we were all drunk. I know it was stupid ... I think maybe I was feeling a little self-destructive.'

'A *little* self-destructive? Victoria, you could lose everything, *everything*, if someone found out what we did.'

'You mean what *I* did. And maybe I deserve to lose everything.'

'Stop it. No, you don't.'

'I just feel like I've been living on borrowed time for the past twenty years. Like it's constantly hanging over me and any day, someone is going to knock on that door and tell me I'm going to jail.'

'Vic, no. Apart from you, there is only one person in the world who knows what happened that night, and I'm not planning on telling anyone. Well, as long as you don't *really* piss me off one day.' Harriet gave her a sly grin.

'Harriet! That's not funny.'

'Okay, I'm sorry, I didn't mean it. Bad joke.'

'Not just a bad joke, that's a horrible thing to say. My life is literally in your hands and it's not fair to joke about that. Do you realise I struggle to sleep every single night? Or that I have this constant sense of paranoia? Even when that dad from your school mentioned he was from Queensland I felt this jump in my gut.'

'Vic, that's ridiculous. You can't be scared of everyone from the entire state of Queensland.'

'You think I don't know that? It's ridiculous, but it's like I said, I'm always waiting for the past to catch up with me. I hate it, it's like I'll never be able to relax completely.'

'Well, no need to worry about Cosmo, anyway. I don't think he is from Queensland.'

'What do you mean?'

'I mean I ran into him recently and I was asking him some questions about which part of Brisbane he was from. He got nervous and couldn't answer and eventually mumbled something about having only been there a really short time and moving around a lot. Weird, but whatever. Maybe he has some sort of dodgy past. Besides, if you're that worried about mixing with anyone from Queensland, maybe it's not such a good idea for you to be so friendly with Karen. Her brother, Doug, lives up there and he's a cop.'

'Seriously?'

'Yes. So maybe stop messaging her so much.'

'I'm not messaging her that much! I just got along better with her than I usually do with your other mum friends, and she seemed like she was going through a tough time with her daughter, so we've been chatting.'

'Yeah, well, what if the reason she's being friendly with you is 'cause she's scoping you out as a suspect for her brother?'

'Harriet! Stop making jokes like that. Don't make fun of me.'

'I'm sorry, I'm sorry, I was just trying to show you how ridiculous you're being. Nothing is ever going to happen. It's been almost twenty years. Besides, I was being mean because I'm jealous. I don't like you messaging another woman so much.'

'Is that why you made up that story about Karen's husband? Because the two of us were getting along so well and you got jealous?'

'What? No! Of course not. I told you, I was drunk, that's it.'

Victoria hesitated for a moment before asking her next question. It had been playing on her mind since that night but she had never found the right time to ask. Now was probably as good a time as any, since they were already on the subject.

'Harry,' she said, 'there's something I've been meaning to ask you about that night. When Cosmo told his two truths and a lie, why did you say that your brother was —?'

'I know, I know,' Harriet said, holding her hands up, a look of defiance on her face. 'Obviously I shouldn't have implied that he was dead, but for Christ's sake, he may as well be.'

Victoria raised her eyebrows and for a moment Harriet held her gaze, but then her shoulders slumped.

'Sorry, that sounded awful, didn't it? I don't mean that. It's just … you know how I get when it comes to Eddie.'

'Of course I know.'

'I really am sorry. And I do appreciate that you didn't out me to everyone at the time.'

Victoria turned away to place the lid on the container of iced cupcakes. Should she admit that she actually had outed Harriet to Karen that night? Maybe not right now, not when Harriet was already jealous of Karen.

She turned back and stepped in close to Harriet, placing her hands on Harriet's arms. 'It's okay, you don't have to apologise to me, I was just … shocked. Although maybe you owe an apology to Cosmo. I don't think it was right that you lied and said you understood how he felt.'

'But we don't even know which of his statements were truth or lies! So maybe his brother hasn't died either. In which case, no harm, no foul.'

'Harriet, it's still concerning. You haven't mentioned your brother in such a long time. Has something else happened … have you heard from your mum or dad recently?'

Harriet shook her head. 'Of course I haven't. But I saw that Malek tried to secretly invite them. For tonight. It was sweet of him, but I wish he hadn't. I knew they wouldn't come.'

The slight quiver in Harriet's voice broke Victoria's heart.

*

Victoria hurried around the living room, snatching up case file notes and searching for her shoes. Harriet had left for work fifteen minutes earlier, but Victoria was feeling scattered as she tried to get herself out the door. She was late, on edge. Why did Harriet get into her head like this? Every time Victoria was starting to get frustrated and fed up with her, every time she began to think enough was enough, Harriet would show her a flash of vulnerability. A reminder that there was so much more beneath the surface. That her moments of arrogance and selfishness were a defence mechanism that she had learned to use.

She stopped in front of the mirror by the door and saw that the bags under her eyes were looking even worse than usual. God, she was so desperate for just one real night's sleep. She dropped her things on the hall table and raced back into the bedroom. A quick dab of concealer would have her looking a bit more human.

As she dotted the makeup under her eyes, she wondered how much she was really supposed to take from Harriet.

Because as much as she had always loved her, surely there was a point where she had to stop letting Harriet take advantage of her. Where she had to speak up and say: *I deserve more. I'm worth it. I'm worth being number one in someone else's life instead of always playing second fiddle.*

But Victoria didn't truly believe that. Because how could someone who had once done what she had done ever be worth more? And if Harriet knew her darkest secret and was still willing to be with her, then how could she give that up?

She finished with the makeup and examined her face in the mirror. Better. But she still looked like death warmed up.

Maybe that was why she kept being drawn back in by Harriet. Because Harriet had been there for her at that point in her life when everything could have gone wrong. Harriet might have been a lucky charm for Malek, but she'd been Victoria's salvation. And luck had had nothing to do with that situation. She would always be grateful to Harriet for saving her that night – even if she still questioned whether it was the right decision.

The fact was, Victoria would never have been able to work in this job that she loved so much if Harriet hadn't done what she'd done – you couldn't get a government position with a criminal record. And her job was important to her. Everyone deserved a chance at rehabilitation. Everyone deserved a chance to change. Not just for themselves, but for the sake of their future victims. Every person that Victoria got through to, every time she kept them off the drugs or the drink for even one day longer than the last time they'd been sober, every time they held down a job or turned up for therapy or study was a win – and that win meant there was a chance that another young girl was not put in the position that she had been put in when she was younger.

Because maybe if someone had stepped in with Dion, if they'd worked harder with him, if they'd made the effort to get him to turn around after his first offence, maybe he wouldn't be dead. And Victoria wouldn't be responsible for his death.

There was a fine line between self-defence and assault. And Victoria knew from experience that, had her case ever made it to court, she would have been in for a tough battle to plead self-defence. Didn't matter that it was an accident, proving it would have been difficult. But she never had to, because Harriet had made sure it wouldn't make it that far.

Victoria was twenty when it happened. She and Harriet had taken a trip to the Gold Coast to celebrate the end of their degrees. It was the closest they'd ever come to being an actual couple and the only time that Victoria thought they might really end up together.

They met Dion and his mates at a nightclub on the main strip. He'd told them outright that he was out on parole after some sort of minor assault – as if he was proud of it. 'Not even meant to be out drinking in clubs,' he'd added, 'but they can't tell me what to do.'

At first Victoria thought he was interested in Harriet. And then when she realised he was starting to make the moves on her, she couldn't help laughing as she told him she was gay. Maybe if she'd noticed the change to his demeanour then and there, the way his face twitched, the way his voice shifted in tone, she would have been more cautious. But the nightclub was dark and loud, and Victoria had had one too many Vodka Cruisers, so she didn't pick up on the signs.

She and Harriet ducked out the back door into the alleyway behind the club for a cigarette. Victoria didn't realise Dion had followed them – until he started yelling at her.

'You think you can embarrass me in front of my friends? You think you can say no to me because you want to be with this stupid slut? You fucking dyke. You stupid lesbian bitches.'

Victoria had always known she was gay. And she'd been fortunate to have parents who were open-minded and totally accepting when she'd first come out to them, despite it being the early nineties, when far too many people still judged what they didn't understand. What she hadn't known was how long the rest of the world would take to grow the hell up and accept her for who she was. She'd dealt with her fair share of homophobia over the years.

Harriet was first to respond. 'Fuck off,' she'd said. 'Don't talk to my girlfriend that way.'

Victoria still remembered the warm feeling of bliss that had swirled in her chest at hearing Harriet describe her as her girlfriend.

'You can't tell me to fuck off. You two are the ones who've been throwing yourselves at me all night. Now you think you can change your mind? Laugh at me?'

He pushed Victoria first, hard enough that she stumbled and almost fell. 'Hey!' she said, reaching out for the wall, trying to regain her balance. But then he was lunging at Harriet and Victoria felt a rage swell up inside her. 'Don't you touch her!' she screamed as she tried to block him from getting to Harriet.

It was all over in less than ten seconds. One moment he was trying to shove past Victoria to get to Harriet, the next, Victoria had somehow managed to twist sideways and use his own momentum to cause him to fall. He pulled Victoria down with him and they both landed sideways, facing one another. She would never forget the look in his eyes when the side of his head struck the concrete kerb. The cracking sound of his skull. The way his face went slack.

The realisation that this was serious, that he might not get back up.

She'd scrambled away from him in terror. 'Harriet, *Harriet*! I think he's … I think he's really hurt.'

Harriet had grabbed her hand and pulled her to her feet. 'Let me check,' she'd said.

Victoria had turned the other way while Harriet crouched next to Dion.

A moment later, Harriet said, 'No, I don't think he's hurt. I think he's dead.'

'We have to find help. We have to get someone to call an ambulance.' Victoria's hand was on the door that led back into the nightclub when Harriet grabbed her.

'No,' she said. 'Go back to the hotel. I'll deal with this. Just run.'

'But, but I can't … I can't leave! It was an accident, I need to be here, to explain …'

'Victoria! This is bad. What if people think we killed him? We'll be arrested. And you're the one who pulled him down. You have to go.' She held Victoria by the shoulders and stared into her eyes. 'You need to trust me, Victoria. Get the hell out of here. I've got some mates up here, there are people I can call and ask for help.'

Harriet was gone all night. Victoria packed their things and cried and paced around the hotel room, wondering if she was ever going to see her friend again. Harriet finally showed up at dawn, looking tired but satisfied. She refused to tell Victoria exactly what had happened.

'It's better you don't know,' she'd said. 'I took care of it.'

They were on a plane back to Sydney that day, cutting their holiday short.

Victoria tried several times to get Harriet to explain. 'But what does that even mean, you took care of it? What kind of friends do you have there? Harriet, you have to tell me.'

Images of Harriet dumping a body in the ocean or dissolving it in a bath of acid plagued Victoria's thoughts and dreams, but Harriet wouldn't budge. She told her that Dion was a bad guy. She said she'd overheard some of his mates talking earlier that evening. They'd said that his previous assault charges were worse than he'd let on; that he'd put a girl in hospital when she'd turned him down. That knowledge didn't make Victoria feel any better. It didn't matter what kind of a person Dion was, no one deserved to die. It only made her more determined to make a difference with her job.

The incident also seemed to spell the end of the relationship that had barely even started between Victoria and Harriet. They went back to being just friends, and then a year or two later, Harriet met Malek.

For the next few months after she returned to Sydney – maybe even years – Victoria was convinced that any day she would open her door to a police officer who'd finally tracked her down and had come to arrest her. But it never happened. And despite scouring the news, she never saw reports of Dion's death. It was as though the entire incident had somehow been erased from existence. It made no sense. All she knew was that Harriet had somehow saved her from a potential murder charge.

CHAPTER TWENTY-THREE

In the car on her way to her first appointment, Victoria started mentally checking through today's schedule. She had four parolees to check on, three at their own homes and the fourth was coming into the office for a meeting with Victoria and their in-house recruitment officer. She had the containers of extra cupcakes next to her on the front seat. Was it going to be odd to turn up to her visits today with baked goods for her parolees? It certainly wasn't her usual MO, but she was only supposed to bring one cupcake to the party tonight and maybe they would make for a nice icebreaker with her clients.

First up was Hamish. Sweet twenty-year-old kid who'd gotten caught up with the wrong people. He was unlikely to reoffend as long as he stayed away from the old crowd. Victoria could tell his brush with the law had really rattled him and he wanted to turn his life around. This was Victoria's favourite kind of case because there was good chance of full rehabilitation. Hamish would most likely be completely reintegrated into society within the year. He was already doing well at his new part-time job, he was staying on top of his studies and he was even dating a great guy who was willing to look past his short stint in prison for break and enter. Why couldn't all her parolees be more like Hamish?

She pulled up at the traffic lights and flicked her indicator on. Sadly, almost fifty per cent of Victoria's parolees would end up reoffending and find themselves back behind bars. Usually, it was just a matter of time. That's not to say that Victoria ever gave up on them. She always put everything into trying to keep them on the right side of the law. Even the ones who distrusted her, thought she was out to get them, that she was always waiting for a chance to catch them out. Which was ridiculous, if only for the reason that there was way more paperwork involved if she had to write them up, so it was in her best interest to help them succeed. It was just hard to get them to believe that. The main reason she worked so hard with them though was because she bloody well cared. Victoria was acutely aware of the fact that she could easily have ended up in their position had things been different.

After Hamish was Kayla. Victoria sighed. Kayla was basically a ticking time bomb. Victoria wasn't going to give up on her, but she was resigned to the fact that any day now, Kayla would explode again. It was funny how Kayla always thought she was getting away with her lies, while Victoria could see right through them. She wished she could make her realise that she only had one life and that she was worth more than she thought. That her current trajectory meant, statistically speaking, she wasn't likely to reach her thirtieth birthday. But you couldn't force someone to change. All you could do was keep guiding and hope that one day it clicked.

She would have to remember to leave her new script for her sleeping pills in her car when she went in to see Kayla. She definitely couldn't be trusted not to try stealing stuff from her bag and Temazepam was the last thing that girl needed.

After Kayla, she would head back to the office to catch up on some paperwork and have a meeting with parolee number three, Tina, and the recruitment officer to see if they could find the right career path for the young girl.

And then … Dex. There weren't many parolees who made Victoria nervous, but Dex was on a whole new playing field. She'd dealt with hundreds of pumped-up men who thought they could intimidate her and she knew how to handle them, how to bring them down a peg or two when needed. How to show them who was boss. But Dex was different. Victoria had always considered herself to be a brave person – it took a lot to scare her. Dex scared her.

She couldn't quite put her finger on what it was that unsettled her so much when it came to Dex. His actual conviction wasn't even close to the worst she'd seen. He'd been arrested for intimidation and harassment of his ex-girlfriend. It was more a case of what he seemed capable of. He had a deceptively quiet air about him that felt very, very dangerous. And Victoria had a feeling that, had he not been picked up when he was, caught following his ex late one night by a cop who pulled him over for a broken tail-light, that night would have ended much worse. There was no direct evidence that showed he'd been planning something more sinister, no weapons in the car, not even a history of violence, yet there was something about him that gave Victoria a gut feeling.

It wasn't unusual to partner up for particularly high-risk offenders. With no actual proof that he was dangerous, though, Victoria couldn't really expect someone to come along with her for her visits with Dex. If she told one of her colleagues that she wanted a bit of backup because she had a bad feeling, they would have been there for her, but she didn't want to ask when she knew everyone was already stretched so thin. It wasn't fair on the others. She would watch her own back.

*

'Black, no sugar, right?'

Victoria smiled. 'Good memory.'

Her umbrella stood in a corner by the door, a small puddle forming around it. Aarnav took the jar of coffee from the high shelf above the sink with ease. He was tall and slender and pretty much the complete opposite of his boyfriend, Hamish, in appearance. Hamish was short and stocky with a low, gravelly voice, pale skin and freckles. Aarnav looked like he could have been a ballet dancer in another life with his graceful movements, delicate features and gentle, softly spoken voice.

'You keep Hamish on the straight and narrow, the least I can do is remember how you like your coffee.'

'Nah, I'm not the one doing that, he's got it in hand on his own. Three more months and you won't even need to remember how I like my coffee. I'll be out of your lives. And in the nicest possible way, hopefully I'll never see you guys again.'

Aarnav laughed lightly as he placed heaped spoonfuls of instant coffee into three mugs. 'In the nicest possible way, I hope we'll never see you again too. Although if you start bringing cupcakes to every visit, I might not be so keen on saying goodbye!'

'Ha.' Victoria drummed her fingers on the top of the small plastic container of cupcakes that she'd placed on the table. 'I promise this is a one-off. Extras that shouldn't go to waste.'

Hamish appeared from the bedroom wearing his neat work uniform and drying his strawberry-blond hair with a towel. 'Sorry, Vic, lost track of time.'

'All good, your lovely partner here is taking care of me.'

Victoria didn't usually let any of her parolees call her Vic. It was too familiar. And it was important to keep boundaries. You could be friendly, but you couldn't be *friends*. Even with the nice ones. It was one of the first things Barb, her unit leader, had taught her when she started in this job. 'You're going to have to learn to walk a fine line with these people. You need to be able to build a rapport with them, they need to know they can trust you. But at the same time, you can't be their mate.' Everyone in the office knew the story of Matt, the officer who'd grown too close with his parolee, Vanessa. The relationship had turned romantic – a massive violation of trust and abuse of power. These days, the story of Matt and Vanessa almost seemed like an urban legend and if Victoria hadn't seen him walked from the office eight years ago on the day he lost his job, she probably would have thought it had been made up as a warning. But somehow, she'd let her guard down that little bit more with Hamish.

'Right,' said Victoria, sitting down opposite Hamish at his dining room table and accepting the mug of coffee that Aarnav placed in front of her. 'I take it from the fact you're in uniform that the job's still going well?'

'Hundred per cent. Boss is an absolute legend. Reckons he'll be able to promote me when I finish my holistic therapy course.'

Victoria grinned. 'Mate, that's awesome news. Congratulations.' She glanced at Aarnav, who was back at the kitchen bench collecting the other two coffees. 'Any contact with the old crew?'

'Nada,' said Hamish. But Victoria didn't like the way he didn't meet her eye when he spoke.

'Hamish, I'm talking *any* contact, even if it seems harmless. Even if they instigated it and you didn't respond. I need to know.'

Hamish dropped his shoulders and ran his hands through his hair. 'It was nothing, really.'

Aarnav set down the mugs, pulled out a chair and sat next to Hamish. He placed a hand on his arm. 'What was nothing?' he asked.

Hamish unclipped the lid from the container, pulled out a cupcake and peeled off the wrapper before shoving it whole into his mouth, stalling for time.

'Hamish,' said Aarnav, 'tell us what's going on.' And Victoria couldn't help noticing how his voice had a quality that was somehow both soft and commanding all at once.

Finally, Hamish finished chewing and swallowed. 'Okay ... One of the guys came into the shop last week, tried to get me

234

chatting ... But there were no issues. I told him to piss off and he did. It's all good.'

Victoria felt a jolt in the pit of her stomach. 'Which one was it?'

'Damien.'

'Was he hostile when you asked him to go?'

'No more than the usual. Trust me, it's fine. They know I'm out.'

'Then why didn't you mention it to me?' said Aarnav quietly.

'Because I knew you'd get worried.'

Victoria knew why Aarnav was concerned. While Hamish's past transgressions hadn't been especially serious, some of the people in his old circle had much heavier crimes on their record. Keeping this visit to himself was a red flag and officially constituted a breach of his parole, but she didn't want to write him up. Not when he'd been doing so well. A verbal warning to remind him of his reporting responsibilities was enough for now. But this was something she needed to keep an eye on. She'd seen better people dragged back under by the pull of an old friend. And she really didn't want to lose Hamish after he'd come so far.

'Alright, Hamish, sounds like it's all under control, but you need to remember to let me know if any of them contact you again, okay? That's really important, you understand?'

'Yeah, I know. All good. Promise to tell you. But I don't think he'll be back.'

Victoria finished up her questions, drank the rest of her coffee and left them to it. She could tell from Aarnav's expression that he would continue to reiterate the importance of full disclosure for her. Hamish was lucky to have such a caring boyfriend who'd stayed by his side despite his near-brush with jail. He was going to be fine.

*

Driving through the pouring rain back to the office after her appointment at Kayla's apartment, Victoria felt a lot less confident than she had when she'd left Hamish. While Hamish was dressed and ready to head out to work, Kayla had answered her door in a thick dressing gown that was far too hot for the steamy summer's day. Her eyes were sunken and her hair was greasy.

Victoria had tried to call her out on her bullshit answers, but Kayla wasn't budging today. She was going with the polite, sickly sweet, 'yes ma'am, no ma'am', responses to everything Victoria said and even Victoria's most authoritative tone couldn't provoke her into dropping her façade. Meanwhile her roommate had sat in the corner, watching the two of them in idle fascination. Victoria wanted to shake the both of them. *Wake up! See what you're doing to your lives!* She could tell that Zoe, the roommate, thought she had her own life under control because she was a high-functioning addict, but Victoria knew better. It wasn't going to last. One day soon she was going to end up just as bad as Kayla. Victoria had also clocked the derisive look on Kayla's face when she'd handed over the cupcakes and had felt a little embarrassed. She should have realised that home-baked treats weren't going to be appreciated by all her parolees.

Her phone ringtone cut through the music on the car stereo and she pressed the button on the steering wheel to answer.

'Victoria Suffield speaking.'

'Ooh,' said Harriet, 'you sound so sexy when you're in professional work mode.'

'What's up? I'm busy.'

'You're always all business when you're at work.'

'Yeah, that's kind of the point. Same as you should be. Aren't you out on jobs right now?'

'Rick and I stopped for an early lunch between houses. Wanted to check where you'll be this afternoon around five-thirty?'

'Five-thirty? Um, by then I'll be finishing up with my last parolee out at Burwood. How come?'

'Oh, that works out perfect. The last house I've got is only fifteen minutes away from there. I never picked up my car today, so I'll get Rick to drop me to you. I'm getting ready at your place tonight so we can turn up together after all the other guests for the big surprise moment.'

'Wait, Harriet, I don't think it's a good idea for you to meet me near one of my parolees.'

'Don't stress, I'm not going to go inside and ask for a cup of tea! I'll meet you out front when you're finished. Text me the address. Have to run, bye!'

Harriet had disconnected before Victoria could argue further. She squeezed the steering wheel and made a growling sound in the back of her throat. Why was Harriet like this? So flippant; never taking Victoria's concerns seriously. She didn't like that Harriet would be dropped off right near Dex's place. It was a clash of her personal and professional life that made her uncomfortable. Of course it had to be Dex she was seeing last. The worst possible parolee she'd want Harriet to run into. At the same time, though, she knew Harriet was going to get her way.

Harriet always got her way.

*

'Sandwich? Trav is heading down to the shop.'

Victoria glanced up from her desk at Barb. She was exhausted after the meeting with Tina. 'Yes, please, you're the best. Egg and lettuce?'

'Done.'

Barb turned away to pass the order onto her assistant, Travis, and Victoria took a moment to tilt her chair back, close her eyes and run her hands through her hair.

'What's up, darl? You're looking stressed,' said Barb when she was finished with Travis. She walked around and rested her hip against Victoria's desk. 'Tell Aunty Barb what's going on.'

Victoria smiled. Barb was always there for anyone who needed her in the office. She could turn steely in a second if the situation required it, but underneath, she was a softie. She had short, white-blonde hair with orange-brown tips that always made Victoria think of crème brûlée – not that she'd ever say that to Barb. She doubted her boss would appreciate being likened to dessert.

'It's nothing really. Had a recruitment meeting for Tina. She's not a bad kid, but, God, it was like getting blood from a stone, trying to encourage her to interact with Renuka. And every job Renuka suggested was either too hard, too easy, too boring or not enough pay. I just want her to realise that she has to start somewhere.'

Barb patted her on the back. 'You'll get through to her, you always do.'

'Do I? I'm also worried about one from this morning. Hamish Duncan?'

'Oh, yeah, the Scottish lad, I remember him. Why are you worried? I thought he was doing well.'

'He is. I mean, he's doing great at work, good relationship, all of that … But he had an old "colleague" drop by on him the other day. He said everything was fine, but you know when you get that feeling? I don't even know what it was, something about the look on his face when he told me? Something's not right.'

Barb rubbed her chin with her hand. 'Interesting. Look, I hate to say it, but I've noticed with you, your instincts are pretty much always spot on. So if you think there's something to worry about, maybe it's worth an extra follow-up. No harm in being sure.'

'Apart from the harm to my paperwork. If I run around making extra appointments just to satisfy bad feelings, I'll never get on top of things.'

'True. But how's that different to any other day here? We're always swamped. If it gives you peace of mind, it's worth it. And I can get Travis to help you out on Monday if you like? You're in the office in the morning, aren't you?'

'Yep, I'm planning on coming in early on Monday. A bit of help would be great.'

'No problems, consider him yours.'

'Thanks, Barb.'

Barb squeezed her arm. 'No worries, always here when you need to talk.'

Victoria turned back to her computer and opened up her online diary to look at the rest of her plans for the day. If she moved a few things around, she should be able to check briefly on Hamish at his work on her way to Dex's place. She wouldn't hassle him, literally just pop her head in and make sure everything was okay. He wouldn't mind.

*

Cynthia

Nutri-Vit Health Food Store

It was the sound that Cynthia would never forget. The *ffft, ffft, ffft* of the knife plunging in and out. And it was so fast. He must have stabbed the other young man seven or eight times in only a few seconds. Of course she didn't know that that was what had happened at first. It was all so … unexpected. So unlikely. One moment the shorter of the two, maybe nineteen or twenty years old, head down, hands stuffed in his pockets, cap pulled low over his head, was shuffling through the store, the next minute, he'd crashed straight into the staff member that had been helping Cynthia choose her echinacea tablets only two minutes earlier. There was nothing all that unusual about him, apart from the fact that it was far too hot for that thick jacket, even with the constant rain lately. At first it looked like the collision was a simple mistake, like he wasn't watching where he was going and he'd run into the other man accidently. Cynthia expected the two of them to step back and apologise, maybe chuckle about it.

But that's when the shorter man's arm started pumping back and forth. What was he doing? Then Cynthia heard the sound: *ffft, ffft, ffft.* She couldn't make sense of it. Later, when she understood it was the sound of the knife tearing through flesh and material, she felt physically ill.

The entire altercation was over in less than thirty seconds: crash, stab, flee. The staff member didn't even hit the floor until the perpetrator had disappeared out the front door. And it took everyone in the store several more moments to come to his aid because, at first, no one realised he was so badly hurt. Not until the red stain began to bloom across the front of his white uniform did other staff and customers start rushing over to help him.

All she could think as she stood there was: *That young man was helping me choose my health supplements just two minutes ago.* And behind that thought, the sound played over and over: *ffft, ffft, ffft.*

She had a terrible feeling he wasn't going to make it.

CHAPTER TWENTY-FOUR

Victoria knew the moment that she turned the corner and saw the flashing red lights right out the front of the health food and supplements shop that it was going to be Hamish. *Goddammit.* Why hadn't she trusted her instincts sooner? Why hadn't she grilled him more about the old friend who'd dropped by? She didn't know exactly what she was going to find when she arrived, but she knew it wasn't going to be good. Either Hamish had done something – or something had happened to Hamish.

After she parked and dashed through the rain, she saw that a small crowd had gathered near the front of the shop. She was relieved to see no police tape up yet; that would make it easier to gain access and find out what was going on. While their jobs crossed over sometimes, police weren't always willing to share information with corrections officers. They were often under the impression that corrections officers were too sympathetic to their parolees.

A staff member was temporarily posted at the doorway to stop onlookers from getting too close. Victoria went up to him and checked his name badge. 'James, hi,' she said, pulling out her identification to show him. 'I'm Victoria Suffield, Hamish Duncan's corrections officer. Can I come through, please?'

The look that crossed James's face when she mentioned Hamish told her what she dreaded. Her professional demeanour slipped.

'How bad is it?' she asked, unable to stop the crack from creeping into her voice.

James's eyes flew to the ground. 'I don't know,' he whispered. 'But it wasn't good. They're saying someone stabbed him. I didn't see it happen.'

Victoria placed a comforting hand on James's arm. 'Okay, thank you. I'm sure the paramedics are doing everything they can.'

She walked past him and into the shop. Outside she could hear more sirens. That would be the police now. They'd clear the area and then they'd want to interview witnesses. She just wanted to get one look at Hamish before she was ushered back outside, to see his face for herself. Get some kind of reassurance that he was going to be okay.

She sidestepped around customers who were standing in a small circle, speaking in hushed tones, and then down an aisle and around a corner until she saw the stretcher and the paramedics leaning over Hamish, working urgently yet somehow still with a sense of calm and ease. She'd always been in awe of ambulance officers, of the way they could take charge and deal with the most horrific of situations all while keeping everything smooth, relaxed and completely under control. She took one more step so she could see Hamish's face and when she did, she let out a small noise of relief.

He was alive. There was colour in his cheeks. He hadn't given up.

She was desperate to move in further, to let Hamish know that she was there for him. To hold his hand or tell him to hang on, to tell him to fight. But she couldn't get any closer, not without getting in the way of the paramedics. The sense of powerlessness at not being able to do anything to help made her want to drop to the floor, curl up and hide from the world for the rest of the day. But she couldn't. She needed to keep moving.

Outside on the footpath, under cover from the rain, she wondered if she should call Aarnav to let him know what had happened, but Hamish's boss would likely have already contacted him. Besides, she wanted to make sure she caught one of the police officers when they started taking statements from witnesses. She could give them the background information on Hamish. Let them know the names of the crew Hamish used to run around with and tell them which one had been by to see him the other day. Hopefully it would give them a head start on catching the person who'd done this. Although she already knew who it was. There was no doubt in her mind that Damien had returned to punish Hamish for turning him away.

*

Victoria didn't even think of Harriet until she was on her way to Dex's place. With the time it had taken to pass everything she knew that might help onto Constable Feltrin – who thankfully had been appreciative of her insight instead of being arrogant and telling her to stay out of this side of things, as some officers would – she was half an hour late for her appointment with Dex. That wasn't ideal. Parolees were distrustful at the best of times. And someone like Dex wouldn't like to be kept waiting. *They* could run late and skip appointments all over the place, but they didn't like it when they were the ones being inconvenienced. Throw Harriet standing out the front of his house into the mix, and Victoria didn't even want to think about all the things that could go wrong. What if Dex looked outside, saw Harriet watching his house from the street and got paranoid? What if Harriet got impatient and decided to go and knock on his door in search of Victoria? It was just the kind of reckless thing she would do.

Victoria tried calling Dex first, to let him know she was on her way and apologise for being late. But his phone rang out and disconnected without allowing her to leave a voicemail. Next, she tried Harriet, but she didn't answer either. At least she was able to leave Harriet a message.

'I'm so sorry, I got caught up on another case … it's been … it's been a really rough day. I'm on my way now but I still have to go in for the check-up with my parolee. If you're still waiting out the front there, I think it's better if you take an Uber home and I'll meet you at your party later, okay? Sorry, I know the plan was to get ready at my place so I could take you after everyone arrives but seeing as it isn't an *actual* surprise party, it doesn't really matter, right? I'll explain everything later.'

She hung up and pressed harder on the accelerator, letting the speed creep up over the limit despite the wet road. There was a bad feeling in her gut again. She'd been right about Hamish. Was she right about this too?

'Come on,' she murmured to the red traffic lights up ahead. 'Turn green. I don't have time for this.'

*

When she pulled over on the opposite side of the road to Dex's home, at first she thought she'd spotted Harriet sitting under a nearby bus shelter to keep out of the rain. But when she got out of her car and walked closer, she quickly realised she was mistaken. The woman had similar hair to Harriet, but it definitely wasn't her. Victoria surveyed the area, checking up and down the street and then tried to call Harriet again. Once more it went to voicemail. Maybe she'd already received the message and taken her advice and left? But then why wouldn't she answer? Or call her back or send her a text? Could it be because she was sulking about being stood up? Or had something gone wrong?

Victoria half speed-walked, half ran up to Dex's single-level red-brick rental, ducking her head from the rain. She pressed the doorbell. Several agonising seconds passed and then, finally, there was the click of the door opening and it swung inwards. It was dark inside the home and she could just make out Dex's tall, hulking shape standing back from the door. He didn't say hello, but that was normal. He wasn't big on social niceties.

Victoria held out the plastic container. 'I brought you some cupcakes,' she said.

Dex stared back at her for a beat before responding.

'Now why the fuck would you do that?'

*

Usually, Victoria wouldn't have any issue asking for the music to be turned down, but she was getting the sense that Dex was in a bad mood and so she wanted to be careful about which battles she picked. If she needed to strain a bit to have a conversation over the heavy bass, then she could manage that.

She was also feeling out of sorts. She was sitting on the edge of the worn leather couch and Dex was slouched in an armchair opposite her, one of his legs lifted up over the side. The container of bright red-iced cupcakes sat on the scratched coffee table between them, looking garishly incongruous. It was stiflingly hot and the air was hazy with cigarette smoke. A black and white poster of *The Godfather* caught her eye, and she was mildly irritated that she had the same taste in movies as someone like Dex.

She stood up from the couch and took a few steps over to a window. 'Should we open this up?' she asked, unlatching the lock. 'Get some fresh air in here?' She knew it was an absurd suggestion with the rain still pouring outside, but between the humidity and the smoke, her throat felt like it was closing over.

'No,' said Dex, eyeballing her.

'Fair enough.' She backed away from the window, not bothering to relock it, and sat down on the couch again, trying to sit more comfortably this time, to seem like she was relaxed and at ease. She opened her folder on her lap and then spoke with as much faked bravado as she could muster. 'How's the job going? Still on the apartment building site at the moment?'

'Nuh. Quit.'

Victoria looked up from her notes in surprise. 'You quit? When? I'm sure I spoke to your supervisor just two days ago.'

'This morning. Got into a bit of a biff with a couple of the lads. I don't need that shit.'

Dammit. This wasn't off to a good start. Leaving his job, fighting … Dex was in trouble. No wonder he was in such an antagonistic mood.

She thought she heard a thud from another room, but it was hard to know for sure with the music. Her head snapped towards it. 'Someone else here?' she asked.

Dex didn't turn to the sound, he just kept staring right at Victoria. 'No,' he said.

'Okay … what was that noise?'

Dex shrugged. 'Beats me,' he said.

A sick feeling was twisting at Victoria's guts. 'Dex, there wasn't a woman here earlier, was there? Someone looking for —'

'Fuck's sake. I haven't been anywhere near Shailene.'

Victoria's focus sharpened at the unprovoked mention of Dex's ex-girlfriend. All thoughts of Harriet left her mind. Shailene had an AVO out against Dex. He wasn't supposed to have any contact with her. Suddenly, she felt clearer.

'Of course you haven't,' she said calmly. 'Because you know that if you went anywhere near her, that would be a serious breach and you wouldn't risk landing yourself back in prison for that, right?'

'Exactly.'

'So why are we talking about her?'

''Cause you brought her up.'

'No, I didn't.'

'Whatever. She's not here, alright?'

The hairs on Victoria's arms stood up. Why did he keep denying things that she hadn't actually asked?

She was trying to stay calm, but felt on edge. First with Hamish being stabbed and then with Harriet not responding to her calls or messages. Now the thud from the other room had her nerves on fire. She was straining to hear any other sounds, but the music was too loud for her to focus. She needed to find out what the hell was going on.

'Dex,' she said firmly. 'Who's in that room? Tell me right now and I'll do what I can to help you.'

Victoria knew Dex wasn't going to take kindly to the accusation but being direct with him was the only way to go.

Dex didn't respond right away. He was still staring at her and without breaking eye contact, he lifted his leg off the side of the chair, leaned forward, stood up and took a step towards her. Victoria held still. There was no point standing up to try to match his height, he would still tower above her. She knew not to speak, not to start back-pedalling or apologising for the accusation. She was better off waiting to see what he was going to say.

Dex stood in front of her for several seconds, then turned sharply and walked out of the room.

Victoria sat still, her heart thudding in her chest. Thirty seconds later, Dex reappeared with a huge, light grey Staffy by his side.

'There you go,' he said. 'I haven't got any fucking ex-girlfriends in the house, it's just me fucking dog.'

Victoria exhaled with relief.

But, God, how long was it going to take to repair her relationship with Dex after making an accusation like that?

Bloody Harriet, if she hadn't been so demanding about meeting her here, Victoria never would have been so rattled. She could kill her for getting in her head like this.

*

Evan

Mile End Skate Park

At first, Evan thought it was awesome that Serge had talked some girl into sending him a topless photo. For one thing, it might give him leverage to talk Sophie into sending him some nudes. Kind of like, *See! Everyone's doing it, Soph, it's no big deal.* But he was surprised to find he felt uncomfortable when Serge passed the phone around for all the guys to gape at.

Of course he looked at it. Just because he felt a bit weird about it didn't mean he wasn't going to look. But the uncomfortable feeling grew. His neck prickled. His gut was all coiled up. What the hell? Why was he getting like this?

He shouldn't have focused on her face. Obviously, she didn't know that the norm was to crop out your face. But it was her expression – it was sort of nervous and hopeful. Like she was saying to Serge, *Am I good enough? Is this right?*

And there was no way that girl would have thought eight other guys were going to be rating her tits. She would have thought it was just for him.

For one fucked-up moment, Evan thought he might actually punch Serge in the face. But that would have been suicide. Serge was built like a boxer. He wasn't huge, didn't have those puffed-up muscles like you'd blown your biceps up with a bicycle pump. No, Serge was more compact and powerful. He'd drop Evan in an instant.

So instead, he'd passed the phone on and then silently clenched and unclenched his fists. *Come on, Evan, snap out of it. This is nothing to you.*

Harriet

It probably seems like Victoria should have been suspect number one, right? Considering everything that happened with Dion.

But you know the truth, don't you? There's a lot more to that story.

You really do love her. You always have. But admitting that isn't going to change anything now. You're dying. And it doesn't matter that you had a plan, a way to make it all work out between the three of you. You, your husband and your lover.

Deep down, though, you know your plan never would have worked.

So, did Victoria give you the poisoned cupcake? Because if she did, then you have your answer. She's got some powerful drugs on hand – didn't she say her new sleeping tablets were a lot stronger than the ones she used to take?

You were with her this morning, but what happened next? You had breakfast ... coffee ... she was making cupcakes, wasn't she? For the party. But did she give you one?

You need to work this out. You need to work it out fast.

It's just that you're really starting to feel sick. Is that the poison? Or nausea from the pain? The blood loss from the wound on the back of your head?

Okay, so these are your three main suspects, your whole list: Malek, Karen and Victoria. All potential killers, all with motive, all with means. And you're still nowhere near an answer. So what now? Keep investigating the three of them? Go back through it all again? Or extend the list?

Think, Harriet. Who else could it have been?

There's that woman at the coffee shop who's got a thing for Malek. What's her name again? Colleen. He doesn't think you know about her, but you see things. What if she decided she was really into him and she needed to get you out of the way? Funny thing is, if Malek was a bit more up-front about the open relationship, she'd know there was no need to get rid of you.

But why now all of a sudden?

Because something changed. What's different? What's new? Who's new?

There's Cosmo. He's new.

Why didn't you think of that sooner? Just because he's recently moved to the area and has a son at the same school as Farrah, you assumed you could trust him and took it upon yourself to show him around. What are you? The bloody welcoming committee? For God's sake, you hardly know anything about the guy. When you tried to chat to him about which part of Brisbane he was from, he became uncomfortable. Why was that? What if he got flustered because you caught him out in a lie? And if he lied, then the important question is: Why? What's he hiding?

An image is coming back to you now. Cosmo's face. He looks angry. His hands are gesticulating and his voice is rising. When was that? Did that really happen or are you imagining things?

Anyone else? Who else did you see today? What did you do? You had work, right? And you didn't have your car, so you needed ... you needed ... Oh, yes, you needed Rick to help you get around. Rick the Dick.

Rick's always had a bit of a thing for you. May as well add him to the list. He's always been creepy. When did you last see him? Think. You had the house on Laurel Avenue first up. Then that dodgy little apartment near the beach. Size of a broom closet, but it'll still sell for over a mil just 'cause of the location. Then coffee break. After that ...

Why can't you remember what happened next?

PART FOUR

the party

CHAPTER TWENTY-FIVE

Malek

Malek needed to pull himself together. Guests were arriving and it was far too obvious that he was rattled. People kept shaking off their umbrellas and commenting on the weather, usually making the same jokes like, 'At this rate we'll be swimming home, ha ha ha'. But then they would give him a strange look when he didn't react appropriately. He wasn't a good enough actor for this. Besides, it felt weird to be welcoming Harriet's friends into their house without her there. The more people that arrived, the more Malek was realising that there really weren't that many of her friends that he actually liked.

He was also noticing that people had very different ways of interpreting the 'splash of red' dress code. Some people were in full red dresses, some just had a red tie or a red ribbon in their hair. One guy had a pair of bright red sneakers. Unfortunately, there was also the odd guest who apparently didn't get the memo that the theme had changed from bling. One man was particularly incongruent in a gold sequinned jacket.

Malek needed a bloody drink to calm his nerves, but the doorbell had just gone again so he excused himself from the most recent arrivals and shuffled past the growing number of people spilling out of the lounge room.

It was his sisters, Lina and Nadia. For a second, Harriet's nickname for them flashed through his mind: Bert and Ernie, because Lina was tall and skinny and Nadia was short and plump, and they were always side by side. He sucked in his cheeks to stop himself from smiling. Honestly, it wasn't even that funny, it was just that ever since Harriet had first started calling them that, he always pictured Bert and Ernie in his mind when he saw his sisters.

'Did we miss it?' Lina asked, without even saying hello. 'The part where Harriet turns up and we all have to shout surprise?'

He stepped back to let them walk through and they shook water out of their hair and brushed droplets off their arms. 'No, no, we're not doing that, she doesn't want us to.'

'Well, that makes sense considering it's not really a surprise party, is it?' There was a derisive note to her voice and Malek eyeballed her.

'*Lina*, don't start.'

'What? What did I say? Anyway, where is the birthday girl?'

'Uh.' Malek rubbed his hand on the back of his neck. 'She's … She's not here. Won't be for a while, yet.'

'There you go, Lina,' said Nadia, 'you can have a couple of drinks first and work on dropping that tone from your voice.'

'Seriously! What tone? You both know I'm over the whole fun-run thing. I'm *fine!*'

'Here's our cupcakes,' said Nadia, holding up a large Tupperware container with a dozen cakes inside.

'You were only meant to bring one each!'

'One cupcake is weird. What was I meant to do with the rest of the batch? Although the whole cake concept is already weird anyway. Doesn't seem very hygienic to me.'

Malek shrugged. 'She saw it on Pinterest or something. Where's Dad, he's not with you?'

'No … he needed a bit more time, he was waiting for the oven to finish.'

'Lina! You were meant to stop him from bringing food!'

'I tried! But you know what he's like. When I asked him if he was cooking anything he said, "No, of course not." Five minutes later, I catch him putting the trays in the oven and he says, "I'm not! Sambusaks don't count."'

Malek shook his head but smiled. At least thinking about his dad took his mind off everything else. 'Fair enough … but he's not driving by himself in all this rain, is he?' Their father was still a decent driver despite his age, but he refused to admit he needed glasses. Malek was convinced he must have slipped someone a fifty to be allowed to skip the eye test the last time he renewed his licence. But Hassim claimed he passed it with flying colours.

'No, Aunty Ley and Sareena are driving him.'

'Wait, they weren't on the list. We weren't doing extended family for tonight.'

'Oh, Malek, my sweet, dumb brother. You really think you could get away with a party this big and not have all the aunties and uncles here? Dad told them weeks ago.'

'Oh my God. They're *all* coming?'

'Of course they are. I assumed you knew.'

'Shit. Our house is not big enough for this.'

'We'll manage, doesn't matter if we're packed in like sardines. As long as there's food and music and alcohol. Speaking of which, where are the drinks?'

Malek pointed them through to the makeshift bar in the living room where one of the catering staff was pouring drinks. 'I'll catch up with you later. I can see more people coming up the driveway.'

*

Karen

Karen felt slightly sick as she and Robert headed up the steep driveway to the front door, Robert carefully holding the umbrella over her. She had the container of cupcakes tucked under one arm and a battle was taking place in her mind.

Take off the lid and tip the cakes into a bin. Now. It's not too late.

No, Harriet deserves this. She deserves to pay for the way she treated me.

You're not in high school anymore. You don't need to get revenge. Be an adult. Take the higher ground.

Fuck the higher ground. I'm going through with this.

'Did I tell you that you look absolutely stunning in that dress?' Robert asked as he placed one hand on the small of her back to guide her up the slippery driveway.

Ah, Robert was getting into attentive-husband-in-a-social-setting mode. No, he hadn't mentioned that she looked stunning in this dress as they'd got ready and left the house. To be fair though, Ralph had followed them around as they'd tried to get out the door, asking for McDonald's for dinner, asking why he had to have a babysitter when at least *two* of his friends were allowed to stay home alone when their parents went out, and asking for the screen-time limit to please be taken off his gaming PC because otherwise he would have *nothing* to do tonight. By the time they finally left Ralph in the care of Annabelle from two doors up, Karen was desperate for a drink.

'Thank you,' she said, even though what she actually wanted to say was, *If you think I look so stunning, why don't you ever kiss me anymore? Why don't you look at me the same way you used to? Why don't you want me? And where the hell did you take off to this afternoon when you were meant to be at home?*

She glanced down at her outfit – a classic little black dress. Knee length and sleeveless to show off her shoulders. Strappy black sandals. Toenails and fingernails painted crimson as per the dress code. At the last minute, she'd found a blood-red lipstick in Tallulah's bedroom and drawn it across her lips, having to immediately resist the urge to wipe it straight off. She would usually find anything that bright far too bold.

She looked up as they reached the steps to the porch and saw Malek standing at the open front door. Oops, how long had he been waiting there for them?

She adjusted her face, trying to appear as though she was excited to be there and waved at Malek. 'Hi! How'd you go with your delinquent teen this afternoon?'

Malek laughed, but she couldn't help noticing that it was a little forced. 'Yeah, not too bad,' he said. 'And yours has been a big help over here getting everything ready; thanks for loaning her.'

She also noticed that Malek ran his eyes over her body as they took the last step. She supposed she should find it objectifying, but she was too busy feeling pleased that at least someone wanted to check her out. She also noted that Robert didn't seem to clock it at all.

'No problem,' said Karen. 'Glad to hear she was helping not hindering. This is Robert, not sure if you've met?'

Robert stepped forward to shake Malek's hand. 'Nice to meet you, mate.'

'You too, come on in out of the rain, guys, no, no, don't worry about that,' he added as Karen motioned to her shoes. 'Trust me,' he said, 'there's plenty of wet footprints tracked through here already. Let me show you where the bar is.'

CHAPTER TWENTY-SIX

Malek

Malek hadn't really intended on having that many drinks that quickly, that early. But when he'd finally had the chance to escape the duties of welcoming people through the front door and get himself a Scotch, he'd made a joke to the bar staff to 'Keep me topped up, would you?' Now it seemed like one of the young blokes had taken him so seriously that every time he turned around to talk to someone, he'd look back at the glass in his hand to discover it full to the brim again. It was handy, he quite liked the service – but it was making it difficult to track his intake. And he needed to keep his head. Too many things had taken a wrong turn this afternoon and he wasn't proud of the way he'd behaved. That simmering rage had been affecting him all day, exploding when he'd put his fist through the door.

And then the shame of what had come after that. He should have known Harriet was going to push him too far one of these days.

True to Lina's word, his dad and a good three car loads of his relatives had shown up soon after his sisters, along with several trays of homemade appetisers. He was starting to think he'd need the extra food with all of the surplus guests. None of his aunts, uncles or cousins seemed aware of the fact that they weren't originally invited – otherwise he would have been clipped over the head at least four times by now. Thankfully, the caterers hadn't seemed too put out by the new dishes that were now circling the room along with their own canapes.

One of his aunts had brought a tray of warak enabs and the sight of the stuffed vine leaves took Malek straight back to the days he'd spent as a kid, picking the leaves from the climber in their backyard with his sisters. His mother would then fill their bathtub with water to wash and soak them for a couple of days until they were soft enough to use, and Lina would complain that she couldn't take a bath. His favourite part was helping his mum roll the rice, mince and spices up in the leaves. He ought to make those with Farrah one of these days.

He spotted Colleen and wandered over. 'Glad you stayed?' he asked.

She turned out her bottom lip thoughtfully, then nodded. 'Yep. You put on a pretty good shindig. Question though: When's the guest of honour going to show up?'

Malek checked his watch. 'Uh, she's not due just yet.'

His tone must not have sounded as confident as he'd thought, as Colleen was giving him a strange look. 'Really? It seems like all the guests are here now. Won't she miss too much of her own party?' she asked.

Malek swallowed. How could he explain that there was every chance Harriet wouldn't even make it tonight? Or that it was all his fault? No … he couldn't think that way. She would still get here, despite what he had done. The woman was too damn stubborn to let anyone stop her from being the star of her own night.

'Yeah, but she likes to make an entrance,' he said.

Colleen nodded in the direction of Brad, who was sitting on a couch chatting to a group of school mums. 'How's the feelings around the non-cousin situation? Will you confront her about it when she arrives? Or leave it for another time?'

For a moment, Malek felt another stab of guilt at the way he'd acted this afternoon, but then he thought again about all the things Harriet had done. About the lies she'd told and the plans for Victoria to move in. The guilt shifted back to frustration, and he downed his drink in one go before responding.

'Think I might just have to play that one by ear,' he said. 'But these are going down a bit too easy, so who knows what might happen,' he added, holding up his glass to show her and catching the attention of the waiter, who immediately stopped to refill his glass again.

'All good, mate,' Malek said when he was done. 'You can ease up on mine now if you like.'

'I don't mind!' said the waiter cheerfully, before weaving off through the crowd back to the bar.

'You really do look great in that scarf,' Malek said to Colleen, leaning in a little closer.

'Who's this?' said Lina from behind him.

Malek spun around and took a quick step back from Colleen. 'Ah, Lina, this is Colleen, you've met before, she runs the little café near Farrah's school. She fixed the macarons for me. This is one of my sisters,' he said to Colleen.

Lina eyed Colleen up and down, then stared pointedly back at Malek. 'You're right,' she said, 'she does look better in that scarf than Harriet.'

Malek's drink sloshed over his hand. 'Lina! That's not what I said, I said she looks great, that's all. You told me you weren't going to cause trouble.'

'What? I'm not causing trouble. I'm just making an observation.'

'No, you weren't, you were putting words in my mouth.'

Colleen scrutinised the back and forth between Malek and his sister with pursed lips. 'Ah, Malek, I thought you said this was Farrah's scarf.'

Malek winced. 'I was worried you wouldn't wear it if I said it belonged to Harriet.'

Colleen's hand flew up to touch the scarf around her head and for a moment he thought she was going to pull it straight off. But then a wry smile appeared on her face.

'You're right,' she said, 'I absolutely would not have worn it. Next time you want to use me to make your wife jealous, give me a heads-up first, would you?'

Lina's eyes widened and Malek's face warmed. 'No!' he said. 'That's not what I was doing! Harriet doesn't even like that scarf anymore ... and I knew it would suit you.'

'Relax,' said Colleen with a laugh. 'I'm only joking. Well, half-joking. I know you've had a rough afternoon.'

Lina prodded him. 'What does she mean? What happened this afternoon?'

'It's a long story,' said Malek. 'Don't worry about it.'

'Something to do with that ridiculous new-age open relationship of yours?' Lina asked.

Malek jolted. What the hell had Lina just said? 'What are you talking about?'

'Oh, come on, baby brother. You really think Nadia and I are that clueless? You can't keep secrets from us. We've known for months.'

Malek decided not to point out that if she'd only known for months, then she'd actually been clueless for some time considering how many years this had been going on.

'Shit, does Dad —?'

'Of course not. You think we want to give him a heart attack? Neither do any of the aunties, but you know if it gets to them, it'll spread like wildfire.'

'Fark. This is a nightmare.'

'It's fine, maybe just lay off flirting with Colleen here before one of the aunties spots you and starts whispering.'

Once again, Malek felt his face redden. 'What? No! I wasn't —'

'Like hell you weren't.' Lina examined Colleen. 'For the record, I like her. She has a good aura around her. It's way more compatible with yours than Harriet's is.'

'Oh, for God's sake, not your aura bullshit again.'

Colleen was clearly amused. 'Wow, Malek, your family has some serious *drama*.' She turned to Lina. 'Don't worry, I won't let him start snogging me in a corner of the room while all of your aunties watch on.' She smirked. 'Now, if we find a private spot out in the backyard, that might be a different story.'

Lina burst out laughing and Malek found himself backing away from them. This was all too much to take. Not only did his sisters know about his open marriage, but it seemed like Lina was playing wing woman and that was all kinds of wrong. And now he couldn't tell if Colleen was actually flirting with him or just making fun of him.

Clearly, he'd told the waiter to ease up on his drinks a bit too prematurely.

*

Victoria

Victoria was late, stressed, exhausted and agitated. The meeting with Dex had run long as she'd tried to smooth things over with him. As uncomfortable and intimidating as it had been, she'd felt a lot better once he'd brought out the dog and she'd stopped imagining that his ex-girlfriend – or even Harriet – was somehow trapped in his bedroom, banging on the wall, desperate for help. So she'd decided her first instinct – that Harriet had become fed up waiting for her and left in an Uber – must have been right and there was no danger that she'd run into trouble with Dex. Although there was something niggling at her about that dog that he'd brought out. Why was that making her feel uncomfortable? The dog was friendly enough, so what was bothering her? Whatever it was could wait until Monday.

On the way back home to get ready, she'd seethed with frustration at her best friend. Why did Harriet always have to be so demanding? And she still hadn't returned any of Victoria's calls or messages to make sure everything was fine after the change in plans. Obviously, Harriet was ignoring her, but for crying out loud, the woman needed to grow up and stop sulking. These things happened!

What if there was actually nothing good about her relationship with Harry? What if their friendship was toxic? What if it had always been toxic? What if it was time for something to change?

As the anger built up, Victoria briefly considered ditching the entire party, popping a couple of sleeping pills into her mouth and crashing out for the night. But by the time she'd arrived at her place, she knew that wasn't going to happen.

Getting ready took longer than expected as well. She'd completely forgotten that the dress she'd been planning on wearing tonight was suited to the original gold and silver bling theme, not the updated red velvet theme. By the time she'd chosen something else to wear – black leather pants with heels and a cherry-coloured halter neck top – and was ready to head back out the door, she was over an hour late to her best friend's surprise fortieth party.

The roads were slow with all the rain and as she drove, her thoughts turned to Hamish – another source of stress and worry. She still hadn't heard any updates on how he was doing and every passing minute without news made her more convinced that it was going to be the worst possible outcome.

Running so late meant Victoria had to park miles away around the corner. And then she had to make a dash through the pouring rain. When she finally got to the front door, she didn't bother knocking. The music and chatter inside was so loud, it was doubtful anyone would hear her. She tried the door, found it unlocked and headed in to discover a house absolutely packed with people. She'd never seen this many people in Harriet's home. Jeez, how many had Malek invited?

Then she realised. Of course Harriet would have added to the guest list herself after asking Malek to organise this party for her; she wouldn't have been able to help herself.

Victoria moved through the crowd, searching for the birthday girl.

*

Karen

Karen had been watching Malek flirting with a woman with a red scarf tied around her head and for some reason, she was getting a strange sense of déjà vu. But it was mixed up with something else … jealousy? Was she jealous of that woman getting Malek's attention? Or was the jealousy somehow linked to the déjà vu? She couldn't quite tell. She and Robert had been hovering on the edges of various groups, with Karen never quite feeling like any of them were welcoming them into their conversation. Robert hadn't seemed to notice, he appeared all too comfortable with a napkin stacked with canapes in one hand and a drink in the other. She was looking forward to seeing Victoria, then she'd relax a bit more.

Robert elbowed her and leaned in. 'Is it just me, or is there a real buzz around everyone anticipating Harriet's arrival? It's like she's some sort of celebrity to these people.'

Karen grimaced. Was he sounding a bit too star-struck himself?

'I've told you before that half the parents at this school idolise her. But I've also told you that she acted like a bitch to me at that karaoke night, so she's not all she's cracked up to be.'

Robert seemed shocked by her candour. 'Hey,' he hissed, 'lower your voice; you can't say that while you're at her party, surrounded by her friends. Anyway, you told me she apologised for that. If you really feel that way, why are we even here?'

'You know why we're here,' Karen said with a huff. 'I'd look like a bad sport if I didn't accept her peace offering. Besides, the moment I told you we were invited, you acted like you'd won the lottery.'

For a moment she just wanted to blurt it out: *Hey, honey, was the reason you were so excited to come to this party because you fucked the guest of honour?* But of course she wasn't going to do that. Sometimes she wondered if she was ever going to have an honest conversation with Robert about all of this. Was this an inevitable part of marriage? At some point, you just gave up and accepted mediocrity?

She glanced over at the corner of the room and saw a bright red papier-mâché heart hanging from the ceiling. Was that a piñata? Yes, she realised, it was, because there was a baseball bat resting against the wall below it. For goodness' sake, was this a children's birthday party or a grown woman's fortieth? Besides, with guests packed in this tight, there was no way anyone could take a swing at that piñata without clocking someone else over the head. With the way she was feeling right now, she wouldn't mind picking up that baseball bat and smashing the heart over and over until it broke. She couldn't help smiling as she realised how perfectly poetic and fitting that image was.

She ran a finger around the neckline of her dress. It was getting stuffy inside with the body heat of so many people crammed into the house, along with the steamy, humid weather.

'Do you want to go out on the back deck and get some air?' she asked.

Robert made a face. 'Out in the rain?'

'Well, no, it's under cover.'

'You go ahead,' he said. 'I might get a top-up.' He held up his glass, which was actually still half-full, and then headed off to the bar.

Karen tried not to feel rejected as she weaved her way through groups of people to the back door and then onto the deck. There were a few other people out there that Karen didn't recognise. Two of them were blowing white clouds into the air from their vapes. Karen could smell a scent of blueberry.

The rain was continuing to pour down, but at least there was no wind blowing it sideways, so it was dry under the cover on the deck. Fairy lights were wound around each of the posts and a very full swimming pool was lit up with turquoise lights. It was really lovely out here. Such a shame about the rain. She moved to a spot down the other end of the deck so she could be alone. The music was still loud out here, but it was easier to think without the heat clouding her mind.

She was starting to lose her nerve. Maybe she should go and talk to the catering staff, tell them she realised she'd left the sugar out of her recipe or something like that and that she needed to take her cupcakes back.

'What are you doing out here all alone?' said a voice from behind her.

She swung around and saw Victoria walking towards her from the back door.

'Oh, hey, I was beginning to wonder if you were even coming tonight.'

'Yeah, ran a bit late – but apparently I still beat the birthday girl. What's up, are you okay?'

'I'm fine, getting some fresh air.'

'Are you sure? You look a little pale.'

'Do I? I guess I'm just a bit …' Karen stopped. She had spotted someone through the glass door. Someone very familiar. It couldn't be … could it?

'Karen?' Victoria prompted. 'What's wrong?'

The person inside turned and Karen could see her face clearly.

'Sorry,' she said, 'I'm just wondering what the hell my sister is doing here.'

CHAPTER TWENTY-SEVEN

Malek

He'd bailed from the conversation with Lina and Colleen – that was far too weird and intense for his frame of mind tonight. He was wandering through the party, trying to see if he could spot the warak enabs making the rounds, when he heard Harriet's name mentioned along with the words *the most unbelievable prank.*

He stopped short and hovered on the outside of the circle of school parents, listening in on their conversation while trying to appear like he wasn't eavesdropping.

'... all started with this game. Two truths and a lie,' a woman was saying. 'And look, I know it sounds mean, but you have to understand that sometimes Karen can be a bit of a ... well, you know, a *Karen.*'

The voice continued but he missed the next few words as Farrah and Tallulah appeared in front of him.

'Dad, I have a stomach ache,' said Farrah. 'So we're going to hang upstairs in my room now, okay?'

Malek raised his eyebrows. 'Farrah, have you guys had any of the alcoholic drinks?'

'Oh my God, Dad, no! You already said I couldn't and as if we'd try and drink in front of this many adults!'

'Alright, you need anything? Will you be okay?'

'Yeah, yeah, I'll be fine. I think I just ate too much. But Tallulah's taking care of me.'

'Fair enough.' He brushed his daughter's cheek but couldn't help noticing a funny look on Tallulah's face as she was led away by Farrah. What was that? An expression of ... guilt? Maybe they *had* snuck a flute of champagne or something. Not ideal, but not the end of the world. Even though he'd told Farrah she was too young, the truth was, he'd been drinking arak with his older sister when he was fourteen.

Although there was something more to Tallulah's expression than that. Did she seem a little worried? Scared? Or maybe he was imaging it and reading into things because of the girls' fight today. He was sure everything was fine, but he'd go up and check on them a little later, make sure.

He tried to tune back in on the conversation, but now that group all seemed to be talking at once and he could only get snippets of half-sentences accompanied by peals of laughter.

'... I heard she had to call and apologise!'

'... I mean, take a joke!'

He *knew* something had happened between Harriet and Karen. What had she bloody done? He wondered if he should try to find Karen and sus it out from her. He'd liked chatting to her today, she was nice. Although maybe that was a bad idea. What if his sister accused him of flirting yet again? To be fair, he had checked Karen out when she arrived tonight – she looked great in that tight black dress. He just hoped her husband hadn't noticed him staring.

He glanced down at his glass and saw it was full again, despite him taking several large sips while standing there trying to listen in. That sneaky bastard had topped him up again. Ah, well, he couldn't fault the guy's style. He took another large gulp and moved off through the room. He didn't really want to hear any more of what that group was saying.

*

Victoria

'Your sister? How does she know Harriet?'

'I wasn't aware that she did.'

'Does she have kids at your school too?'

'Nope, Ariella doesn't even have kids.'

Victoria squinted at the crowd of people inside. 'Which one is she?'

'Curly hair. Long skirt.'

Victoria spotted her then. A petite woman with long curls and a loose white shirt hanging off one shoulder, a swishy red skirt and an oddly familiar face. Of course it was familiar, it was a slightly rounder and younger version of Karen's face.

'You want to go and say hi?'

'I … I'm not sure.'

'Don't get along with your sister?'

'Sort of ... I mean, it's not like we're constantly at each other's throats or anything, we just don't really click, if you know what I mean?'

'Yeah, I get that.'

'I'm so confused. I saw my mum today and she knew about the ... altercation I had with Harriet at the karaoke night – apparently, she heard it from Ariella. And I was trying to figure out how the hell Ariella knew – but now it seems like she must have heard about it from Harriet.'

'As in, she knew that Harriet had lied and said she'd slept with Robert? She's your sister! Surely, she should have called and checked on you. I mean I know you said you're not super close but still ...'

'I'm not sure exactly how much she knew ... my mum didn't seem to know all the details. But, I have to admit, if Ariella did know, that's kind of bothering me too.'

'Right. Why don't you go and ask her then?' Victoria moved towards the door, but Karen grabbed her hand and pulled her back.

'Wait, look.' Karen pointed and Victoria saw that Ariella was now talking with a tall, bearded man. She was leaning in close and having what appeared to be an intense conversation from the way they were both gesturing.

'Who's that she's with?' Victoria asked.

'That's Robert. My husband.'

*

Malek

The constant top-ups to his drink were adding up. Malek was feeling tipsy and relaxed. His inhibitions were beginning to fade. Maybe he would quite like for Colleen to find a private spot somewhere and kiss him. What was the point of having an open marriage if you hardly ever took advantage of it? Or maybe he'd like to find Karen, flirt with her a little, no harm in a bit of innocent banter, right? Although perhaps Karen's husband wouldn't agree.

He spotted Karen coming back inside from the deck and was about to head over and chat to her when a man he didn't recognise stopped in front of him.

'Hey, mate. I'm Cosmo,' said the guy, shaking his hand. 'Thanks so much for having me tonight. Great spread.'

'Right … nice to meet you. Sorry, I was just about to —'

'When's Harriet going to arrive? Seems like she's missing a lot of her own party.'

'Oh, right,' said Malek. He made a show of looking at his watch. 'Um, should be any minute now, I'm sure.' Malek started to move away, but Cosmo grabbed his elbow.

'Listen,' he said, 'there's actually something I'm a bit worried about.'

Malek turned back, but at the same time, Brad appeared next to them.

'Malek, I need to talk to you,' he said.

CHAPTER TWENTY-EIGHT

Karen

As she approached Ariella and Robert, Karen caught a snippet of hissed words.

'You need to trust ...'

'You're being hysterical ... Anyway, this isn't the time ...'

With a start Ariella noticed Karen and prodded Robert before quickly composing herself. Robert instantly snapped his mouth shut.

'Kaz! Hey!' she said, far too brightly.

'Ariella, hi. What are you doing here?'

Ariella hesitated and Robert stepped in. 'Apparently she met Harriet through book club. Small world, hey?'

Karen's brow furrowed. She wouldn't have picked Harriet as a book club kind of person.

'Why didn't you say anything about us having a mutual friend?' Karen asked.

'Only just realised,' said Ariella.

'No, you didn't. You told Mum about the fight I had with Harriet at the karaoke night.'

'Oh … um, I meant, I only realised quite recently. And then I didn't say anything to you because I thought maybe you wouldn't want me to bring it up.'

'Right.'

Karen paused. She wanted to ask the two of them what they'd been talking about before she'd walked over, but she didn't know how to say it in a natural way.

Before Karen could say anything else, though, Ariella beamed at her and said, 'Speaking of Harriet, I haven't even said hi yet, I'm going to go and find her.'

'I don't think she's here yet,' Karen tried to tell her, but Ariella was already walking away.

*

Malek

Brad had won out, pulling Malek away from Cosmo and suggesting they go into Malek's study for a quiet word away from the noise and the music.

'Listen,' he said once there were inside the room with the door shut. 'I know I'm not your favourite person just now, but I'm getting a bit concerned. I've sent Harriet several messages and tried to call her but I'm not getting anything back. I can see that she hasn't even opened my messages and that doesn't seem like her.'

'Okay, but why are you trying to contact her anyway? She should be here any minute.'

'Originally, I was texting her to warn her that I'd … you know, ballsed up and accidently spilled the beans on a few things with you, but, mate, have you even noticed the time? I know you said she wanted to make an entrance, but I also know how much she loves a good party. She should be here by now.'

Malek's head dropped. 'You're right,' he said. 'She should be here … and it's my fault that she's not.'

Brad frowned. 'What do you mean?'

Before Malek could answer, the door swung open and Victoria appeared.

'Hi,' she said. 'I'm really sorry to interrupt but I saw you two come in here and I need to speak with you, Malek.'

Malek felt like telling her to take a bloody number. What was with everyone having important things to speak with him about tonight?

'What is it?' he asked.

'I've been hearing lots of people out there asking where Harriet is and some of them are getting a bit worried. Is everything okay?'

'Well, if anyone was going to know, I would have thought it would be you, Vic,' Malek huffed.

'What's that supposed to mean?'

'It means I know about Harriet's ridiculous plan.'

'What plan?'

'Inviting you to move in with us. And it's probably why she's not here right now.'

'Move in? What the hell? Malek, I don't know what you're on about. And what do you mean that's why she's not here?'

'I mean I lost my bloody temper with her when dickhead over here told me about her big surprise,' he said, jerking his thumb at Brad.

'Malek. What did you do?'

*

Karen

She probably should have knocked first, but she was too impatient and was feeling bolder after a few drinks. Besides, she didn't know who else to talk to. She'd seen Victoria disappear into this room, but she stopped short when she opened the door and saw Malek, Victoria and another man standing together.

They all swung around to look at her.

'Sorry,' she said, 'I didn't realise … I just … I wanted to talk to Victoria.'

Victoria stepped forward and shut the door behind her. 'One second, Karen,' she said. She turned back to Malek. 'Malek, what's going on?'

Malek's shoulders slumped. 'I called Harriet earlier, left her a voicemail. I think that's why she's not here yet. I really let loose. Told her I was fed up with the way she walks all over me, told her announcing to everyone, including my family, that she wanted her girlfriend to move in was incredibly selfish and that she didn't deserve this party tonight and she shouldn't bother showing up. I was awful. But I didn't really think she would listen. I mean, it's Harriet. *No one* tells Harriet what to do.'

Karen was taken aback. This didn't sound like the Malek she'd met earlier today.

'Oh, Malek,' said Victoria. 'Listen, I don't know anything about this supposed plan for me to move in, but if that's something Harriet was intending, you need to know two things. First, you have every right to be angry. I know you guys have an open relationship, but I also know she's the one driving it and you've always been very patient with that. But asking me to move in would be taking it way too far. And secondly, I would have said no. This isn't what I want either, and Harriet should have known that.'

Karen was trying hard to play catch-up as she listened to the conversation.

'He's right, though,' said the other man, who'd been standing listening to the two of them. 'Harriet doesn't let anyone tell her what to do. There's no way that voicemail would have stopped her from coming here. I think something else is wrong.'

Karen checked her watch. 'It's almost nine,' she said. 'What time was she meant to arrive?'

'Eight,' said Malek.

'Have you guys got Find My Phone activated? Maybe we could figure out where she is.'

'Didn't think of that,' said Malek. He pulled out his phone and started jabbing at it, but it was clear he was a little drunk.

'Here,' said Karen, 'let me help.'

She took Malek's phone and opened up the app.

'Hang on,' said Victoria as she peered over Karen's shoulder at Malek's phone. 'This is your street, Malek. Look, she's literally arriving right now.'

'Oh, thank God,' said Malek.

'I'll go and meet her,' said Victoria. 'Maybe have a quick word before she comes in and let her know that there will not be any big announcement tonight.' She glanced at Karen. 'Sorry, I know you wanted to talk to me about something. I'll come back to you after Harriet's inside, if that's okay?'

'Of course.'

*

Victoria

When Victoria opened the front door and stepped out to search for Harriet, at first she ignored the guy walking up the driveway, assuming it was a guest who'd arrived late. But as she moved to the side to let him go past, he stopped in front of her.

'This is Harriet's party, right?' he asked.

'Yep. And the birthday girl is just about to arrive, right behind you.'

The guy spun around to look out at the street. 'I didn't see anyone else out there.'

'She must be, we just checked her phone location.'

'Oh! No, sorry, that would have been me.'

Victoria stared back at him. 'Huh? What do you mean?'

'I mean I've got Harriet's phone. She left it in my car, I was bringing it back for her.'

He held out the phone and Victoria took it from him. The guy was tall and lanky with slicked-back hair that looked disturbingly greasy. 'Are you … Rick? You work with Harriet?'

'Yep, that's me. We were on the road together today. Phone must have fallen out of her pocket. I found it down the side of the passenger seat. Only noticed it 'cause I got back in my car to go pick up some takeaway and it started buzzing with all these missed calls and messages.'

'So, wait … when did she leave it in your car? When did you last see her?'

'This afternoon when I dropped her off for some errand. She was supposed to meet me to go to our last job together but she was a no-show. I figured she'd get an Uber and turn up there on her own, but she never did. Tried calling her from the last job, but obviously she didn't pick up, seeing as her phone was in my car. Tell you what though, her junior agent really liked having the chance to run the show without her.'

Now Victoria was starting to feel a bit sick. This was getting weird. Harriet had vanished before her final job of the day, she'd left her phone behind and if she hadn't made it to the last house, where the hell was she?

She was about to ask Rick more questions, but he moved past her towards the front door.

'Think I'll join the party for a bit. Say happy birthday to her when she gets here,' he said, seemingly unconcerned. He vanished inside before Victoria could speak.

She stood still for a moment, staring down at Harriet's phone in her hands and then out at the street, as though she could make her materialise by willing it to happen, but the only movement out there was the falling rain.

She turned and headed back inside. She wasn't looking forward to telling Malek that Harriet was still missing. Inside, she spotted Rick helping himself to a drink from the bar. She considered going straight over to ask him for more specific details about where he'd last seen Harriet, but decided she was better off updating Malek first. Perhaps then the both of them could talk to Rick together. Besides, Rick had an arrogant air about him that she didn't like. Right now, he was pouring himself a Bacardi and Coke while the catering staff behind the bar appeared irritated that he hadn't waited to be served. Harriet had mentioned once before that Rick could be a bit of a sleaze at times. That was why she hadn't invited him to her fortieth in the first place. What kind of a guy goes out for takeaway, then turns up at their coworker's party instead and invites himself in?

Maybe he knew more than he was letting on.

*

Malek

'Well, that was all a bit intense, wasn't it?' Brad was saying to Karen as they walked out of the study. 'I'm Brad, by the way, Harriet's cous—' He stopped short as Malek shot him a look. 'Harriet's mate,' he finished. 'Sorry,' he added to Malek, 'force of habit.'

Nadia was waiting just outside the study and she grabbed Malek's arm as he stepped out. 'Malek, people are becoming concerned. Where's Harriet?'

'All good, don't stress. She's out front, she'll be in any minute.'

'Oh, thank God. I just heard this woman saying that she saw Harriet having a massive argument with some school dad earlier today. Seemed a bit concerning with her not showing up yet, but if she's about to walk in then I guess it isn't a problem.'

Victoria appeared in front of him.

'That was a quick conversation,' said Malek. 'Where is she?'

'Malek, I still don't know. It wasn't her, only her phone.' She held it up, then passed it over.

Malek felt his stomach drop. Just a moment ago, it had seemed like everything was fine, now Harriet was still missing? 'What do you mean only her phone?'

'A guy from her work was returning it. Rick, I think he's one of the photographers, isn't he? He came in and joined the party. He said Harriet must have left it in his car today.'

Malek checked Harriet's phone in his hand. There were several missed calls and unopened messages on the locked screen, including his own voicemail message. At least he knew now that she'd never heard his unkind words. But where the hell was she?

He turned back to Nadia.

'Tell me exactly what you heard about this fight. Do you know which school dad it was?'

'I think the woman said his name was Cosmo.'

CHAPTER TWENTY-NINE

Victoria

There was a mixture of reactions throughout the party. Some people, like Malek's aunties, who'd set up camp in a corner of the living room, hadn't even noticed that Harriet hadn't shown up yet. 'Isn't she here? Oh, I thought she must have been flitting about the house somewhere.' Others were starting to get worried. 'Have you heard about the road closures with the flooding further out west? Maybe she's caught up somewhere?'

Victoria and Malek had split up to search for Cosmo. Victoria was keeping an eye out for Rick as well. She wanted to know more about exactly where and what time he'd last seen Harriet today. Nadia had gone off in search of the woman she'd overheard, to find out more details about the argument.

A hand touched her shoulder and she turned to see Karen behind her. 'How did it go with Harriet?'

'Um. She's not here. It was a work friend dropping off her phone.'

'Shit, really?'

'Sorry, I know you wanted to talk to me, but we're getting really worried now. Have you seen Cosmo? Apparently, someone saw him having a big argument with Harriet today.'

'Oh, no, I think that's my fault.'

'What do you mean?'

'I was talking to Cosmo at school pick-up this afternoon. I told him about how Harriet's brother is still alive. He was angry … I think he felt betrayed because he'd shared about his own brother, and Harriet pretending to know how he felt cheapened it.'

Victoria suddenly thought back to the karaoke night, to that moment when Cosmo had shared his final two truths and a lie. *I'm going to make whoever killed my brother pay for what they've done.*

'Karen. Did he tell you how his brother died?'

'No, why?'

'I … I'm not sure … but there's something weird going on with Cosmo. Harriet told me he was acting cagey when she tried to ask him about which part of Brisbane he was from.'

Karen watched her intently and Victoria could see that she was thinking hard. Suddenly she snapped her fingers. 'I knew there was something bothering me when I spoke with him today. He mentioned moving *up* here to Sydney. Not down.'

'So … what does that mean? He keeps lying to everyone about where he used to live? Why? Why does he want to keep it a secret?'

Karen put an arm around Victoria's shoulders. 'I'm sure there's an explanation for everything.'

'What if ...? What if he came here for a reason, Karen? What if it's all to do with his brother? Oh God, he said he wanted to make someone pay.' Victoria was shaking and her breath was getting short. Her vision was clouding as she tried desperately to understand. To work it out.

'Okay, Victoria, take a breath. What are you talking about?'

She could barely breathe as she tried to speak. She clutched at Karen's arm and dragged in a mouthful of air.

'I think Cosmo is here for us ... For me and Harriet. I think he wants revenge.'

*

Karen

Karen was trying to calm Victoria down, telling her to breathe and rubbing her back. None of what she was saying was making any sense, but clearly the woman was terrified. As she soothed her friend, she looked up to see Cosmo walking towards them.

Karen swiftly stepped in front of Victoria, placing her body between her and Cosmo. She could feel Victoria shaking behind her.

'Hey,' said Cosmo. 'Do you two know where Malek is? I wanted to talk to him earlier, but some other bloke got in first.' His face changed as he scrutinised them. 'Is ... something wrong?' he asked.

Victoria pushed Karen aside.

'Why did you really move here?' she asked. Her voice was wobbly, but Karen could tell she was trying to hide it. 'Tell me the truth.'

Cosmo's face paled. 'What do you mean? What are you talking about?'

Victoria took another deep breath. 'During the two truths and a lie game, you said you wanted to make someone pay for your brother's death. Is that what this is all about? Is that why you're here?'

'Wait, what? My brother?'

'Yes, your brother. His name was Dion, wasn't it? And you came here to get to Harriet and me.' Victoria's voice was starting to crack now, as though she was losing her strength.

Cosmo held his hands up. 'Now, wait just a second. I have no idea what you're talking about. That's not my brother's name and I didn't know who you or Harriet were before I moved here.'

'It's … It's not?'

'No! My brother's name was Nicholas and I lost him to cancer five years ago. Look, when I said I was going to make someone pay for his death, I was telling the truth, but I guess I was making it sound more … melodramatic for that stupid game. The truth is, I've been involved in long-running lawsuit against Nick's GP. He dismissed my brother's concerns when he first went to see him with symptoms. If the cancer had been picked up sooner, he might have survived.'

'Oh,' said Victoria. 'I … I'm so sorry. It's just that Harriet is missing and someone said they saw you fighting with her today. And then I started to think …'

'You started to think what? That I hurt her? Jesus, that's a big leap from two people having an argument.'

Victoria wiped the back of her hand across her nose. 'You're right … I was mixed up. Please, forget I said any of that. I've had a bad day and I haven't been sleeping well and I'm not thinking straight.'

'Look, I shouldn't have had a go at Harriet today, I was just angry when I heard she'd lied about her own brother. It felt like that was one step too far, messing with stuff like that. I'd give anything to have my brother back, so I was upset that someone who still had a brother could wish him away. When I confronted her, she got defensive, acted like it was no big deal – and that only got me more worked up. I was trying to find Malek earlier to explain about what had happened, because I felt bad and I was worried that maybe it was my fault she was running so late tonight. I thought maybe I'd really upset her. She wasn't returning my messages. I think I'd better leave.'

'No, you don't have to go,' Victoria began, but Cosmo was already walking away.

'Leave him,' said Karen. 'It's probably for the best.'

Victoria nodded. 'I really might be losing my mind.'

'Come on,' said Karen, 'let's duck back into the study so we can talk privately for a minute.'

Once they were inside the room with the door shut, Karen spoke quietly. 'Who's Dion?' she asked.

Victoria rubbed at the back of her neck and dropped her head. 'I shouldn't have said that name.'

'Okay, but you did. Come on, who is he?'

'Fuck,' said Victoria. 'I can't … I —'

'The two truths and a lie game,' Karen interrupted. 'You were telling the truth when you said you'd killed someone, weren't you?'

Tears started to slide down Victoria's face. 'Bloody Harriet and that stupid game.' Then she shook her head. 'Why am I blaming her? I was the one who had too much to drink and said it. I don't even know why. Or maybe I do … maybe I can't handle the guilt anymore and I want to be found out.'

'Okay, start from the beginning, tell me what happened.'

'You don't want to know,' said Victoria, her voice cracking. 'You'll have to turn me in. And you'll never look at me the same way again.'

'You've essentially already admitted to it,' said Karen. 'There's no going back. At least this is your chance to tell your side. Talk to me. Trust me. Please.'

She watched as Victoria's entire body seemed to crumple. As though she simply couldn't hold on anymore. Then she opened her mouth and started to speak.

Karen listened as Victoria explained the story about Dion, and then described how she'd started to think that Dion must have been Cosmo's late brother.

When she was done, Karen stood for a moment, thinking. 'Something doesn't add up here,' she said.

'What do you mean?' Victoria asked. 'I'm not lying, that's what happened.'

'No, that's not what I'm saying. I don't think you're lying.' Karen paused.

'Victoria,' she said carefully, 'what if Harriet lied to you? I mean, think about it. A twenty-year-old woman on a holiday in another state somehow manages to cover up a murder in a short amount of time? Then later, when you try to investigate it, you can't find any news stories about him. Not even a missing person's report? I don't buy it. Murders make headlines, especially when they can't find the killer. Look at the way they're reporting about that poor girl down in Melbourne right now. There's no way this wouldn't have made the news.'

'I don't know what to say. That's how it happened.'

'Okay, tell me, do you remember the exact date?'

'Of course I do, it was the third of December, 2003.'

'Can you give me five minutes alone in here? I need to make a quick call.'

'Are you ... are you calling the police? To report me?'

'No. You'll just have to trust me, that's not what I'm doing.'

'Oh ... okay.' Victoria made as if to turn away, but Karen pulled her into a hug.

'I don't deserve your sympathy,' Victoria said, although she hugged Karen back tightly. 'I didn't go through something horrible; I *did* something horrible.'

'Sorry,' she said, 'I should have done this as soon as you told me that story ... I was too busy thinking that it didn't sound right – and I forgot that you probably really need a friend right now. Now, listen, you know as well as I do that what happened was self-defence. But like I said, I think there's more to this than you realise. Give me five, I'll be right out.'

She closed the door behind Victoria, then sat down at Malek's desk and picked up the phone. *I hope Doug is willing to bend the rules a little for his sister.*

*

Logan

Gumnut Place

He stood out on his front porch with his mug of decaf coffee and watched the rain continuing to hammer down. Across the road, at the Osman house, the party was still in full swing. He wondered if those guests realised that they might end up trapped there all night long. He doubted any of them were paying attention to the weather warnings and potential street closures around the area. He could see rivers of water running down the street out the front. Evergreen Road around the corner had already been closed due to flooding. And he figured the bridge down at Manor Creek would have gone under now too.

Once Norton Road flooded, it would be almost impossible for any of the residents of Olive Tree Estate to leave the area. So far, though, evacuation hadn't been recommended because apparently the 'experts' – whoever they were – didn't think Norton Road was in danger of flooding. Logan had a hunch they were wrong. But at least his house was up high at the top of the estate. So while it wouldn't be ideal to be temporarily trapped, they weren't in any immediate danger up here. It was just funny that all those party guests might end up having the longest party ever.

Then again, Mrs Spotswood on the right would likely be banging on their door soon, complaining about the noise. She never bothered to wait until midnight to demand that the music to be turned down. Maybe once that happened, someone would take notice of the weather.

He was about to head back inside when he noticed a dark shape climbing out of one of the second-floor windows of the Osman house. Hello, someone had enough of the party?

He watched as the person easily made their way down the trellis on the side of the house, then jumped to the ground and opened an umbrella. He squinted his eyes. Not an adult, a kid. They had a teen daughter over there, didn't they? He was distracted by a car rolling up the street and then pulling over out front. The girl ran down to the car, collapsed the umbrella and hopped in the back. The car moved away.

Hmm, should he go and knock on the door? Let them know they had an escapee? Nah, nothing wrong with a teenage kid getting up to a bit of trouble while her parents partied. She was probably just taking off to a friend's house. If he was a teen, he wouldn't want to hang around at a party full of old people either. Besides, she was the smart one, getting out of there before the last road closed.

He took another sip of his coffee and turned around to go back inside.

CHAPTER THIRTY

Malek

A hand clapped him on the back and he swung around to see his dad frowning at him.

'Malek, what's going on?' he said. 'No one seems to know where Harriet is.'

'I know, Dad, that's what I'm trying to find out.'

'Well, if she doesn't get here soon, she'll miss out on all the sambusaks. I made those special for her, I know she always loved it when Maryam cooked them. She said Arabic samosas were the best kind.'

For just a moment, Malek thought he might cry, but then he shook himself off. Harriet would show up, she would definitely show up. And he was going to be relieved *and* mad with her all at once when she did.

'Oi,' said Lina, walking over to join them. 'What's up? You're looking stressed. You need a drink? I'll get you a drink.'

'No! That's the last thing I need. I'm trying to sober up.' He hesitated, turning between his dad and his sister. He didn't want his dad to worry. 'Maybe you can put a few of the sambusaks aside, Dad. I'm sure there's still a tray of them in the kitchen.'

Hassim nodded and headed off to the kitchen.

As soon as he was out of earshot, Malek pulled Lina to the side. 'Listen, we think Harriet might be missing. As in properly missing.'

'Well, have you tried calling her?'

'Of course we have! But she doesn't have her phone. Some bloke from her work showed up with it. He said she left it in his car today. And someone *else* saw her arguing with a dad from the school this afternoon. I'm trying to find him to ask what that was all about, but I can't see him anywhere.'

'Okay, calm down, take a breath. I'm sure there's an explanation for all of this. What about the guy from her work? Where was it that he saw her last?'

'I don't know! Victoria didn't get the chance to ask. He's here somewhere, invited himself into the party, apparently.'

Colleen appeared at Lina's side with two drinks. She handed one to Lina. 'Who are you trying to find?' she asked.

'Some party crasher who might know where Harriet is,' Lina said. 'Right, what's his name? What does he look like? We'll help you search.'

*

Victoria

She couldn't see bloody Rick anywhere. Maybe the guy had left, and they were wasting their efforts looking for him.

Was it time to call the police? But Harriet had technically only been missing for a few hours. Was that long enough to involve the police?

She felt a hand close around her elbow and pull her sideways. She turned to see Karen looking at her, her eyes wide.

'We have to talk,' she said.

'What is it? Harriet?'

'No, not that, it's about what you told me … about Dion.'

'Oh …' Victoria bit her lip. 'Did you —? Am I in trouble here?'

'No, it's not that, but I've found something out you'll want to hear. Come with me.'

Victoria followed Karen onto the back deck. The rain was blowing harder onto the deck now, so there was no one else out there. Karen and Victoria stood close to the wall and lifted their hands to try to protect themselves from the spray.

'I'm going to go to jail, aren't I?' said Victoria, raising her voice to be heard above the rain.

'No. You're absolutely not, because you never killed anyone.'

'What are you talking about? I told you what happened that night. It was my fault.'

'Victoria, trust me. My brother, Doug, he's an inspector on the police force in Queensland. I called him and asked him to do a bit of off-the-books investigating for me.'

Victoria felt her throat tighten and her stomach flip with fear. 'You did call the police on me!'

'No, no, you don't understand. Dion didn't die. My brother checked up on the date you gave me. He found an old report about a young guy called Dion Kappas who was assaulted out the back of Galaxy nightclub. But he survived. The report said he claimed someone pushed him from behind and he never knew who it was. He was on the cops' radar because he was breaching his parole by being out at that club. He made a full recovery, case closed.

'Victoria, I'm sorry, but Harriet lied to you.'

Harriet

You really should have told Victoria the truth. You never should have let her believe that Dion died that night.

You didn't do it to be cruel. When you first looked at him, you honestly thought that he was dead. The sound his head made when it cracked against the kerb. His blank face. How could he not be?

And you really were prepared to do anything to cover for Victoria. But then ... you didn't have to. Next thing he was groaning and you realised he wasn't dead after all. God, it was such a relief!

Someone called an ambulance. He got carted off to hospital and you followed in a taxi, just to make sure he really was okay. You had every intention of heading straight back to the hotel and telling Victoria everything. She'd be so happy and relieved to find out that he wasn't dead, that she wasn't in any trouble, and it was all going to be fine.

One of Dion's mates who'd come to the hospital chatted to you on the way out. He was hot, had kind eyes. A much nicer guy than Dion. You were still a little tipsy.

You're not proud of what happened next. One more drink with him turned into two. From there, you ended up at his place.

But you didn't think, did you? You never think!

Because if you had, you would have realised that while you were off sleeping with some boy, poor Victoria was back at the hotel room, terrified as she waited to hear how you'd magically dealt with the 'dead body'.

You realised your mistake as soon as you returned and saw her pale, tear-streaked face, her trembling hands. All of your things packed up into suitcases, ready to leave. And then she did the one thing you weren't ready for. She told you she loved you.

And you just couldn't do it. You couldn't admit that you'd left her alone all night, thinking the absolute worst. You couldn't break her heart by confessing to being with that guy. She never would have forgiven you.

So you let her believe that you had saved her that night.

You really are a monster.

Does that mean you deserve all of this? Does that mean you deserve to die? No. No one deserves this. Come on, keep working. You need to know who did this to you. What if you have it all wrong? What if the person who killed you doesn't even know you?

What else happened today? You were working with Rick. What else? You called Victoria. Told her you wanted to meet up at the end of the day. Did that happen? Did you see Vic?

This shouldn't be so hard!

Where did she tell you to meet her? It was outside one of her parolee's places, wasn't it? Did you make it there?

Think. Figure out where you are.

You open your eyes and look around. It's dark, but there is some light coming through the window. Enough for you to make out shapes.

On the floor next to you is a small plastic container. Why didn't you notice that sooner? There's something about that container ... it's sparking a memory, but you can't quite grasp it.

Next to the container is what you think must be the murder weapon. The blunt instrument that hit you from behind. What is it? A baseball bat? A plank of wood?

And you can hear something ... it's muffled, bassy, a deep rumbling sound. Is that music? Has it been here the whole time and you only just noticed it?

Music means people.

People means help.

Not for you. It's too late for you. You're almost dead.

Work it out, Harriet.

You look at the murder weapon again. The more you stare at it, the more you can't help thinking there's something familiar about it.

CHAPTER THIRTY-ONE

Victoria

'But … but it doesn't make any sense. I saw his face, he *looked* dead.'

'He was probably unconscious,' Karen said, 'and in the shock of the moment, you thought he was dead. I don't know why Harriet let you keep believing you'd killed him, but you didn't.'

'Are you sure? Are you absolutely sure?'

'I am. I'm telling you, Victoria, you never killed anyone.'

Victoria felt her knees go weak.

'He's still alive?' she said.

'Yep, alive and well.'

'Oh my God.' The nightmare was over.

Without thinking, Victoria stepped forward and kissed Karen.

She felt Karen freeze for a split second and then she was kissing her back. After several seconds, they pulled apart and stared at one another.

'I'm so sorry,' said Victoria, 'I don't know why I did that.'

'Um, that's okay … it's fine … I —'

'I think I just got a bit caught up … it's like … it's like you've given me my entire life back. I can't even describe what this feels like.' She paused. There was another feeling underneath all the joy and extreme relief. A sickly sensation of hurt and confusion. Because why the hell would her best friend have lied to her about this all these years?

Karen picked up on the change. 'Hey, are you okay? This is a lot to take in.'

Victoria nodded. 'I am … I just … I'm wondering if I even know Harriet at all. Who would do something like this? Who would let someone believe they were responsible for a death? It's psychotic, isn't it?'

Karen lifted her hands. 'I have to admit, it really is horrendous. But until you talk to her there's no way of knowing what she was thinking or how any of this came about.'

They fell quiet, and Victoria noticed that the wind had dropped, so at least they weren't being buffeted by the sideways rain anymore. She moved around and leaned against the wall, next to Karen.

'Listen,' she said, 'knowing now that Harriet is capable of something so outrageous as this … there's something I need to tell you. I didn't know how to say this, because I didn't want to upset you, but you deserve to know.

'A few days after the karaoke night, I realised something. Harriet's two truths and a lie. When she called you to apologise, she told you that sleeping with Robert was definitely the lie because the blonde hair and blue eyes were actually the two truths – she dyes her hair dark, right?

But here's the thing – Harriet's eyes aren't blue. She wears coloured contact lenses.'

Karen was momentarily confused, then her mouth dropped open. 'Of course,' she said. 'She even mentioned the bloody coloured contacts earlier in the night. How the hell did I miss that?'

'We all did.'

'So, you think that means …'

'I don't know for sure what it means. Maybe she was still lying about sleeping with him. But I just thought you should know.'

Karen pushed off from the wall and walked over to the railing, staring out at the rain. There was a defeated look on her face. 'I think I already knew,' she said. 'I've just been in denial. That's why I kept avoiding asking him straight out.' She turned back around and faced Victoria again. 'But, um, I need to confess something. Because I was so angry with Harriet … I did something stupid.'

'What do you mean?'

'You know how we were all meant to bring one cupcake each tonight? Well, I brought a whole batch, and they all have laxatives in them.'

Victoria clapped her hand over her mouth. 'Oh my God, Karen, you didn't?'

'I know. *I know*. It was childish and rash and a horrible thing to do. But I so desperately wanted to find a way to get back at her.'

'But how does that necessarily get back at her? I mean, how would you make sure she would eat one of your cakes?'

'I guess I couldn't. But I thought if a bunch of people got diarrhoea from her party, then she wouldn't be known for throwing the most amazing parties anymore, instead she'd be known as the woman who made a heap of people shit themselves.'

Victoria couldn't help herself. She burst out laughing. 'Jesus, Karen. That's kind of diabolical.'

'Trust me, I've done worse in my time. I've never been good at forgive and forget. I always find a way to even the score.'

Victoria stopped laughing. 'Ah,' she said. 'Your other "truth" in two truths and a lie. I'd been meaning to ask you about that. You broke someone's fingers.'

Karen nodded. 'I never meant for it to go that far. It was a group of mean girls who bullied my sister. I put quick-dry super glue in the finger holes of the bowling balls they were using. I didn't think it through. I thought they would just be embarrassed about being stuck with a heavy bowling ball hanging off their hand. I figured that eventually there would be a way to get them off. I didn't realise what would happen when one of them tried to bowl. She swung her hand in the air and went to let go, but the bowling ball stayed stuck to her hand and gravity took over. It bent her fingers back and snapped two of them. It was awful.

'Ariella was furious with me. She was always more of a pacifist. And she hated feeling like she was a part of that.'

'Wow. You've got one hell of a dark streak, Karen. Gotta say, you get more and more interesting every time I talk to you.'

'You're not repulsed by me? By these terrible things that I've done?'

'Look, if you'd let me eat one of your cakes tonight without saying anything, I would have been pretty pissed off with you – but no, I'm not. I do, however, wonder if you should go and talk to someone one of these days … maybe just see if you can learn some tactics for dealing with anger without resorting to straight-up revenge.'

They were distracted by the sound of a woman laughing.

'Did that come from the pool?' Victoria asked.

'The pool? In this weather?'

Karen turned around as Victoria joined her at the railing. A fully clothed couple were kissing in the middle of the pool, unbothered by the heavy rain.

'I think that's Rick!' said Victoria. 'No wonder we couldn't find him. Who's he with?'

Karen held her hand up to shield her eyes from the rain. 'I can't tell … I can't see her face.'

'Come on, let's grab Malek and tell him we found Rick.'

Back inside, they found Malek walking out of the kitchen. 'I can't find either of them,' Malek was saying. 'Maybe they both left?' He was holding a cupcake and was lifting it to his mouth to take a bite. Victoria slapped it out of his hand.

Malek winced. 'I know,' he said, 'I shouldn't be eating cake at a time like this … It's just, I eat when I'm nervous.'

'Ah, it's not that,' she said. 'I was talking with one of the caterers. Apparently there's been some sort of contamination in the kitchen between the cakes and the other food. They'll all have to be thrown out. But look, don't worry about that now ... we found Cosmo and he explained what the argument was about today. I don't think there's any issue there. But more importantly, we also found Rick.' She jutted her chin to the back door. 'Come on, he's out in the pool.'

'The pool! Seriously?'

They made it only a few steps before they were stopped by several people approaching them at once. First was Robert.

'Karen?' he said. 'What's going on? People are saying Harriet is missing?'

Second was Brad. 'Malek! When were you going to let me know that it wasn't Harriet arriving earlier? Someone just told me it was some bloke with her phone!'

But before anyone could answer, Malek's sister Lina and another woman arrived, either side of an uncomfortable-looking Cosmo.

'Colleen and I found him,' said Lina. 'Out the front, about to leave.'

'I tried to explain to them,' said Cosmo apologetically.

*

Karen

The entire group were trooping out into the rain to talk to Rick when Karen felt her watch buzz on her wrist. She glanced at it and saw an Instagram notification.

Tallulah shared a photo.

The first few words of the image description just said, *Check this out, my parents have no idea ...*

Oh God, what now?

She pulled her phone out of her jacket pocket as they all hurried down the stairs towards the pool and opened up the notification on the screen. Before she could look at the photo, she heard Robert exclaim loudly, 'Ariella!'

Karen looked up from her phone and then followed his gaze to the couple in the pool. There was a bottle of champagne in the man's hand, which he was holding above the surface of the water. The woman was kissing his neck enthusiastically.

Karen squinted through the rain at her. 'It's not, is it?' she said. Then, 'Bloody hell, it is. Ariella! What are you doing?' She slipped the phone back into her pocket and ran in front of the others to the pool's edge. 'Hey! Ariella!'

Malek appeared next to her. 'Ibn kalb,' he growled. Then shouted out to be heard about the rain, 'Oi! Rick! We need to talk to you!'

Rick and Ariella seemed to suddenly become aware of their audience and pulled apart.

Ariella jerked away from him. 'Fuck!' she exclaimed, at the same time as Rick said, 'Ah, kind of busy here.'

'Yeah, too bad, mate. Come here.'

'Who's Ariella?' Karen heard Malek's sister say behind them.

'That's Karen's sister,' Victoria replied.

'Come on, mate,' Brad called. 'Move it.'

Rick said something quietly to Ariella and then waded over to the edge of the pool and rested his elbows on the side. 'What's up?' He took a swig from the bottle. Ariella remained in the middle of the pool, treading water, a stony look on her face.

'What's up? *What's up?* Who the fuck do you think you are? We've been searching for you half the bloody night. We need to know – when and where did you last see Harriet?'

Karen could see the veins in Malek's neck tensing.

Rick took another large gulp from the bottle. 'She asked me to drop her off around three thirty-ish, maybe three forty-five, before our last job. She was buying flowers, taking them somewhere … I don't know what else. She was meant to meet me after that to get another lift to our next job, but she didn't show.'

'Ariella!' Karen hissed. 'What's going on? This doesn't seem like you.'

Ariella stared back at her sister and then gazed pointedly at Robert. 'Ask your husband,' she said.

Karen blinked and turned to Robert. 'What does she mean?'

'Let's just focus on Harriet for now,' he said, nodding towards Malek, who was still questioning Rick.

'Yes,' Malek said. 'You dropped her off, but *where?*'

'Well, actually —' began Rick.

Then two things happened at once. A woman came barrelling through the side gate, yelling for Malek, and Karen heard her daughter's voice shout from the deck, 'MUM! I need to talk to you!' before Tallulah came racing down the wet stairs towards them, slipping and falling on one of the last few steps.

'Tallulah!' Karen yelled, rushing away from the pool to try to catch her daughter at the bottom of the stairs.

*

Malek

In all the commotion of Karen's daughter falling and his bloody neighbour telling him off for the noise, Malek couldn't hear what Rick was saying. And then he was doing his best to calm down Mrs Spotswood as well as trying to see if Tallulah was okay – she seemed alright; twisted her ankle, but no worse than that. Cosmo and Colleen had been close to the stairs and between the two of them, they were able break her fall. When he finally turned around to keep talking to Rick, the bloody idiot was back in the middle of the pool, kissing Ariella again.

Malek could feel his rage growing and next thing, he was running at the pool and jumping. He landed with a huge splash, grabbing Rick by the back of his shirt and dragging him to the edge.

'Tell me where Harriet is!' he shouted.

'Christ!' said Rick. 'I already told you, didn't you hear me? I said I left her right around the corner from *here*, numbnuts. Didn't even realise it was near her place when she asked me to let her out. She didn't say. I didn't know till I got here tonight.'

'That's not right,' said Malek. 'Harriet hasn't been home all day.'

'What do you want me to say? That's where I last saw her.'

'Malek,' said Mrs Spotswood.

'Not now!'

'MALEK!'

'WHAT?'

'Harriet *was* here today.'

'What? How do you know?' Malek shoved Rick to the side and clambered out of the pool. He wiped the water off his face and stood dripping as Mrs Spotswood spoke.

'Because I saw her. I was looking out my kitchen window this afternoon, and I saw her go into that room there.' She pointed at the door to the granny flat under the house.

Malek eyed the door and for a moment his vision tunnelled. He was about to move towards it when Karen, who had been speaking quietly to Tallulah on the bottom step, jumped up.

'Malek!' she said. 'Farrah is in trouble.'

Malek swung around. 'What?'

'She lied when she said she felt sick,' said Tallulah. 'She's gone out.'

'What do mean? Out? Out where? How?'

'She called an Uber. She went to meet her new boyfriend,' said Karen.

'Boyfriend? Farrah doesn't have a boyfriend.'

'Yes, she does,' said Tallulah. 'And he's not a good guy.'

*

Victoria

Malek looked like he was about to have a panic attack. Victoria could see that he was being pulled in two different directions. She grabbed him by the shoulders. 'It's okay,' she said. 'Prioritise Farrah.'

'But ...' He started towards the door of the flat.

'I'll figure out what's happened to Harriet. Just go.'

Malek locked eyes with her then nodded. He rushed over to Tallulah and disappeared around the side of the house with the girl and her parents, Robert with one arm around his daughter's waist, supporting her as she limped on one foot. Hopefully one of them was sober enough to drive.

Colleen and Lina were helping Ariella out of the pool. Victoria supposed Malek had broken the mood when he leapt on top of Rick and pulled them apart. Now she fixed her gaze towards the entrance to the flat. Brad and Cosmo were standing back from it, waiting for Victoria to take the lead. Next door, a dog had started up a constant stream of barking from behind the fence, the animal obviously disturbed by so much commotion. The sharp sounds seemed to pierce Victoria's skull, making her head throb in time with the yaps.

What the hell was Harriet doing down here today? Even if the neighbour had seen Harriet head inside earlier, why on earth would she still be there? But perhaps they would at least find some sort of clue that would tell them where to search for Harriet next.

She placed her hand on the doorknob, twisted it and pushed the door open. A faint smell of chemicals tickled her nostrils and she paused to rub her nose. Inside, it was pitch black.

'Harriet?' she said. 'You're not … you're not still down here, are you?'

She stepped into the room and felt around the inside of the doorway for a light switch. Her fingers found it and she flipped it on.

Behind her, she heard a scream.

'Someone call an ambulance,' Victoria whispered.

CHAPTER THIRTY-TWO

Karen

'Robert can drive,' she said as they ran down the driveway. 'He's only had a couple. Tallulah, tell us everything you know.'

'I told her not to go,' said Tallulah, through tears. 'I said it wasn't a good idea and we should both stay at the party, but she begged me to cover for her.'

'It's okay, forget about that. We need to know where she is.'

They all climbed into Karen's car, Malek in the front passenger seat, his suit still dripping with water, while Karen sat in the back with Tallulah.

'I think they were meeting up behind the Grove shopping plaza,' said Tallulah.

Robert took a sharp turn at the end of the street to head for the shops and Karen slid heavily across the back seat.

'I tried to get you to come upstairs and catch us before she left, Mum, that's why I put that post up on Instagram. I thought if you saw we had alcohol upstairs on your stupid fake account, you'd come running. It seemed like the only way to do it without straight up snitching on Farrah ... I ... I promised her I wouldn't, and I didn't want to break my promise.'

'What? You know about that account?'

'I've known for weeks. Farrah's mum told her you said you were catfishing me when you guys all went out together. That's why I've been so angry at you. I picked your fake account straight away and I was going to block you, but Farrah convinced me we should use it to mess with you, post stuff to freak you out. But then tonight, I thought I could use it to save Farrah. But you didn't come.'

'Oh, honey, I'm so sorry, I should have been there for you. But I was at a party; why would you think I'd be checking my Instagram? And why wouldn't you just come down and tell me? You know her safety trumps your promise not to tell on her.'

'I did!' Tallulah exclaimed indignantly. 'As soon as I realised you weren't going to get there in time, I ran down and told you! And now she's going to hate me forever because I *did* break my promise and I didn't have her back.'

'Right, of course you did. Sorry. But Tallulah, trust me, if you think this guy might be bad news, then this *is* you having her back. Farrah will understand.'

'Who is he?' Malek interrupted from the front.

'I don't know, Farrah was keeping it a secret ... that's why Farrah and I fought today.'

'You were fighting over him?' Karen asked.

'We were fighting because I didn't want her to send the photos.'

317

'What photos?'

'He asked her to send him, you know … *photos*, of herself. And I could tell she didn't really want to do it, but she felt like she had to, because he said that's what all the girls did. And I just think he's going to make her do more. That's how her phone broke … I was going to delete the photos so she couldn't send them, and she tried to grab it from me. Mum, he's creepy. The messages he sends her … I don't know what it is about them, but something's not right.'

Malek banged his hand against the car door. 'She never keeps secrets from me,' he said. 'Never. Why did she do this?'

Karen reached a hand between the seats to touch his shoulder. 'Because she's a teenage girl, and that's what teenage girls do,' she said. 'But it's okay, we'll find her.'

Robert suddenly slammed on the brakes. 'Shit,' he said. 'The road's closed up ahead.'

'What? Why?' Karen asked.

'It's flooded,' he said.

'I'll bloody well swim through it,' Malek growled.

'No, you won't,' said Karen. 'We can turn down Southgate Street instead, it's fine. Farrah's Uber probably had to do that too.'

Robert did a U-turn at speed and the tyres slid through the water.

'Easy,' said Karen, 'we're no good to anyone if we crash. Take a left up there.'

'Robert,' said Malek, 'do *not* slow down.'

*

Victoria

'Is she …? Is she alive?' Lina asked.

For a moment, Victoria was straight back in that alley behind the nightclub on the Gold Coast. All she could hear was Harriet's voice: *I think he's dead.*

Harriet was lying face down on the floor. Her hair was shiny with bright red blood. Next to her was a bouquet of yellow sunflowers spilling out of purple paper. The sweet scent of the flowers mingled with that strange chemical smell in the air.

But he hadn't been dead, had he? Harriet had lied to her.

Victoria knew she needed to go to Harriet, but she was frozen to the spot.

Then she saw Harriet's fingers move. She ran towards her and dropped to the floor. It didn't matter that she'd lied, it didn't matter that she'd manipulated, she was still her best friend and she needed her.

'Harriet? Harry? I'm here.'

Harriet blinked several times, then tried to lift her head.

'No, don't try to move,' said Victoria, touching her hand to Harriet's back. 'We're getting help.' She looked up at Lina. 'We are getting help, right?'

Lina nodded. 'Colleen is already on the phone.'

She could hear Rick and Ariella outside asking what was happening and Brad telling them to make themselves useful and go upstairs to see if anyone was a doctor or a nurse. Amongst it all was the sound of that damned dog still barking incessantly.

Victoria needed to shut them all out. None of what they were saying mattered, none of it. She had to save Harriet.

*

Malek

'She was upset when she left,' said Tallulah. 'He'd sent her a message to say there was a special cupcake for her in the letter box and when she couldn't find it, she was worried he'd be annoyed with her for losing it.'

Malek thumped the door again with the side of his closed fist. 'Who is this little fucker, making my daughter feel afraid?'

'We're nearly there,' said Karen. 'Tallulah, how long ago did she leave? How much of a head start does she have on us?'

'Not long. I came down to get you almost right away once she was gone, but then I fell, so I guess that slowed us up a bit ...'

'Okay, hopefully they're still there at the meeting place. Robert take a right just here, we can go straight into the carpark around the back.'

Robert spun the steering wheel and again Malek heard Karen grunt as she and Tallulah were hurled sideways. The SUV bumped over the entrance to the carpark and Robert slowed down, turning his lights on high beam to look for Farrah and her secret boyfriend through the pouring rain.

'Do you see them?' Malek asked.

There was no one there.

320

Harriet

You never did make it to the meeting place with Victoria, did you?

It's coming back to you now – snatches of the rest of the afternoon. Being let out by Rick next to the flower stand at the top of Paddington Street. Buying the sunflowers, running into Cosmo, arguing.

And then you were rushing to get home. There was one last thing you needed to put in the granny flat before you presented it to Victoria. A finishing touch. The beautiful bunch of sunflowers you'd bought. Her favourite. You can see them now … They're scattered across the floor; you must have dropped them when you fell. You were meant to leave the flowers in the flat and then head back out to meet Rick on the corner so he could drive you to the last house.

You found the container with the cupcake in the letter box on the way in. Some guest must have been confused about the instructions and delivered it early. You were hungry. You had the flowers tucked under one arm and you were eating the cake as you walked around the side of the house.

Malek and Farrah were inside moving furniture. You watched them through the window, but they didn't see you. He's so good with her. You went into the granny flat and were heading for the cupboard

321

to find a vase for the flowers but you started to feel strange. Your throat began to burn. You were coughing.

The cupcake.

Then a loud thud. Movement out of the corner of your eye. The blow to the back of your head.

Who was it? Think! What are you missing?

One last chance before you go.

Malek.

Karen.

Victoria.

Colleen.

Cosmo.

Rick.

But no. It doesn't add up, does it? And you've just realised why. It's because you've finally recognised the murder weapon.

What if it was never really murder at all?

You look again at the small plastic container next to you. That's what the cake came in. There's a label stuck to the side, a name scrawled on it. It's a school lunch box.

You read the name: Serge.

Cosmo's son.

The pieces fall into place.

What if the cupcake was meant for Farrah?

You need to get them a message. They need to know that Farrah might be in trouble.

CHAPTER THIRTY-THREE

Victoria

She could tell that Harriet was trying to say something and she was torn between telling her to save her strength or encouraging her in case these were going to be her last words. But surely not ... Harriet couldn't die, could she?

Victoria's heart was racing and her hands were trembling. This was her best friend. She could not lose her best friend.

How the hell had this happened?

Harriet was still lying face down on the carpet, her head turned to one side, facing Victoria. Victoria had been too scared to move her in case she made things worse. She was holding a red scarf with white polka dots against the wound on the back of Harriet's head. Colleen had given it to her.

'Just hang in there, Harry,' she said. 'You're going to be okay.'

But then a small smile twitched at the corners of Harriet's mouth, and she said quietly, 'No.'

'Harriet! Yes! You've got this, stay strong for me. You can't let go.'

Lina had been hovering nearby, occasionally moving towards them as though she wanted to help, but then she would pull back, realising she didn't know what to do.

Meanwhile Brad had come into the room, taken one glimpse of Harriet, spun around and headed straight back out. 'I'm sorry,' he'd said, his voice choked up. 'I'm sorry, I can't handle this.'

Victoria looked up at Lina. 'Who did this to her?'

Lina lifted her hands. 'I can't even imagine.'

Victoria felt Harriet's fingers brush her arm. She studied her. 'Yes, I'm here, I'm still here.'

'Need to tell …' Harriet said. 'Cake … poison.'

Victoria felt goose bumps spread across her skin. 'What? What cake?' She scanned the room frantically, spotting the cupcake on the table with a bite taken out of it.

Cosmo walked back into the room with a blanket and a towel under one arm. He looked agitated. 'Listen, I … I got these from upstairs for her, I didn't know what else to do … but I think I have to leave. I just got an urgent call.'

'Thanks,' said Victoria, taking the blanket from him and putting it over Harriet. 'It's fine, go if you need to,' she said. Then she dropped her head down to Harriet's face. 'I'm listening,' she said. 'Tell me again … I don't think I heard right.'

'Him,' said Harriet.

'Him? Him who?'

She felt Harriet's hand move again so she sat back up to see what Harriet was trying to do. Slowly, shakily, Harriet lifted her hand and pointed at Cosmo, who was heading for the door.

Victoria's heart kept thudding. She stared at Cosmo with accusation in her eyes. 'You,' she said. 'You did this to her?'

Cosmo spun around, shaking his head, holding his hands up. 'No!' he said. 'I already told you! I didn't! I couldn't —'

But then Victoria heard Harriet's voice again. 'Not him, not me,' she whispered.

'What do you mean, not him? Harriet, I don't understand.'

'His son.'

'Cosmo's son? What does he have to do with any of this?' Victoria looked up at Cosmo. He was coming towards them again.

'What did she say?' he said.

'I don't know!' said Victoria. 'There's a cake over there and I think she said it has poison in it, but now she's saying something about your son, I don't … I don't understand!'

Cosmo crouched down next to them and snatched up a plastic container. 'Where did this come from?' he asked.

'I have no idea.'

'This belongs to Serge.' His gaze moved from the container to the cake on the table, then he stood and walked over to it. He picked up the cake and sniffed. 'It's not poisoned,' he said. 'I'm not sure why she thought that. Maybe it tasted strange … But this smell – it's a pot cupcake.'

Victoria felt a hand close over her arm. She searched Harriet's face.

'Farrah,' she whispered.

Victoria looked at Cosmo. 'I don't get it, what the hell is going on?'

That's when she saw the realisation dawn on Cosmo's face. 'The boy that Farrah snuck out to meet, it must have been Serge,' Cosmo said. 'I have to go. I have to call Malek.'

'Go, do what you need to do.' Victoria turned back to Harriet. 'We'll get it sorted,' she said. 'We'll make sure Farrah is okay.'

Harriet managed a faint squeeze of her hand.

That was when the light went out of her eyes.

*

Cosmo

Gumnut Place

Cosmo was running out to his car. How many drinks had he had tonight? Two? Three? Was he okay to drive? He had to be.

Why the fuck had he moved to this place? Why hadn't he listened to his wife? If something happened to Farrah, he would never forgive himself.

He checked his phone when he jumped in the car. Serge didn't know Cosmo had set it up so that he could track his smartwatch. He found Serge's location and called Malek as he drove, muttering a small prayer of thanks that he'd saved Malek's number back when he'd RSVP'd to Harriet's party.

'What is it?' Malek asked as soon as he answered.

'I know where Farrah is.'

'Where?'

326

'She's with my son, Serge. I'm on my way. Meet me there. As fast as you can.' He gave Malek the details and hung up. He couldn't bring himself to explain any further. Couldn't handle telling Malek what he was afraid of.

Harriet was right to be suspicious when she'd questioned him about which part of Brisbane he was from and he'd been unable to answer her. They'd never lived in Brisbane, that was just their cover story. The truth was that they'd moved up from Melbourne. Right after that girl went missing.

It was his wife, Alyson, who'd found photos of the girl on Serge's phone, taken the night she'd gone missing. And when the news of the missing girl started to spread, she came to Cosmo with her concerns. At first Cosmo had tried to deny it. There was no way their son could have had anything to do with it. No way Serge had actually done anything to hurt the girl.

'Okay,' he'd said, 'so he was one of the last to see her before she went missing. We'll talk to him. He'll explain. Maybe he can help with the search.'

But when Cosmo had talked to Serge, that's when it all went wrong. 'I can't talk to the police about it, Dad,' he'd said. 'No one knows we were together. She was keeping me a secret because she wasn't allowed to date. If they know I was with her, then they'll think I'm a suspect. They'll think I did something to her. Don't make me talk to them, Dad.'

And Cosmo had believed him. Trusted him. He thought he was protecting his son by taking him and running. Alyson hadn't wanted them to leave; she said Cosmo was doing the wrong thing.

'If our son is innocent, then we have to trust the system,' she said. 'We can't lie about his involvement – we're interfering with a missing person investigation. We have to tell the truth.'

So Cosmo and Serge left without her.

Later, when Cosmo heard the news that the girl's body had been found, his resolve had faltered – did he need to take Serge back? What if he could help identify the murderer? But then, only a day or two later, someone had been arrested for the girl's murder. His son was vindicated. And maybe Alyson had been right, maybe if they'd stayed and told the truth, everything still would have worked out, but that wasn't a risk he was able to take. He asked Serge if he wanted to go back, now that he was no longer in danger of being accused of a crime he didn't commit, but Serge was angry with his mother for not showing the same faith in him as Cosmo had. He wanted to stay in Sydney. He liked their new life.

But then, tonight, Alyson had phoned him.

He'd been about to hang up on her. He was still angry with her for not trusting their son too. Besides, everything was going crazy with Harriet and he needed to help.

'We're not coming home, Alyson,' he'd said. 'Serge can't forgive you for thinking he could —'

'Cosmo! Listen! They've released the guy without charge. They know she was with Serge that night. They were here today, at the house, collecting evidence. Cosmo … you have to accept the truth: our son is not the boy we think he is. You have to bring him back here.'

Cosmo hadn't wanted to believe it. He had hung up on Alyson. He was going to go home and talk to Serge, figure all of this out. It couldn't be true. But then Harriet had whispered those words.

Farrah was with Serge.

And now he knew that Alyson was right.

CHAPTER THIRTY-FOUR

Malek

He hung up the phone and turned in his seat. 'Cosmo says it's his son Farrah is with and he knows where they are. He's on his way too.'

'Serge?' Tallulah asked from the back seat. 'That's why she wouldn't tell me who it was.'

'What do you mean?' Karen asked, at the same time as Robert said, 'Which way?' while pulling out of the shopping centre carpark.

'Left. Towards Parsons Road.'

'Because I told her I had a crush on him, so she probably didn't want to hurt my feelings by telling me the boy I liked wanted her instead. This is all my fault. I was mean to her at first, when she said she liked him. I acted as though he wouldn't like her back, but it was only because I was scared that he would.

'But then she started telling me about this new secret boyfriend, and I thought it was someone else altogether. When I tried to tell her that I didn't think this guy was right for her because of the messages he sent, she got angry at me. She must have thought I knew it was Serge and I was only trying to get between them. But I had no idea it was him.'

'It's not your fault, Tallulah,' said Karen. 'We know who she's with now and we're going to find them.'

'Which way next?' asked Robert.

'Take a right. He says they're down behind the school, near Bellbird Bridge.'

'Bellbird Bridge?' repeated Karen from the back seat. 'What would they be doing there in all this rain?'

'I don't know, but Cosmo sounded confident that's where they were.'

'Wait,' said Robert, 'if Urquhart Road was flooded … does that mean that the bridge …?'

'Just floor it, mate,' urged Malek.

*

Victoria

Victoria and Lina had rolled Harriet over onto her back and were taking it in turns to do chest compressions. But each pump of Harriet's chest felt more and more futile. The towel they had placed under her head was soaked in blood.

'Keep trying,' Victoria said, 'we have to keep trying. Why the hell is the ambulance taking so long?'

'It's the roads,' said Colleen, 'someone said they're flooded so the paramedics will be delayed … but I think they're almost here now, I can hear sirens.'

Lina sat back, breathing hard, as Victoria took over again. 'Victoria,' she said quietly, 'I don't think we can bring her back.'

'No!' shouted Victoria. 'She's not gone. She has to be okay.' She pressed harder and felt a rib crack under her hands. 'Oh God,' she said, as a wail rose up inside her. She collapsed on top of Harriet, squeezing her. 'She can't die,' she whispered. 'She's my best friend.'

'This way,' called out a voice from outside, 'just through here.'

'I know, honey, I know,' said Lina, gently pulling Victoria back. 'But the paramedics are here now, maybe there's something they can …' Her voice trailed off and Victoria knew it was because she didn't really believe anything could be done.

Harriet was gone.

*

Karen

Robert parked as close as he could get to the small reserve behind the school.

'Tallulah, stay here, okay?' said Karen as the three adults got out of the car.

'But I want to help,' she said.

'I know you do, but I need you to be safe. We'll find her.'

Karen slammed the door shut and ran after Malek and Robert, who were already several paces ahead. The ground squelched with mud beneath her feet and made each step feel heavy. They fought their way through bushes and wound around trees, racing to get to the small, hidden picnic area.

As soon as the bridge was in sight, Karen's heart sank. The creek had broken its banks and water was gushing over the top of the bridge. Sticks and other debris rushed along in the flow.

'Malek!' Karen called. 'If the bridge is gone, then the picnic tables will be going under.'

'I know,' he shouted, but she could hardly hear him above the sound of the rain and rushing water. She saw his shoe get stuck in the mud. He wrenched his foot free, leaving the shoe behind.

Finally, they came through the trees to the sloped clearing where the picnic tables were. The water had swelled from the creek and up the hill. It had already crept halfway up the poles of the gazebo that stretched over the picnic area. They could just see the tops of the tables, about to be overcome by the flood.

Standing on one of the tables was Farrah, completely alone and shaking with fear.

'Dad!' she shouted. 'It came up so fast. And Serge just … He just left me here and I didn't know what to do. I didn't know if I should follow him or wait to see if it went back down.'

'It's okay, you're going to be okay. I'm coming to get you,' Malek called to his daughter, moving towards the floodwaters.

'Malek, hang on,' said Karen. 'You could get washed away.'

'I'm not leaving her there for the water to keep rising!'

'Just give me thirty seconds,' said Robert. 'I've got rope in the car, I'll be right back.' He took off at a run.

Malek hovered impatiently at the water's edge. 'It's getting higher,' he said, as the rain continued to pummel them. 'I don't want to wait.'

'You're no good to her if you get caught in the current and end up down in the creek. Robert will be fast, trust me.' She focused on Farrah, who was scared and unsteady on her feet. 'Hold on,' she called. 'Your dad is coming to help you.'

Robert appeared beside them again, breathing hard and putting his hands on his knees. 'Here,' he said, holding the coiled rope out to Karen while he caught his breath. 'Tie this around Malek's waist.'

Karen and Malek worked together to secure the rope tightly. Again, he made to enter the rising water, but Karen grabbed his shoulder.

'Not here,' she said.

'What now?'

'Go in a little higher, that way if the water does push you along, you'll still reach the table.'

'Oh,' he said. 'Good point.'

Karen and Robert took hold of the rope and started feeding it out bit by bit as Malek waded through the water towards the picnic table.

Within seconds they could see how powerful the current was. Malek was having trouble continuing in a straight line and Karen and Robert had to plant their feet and lean back to keep hold of him.

'I can't believe that boy just left her there,' said Karen

through gritted teeth as she pressed her shoulder against Robert's to help keep her balance.

'Probably scared,' said Robert.

'Still, the little bastard should have called someone for help.'

'Agreed.'

They watched as Malek reached the picnic table and gripped it with one hand while taking Farrah's hand in the other. They couldn't hear what he was saying to her, but it appeared she was nervous about climbing down to him and he was having to coax her.

Karen glanced sideways at Robert, watching the determination in his face as he held tight to the rope while they waited.

He caught her looking and gave her a half-smile. 'She's going to be okay, he's nearly got her.'

Karen couldn't help it – the words tumbled out. 'Robert ... Are you having an affair?'

Robert's face changed. 'What? Are you serious?'

'Yes. I'm deadly serious. I need to know. Have you cheated on me?'

'This is ridiculous,' he said, nodding at the water. 'I am not having this conversation right now.'

'But ...' she said. 'What did Ariella mean? When she made that comment in the pool? And why were you two having some sort of secret conversation earlier? And ... and why did Harriet tell me you'd slept with her?'

Robert's face hardened. 'Harriet! Why the bloody hell does everyone keep —' He cut himself off and started over.

'For Christ's sake, Karen. Is this some kind of joke? I'd like to think my wife would know me better than that. I am not going to dignify a single one of those questions with an answer. We are in the middle of trying to rescue a child. I can't believe you would ask me these things any time, let alone *right now*.'

Karen returned her eyes to Malek and Farrah. She could see that Farrah had finally agreed to climb down and Malek was getting her to wrap her arms around his neck.

'Start pulling,' said Robert, 'they're coming in.'

Karen shifted her attention back to the rope and they began to pull, hand over hand, as Malek and Farrah came towards them. But all she could think was, *He never denied the affair.*

*

Malek

The current was stronger than anything he'd ever experienced. Stronger than when he'd been caught in a rip in the ocean. Stronger than any force he'd ever felt against his body. If this water had been any higher, there was no way he would have made it through, not even with Karen and Robert holding onto the rope.

But he didn't want Farrah to know he was struggling.

Fake it till you make it.

Fake it till you make it.

Farrah's face was buried in his neck and her body was shivering. 'Dad, I'm so sorry.'

She'd said it over and over again, and each time Malek shushed her. 'No, baby, this isn't your fault.'

His entire body was aching with the effort of pushing against the rushing water, but the pull of the rope around his waist was giving him extra support to keep moving forward. *Almost there.*

When they finally clambered out of the water and onto the hill, Malek collapsed onto the grass. His legs felt like jelly. He wanted to lie there forever, but Karen and Robert were already pulling him to his feet.

'Come on, I know you're tired, mate, but let's all get away from here in case the water surges higher,' said Robert. 'With a flash flood like this, there's no way of knowing what might happen.'

Karen put her arm around Farrah's waist. 'I think I've got a blanket in the boot we can wrap you in,' she said. 'Let's just get to the car and then you can both rest.'

Malek allowed Robert to support him as they trudged back through the rain towards the car. As they got closer, he lifted one hand to shield his eyes from the bright headlights of a second car that was parked next to Karen's. The driver's door had been left open, allowing rain into the car.

'Where's Cosmo?' Robert asked as they grew closer. 'His car's empty?'

'Gone to look for us?' Malek suggested.

'Wait,' said Karen, her voice rising suddenly. 'Why is our car empty too? Where's Tallulah?'

*

Serge

Apple Hills College bus stop

He really wasn't planning on hurting that girl. She was hot, and she was probably a virgin, and he was going fuck her – obviously. But he wasn't going to *kill* her! The other girl back in Melbourne, Amber, that hadn't even been his fault. It was an accident. She'd changed her mind at the last minute, which was infuriating ... so he'd had to hold her down. He didn't realise he'd squeezed so hard until it was too late.

Farrah was the one who said she wanted to try some weed. Apparently, she'd attempted using a bong with her mate recently, but they hadn't really known what they were doing. She'd told him about the weird thing with everyone taking cupcakes to her mum's party, so he'd said he'd make her a special one. He figured it would be good if she ate it just before they met up, that way she'd be a bit more relaxed too.

It was pretty fucking annoying when she told him she never found the cake in the letter box. More likely she got cold feet and backed out of trying it.

But now the creek had started flooding, right when he and Farrah were about to have some fun. She got all whingy then. She was scared about walking through the water, so he ditched her and took off. Let her figure it out on her own. He had walked up the road and was waiting for an Uber but apparently some of the roads around here were flooded now too, so his ride kept getting cancelled. He was trying to book another one when Farrah's mate came up to him – she was half-running, half-limping and she was yelling at him like she was possessed.

'Dude, chill,' he said as she stopped in front of him. 'What's your problem?'

'Where's Farrah? What have you done with her? Did you hurt her?'

He stared back at her. 'I don't even know what you're on about. Farrah's back in the park.'

'You just left her? Alone?'

'Fuck, she's not a baby. Piss off, I'm trying to get a ride home.'

That was when the girl launched herself at him, started pushing him and crying and shouting. First, he tried to bat her away, but could he really be blamed for putting his hands around her throat? It was self-defence! It was the only way he could get her under control.

And then next thing, *bam*. He didn't even see it coming, the fist that connected with his face. He was knocked backwards, forced to let go of the girl's neck. He stumbled for a few steps and then looked up to see what had happened.

He couldn't believe it when he saw his own dad standing there. 'Did you … did you just punch me in the face?' he asked, turning away to spit blood on the ground.

But his dad was facing the girl. 'Tallulah,' he said, 'are you okay? Are you hurt?'

For a second, Serge considered taking a swing back at his dad, but then he sized him up and changed his mind. One day he could probably take him, but not tonight.

He turned and ran.

CHAPTER THIRTY-FIVE

Karen

The relief she felt when she saw Cosmo bringing Tallulah towards the cars was so overwhelming, Karen's legs almost gave way. Tallulah hobbled the last few steps and flung herself into her arms.

'Oh God,' said Karen, squeezing her daughter tightly. 'I was terrified, what happened?'

'I know you said to wait, but I wanted to come and help,' Tallulah said. 'I was looking for Farrah when I found Serge. I was so angry at him ... I just, I lost my temper and I was hitting him, but then he ... he ...' Tallulah buried her face in her mother's shoulder and her words dissolved into tears.

'It's okay,' said Karen, rubbing her back, 'you're safe now.'

Tallulah pulled away suddenly. 'Wait ... what about Farrah?'

'We have her, she's in the car with Malek, trying to get warm. Come on, let's get you out of the rain too.'

*

Victoria

Victoria was numb. The police had arrived shortly after the paramedics and one of the officers had quickly shuffled them all out of the room, but not before Victoria had seen one of the paramedics look at the other and give a small shake of her head.

'I'm sorry,' the officer had said, 'but this room is a crime scene now. We need all of you to stay out here until we can assess the situation and talk to each of you.'

Lina and Nadia were either side of Victoria, holding her steady. Colleen and Brad hovered nearby, silently waiting to see what was going to happen next.

'What about Farrah?' said Lina suddenly. 'Has anyone heard from Malek? Do we know if they found her?'

'I don't know,' said Nadia, 'are we allowed to go and call him?'

'Oh God,' said Victoria. 'Who's going to tell them that Harriet is ...?'

'Harriet is what?' asked a voice.

They turned to see Malek coming around the side of the house. His face was ashen.

'Harriet is what?' he repeated, his voice cracking this time on the last word.

'I'm so sorry, Malek,' said Lina, going to him. But he brushed her aside and strode towards the doorway. He'd taken half a step inside when a police officer blocked him.

'I'm sorry, sir, but you can't come in here.'

'But that's my wife in there,' said Malek, pushing against him.

'I understand, and I know you want to see her. But this is a crime scene now, and we need to figure out what happened here.'

'I can tell you what happened,' said Malek. 'It was me. I caused this.'

*

Malek

He hadn't let Farrah come down to the granny flat with him, not when he knew there was going to be bad news. She didn't need this tonight, not after what she'd already been through.

He'd known the moment Mrs Spotswood from next door had pointed at the door to the flat and said she'd seen Harriet go in there. He'd known no one had seen her since. Known it – but hadn't wanted to believe it. And it only took one glance around the room for him to fill in the blanks.

How long had she been asking him to get rid of those cockroaches? Weeks and weeks. But he'd finally got around to it today, the day of the party. And because he'd left it so late, he wanted to be sure he did the job properly. Three of the spray bombs instead of the one recommended for the space. Set and forget. But don't go back in there for at least two hours. Otherwise, you risked being exposed to the pesticide.

He hadn't had to worry about it, though. The only other person home was Farrah and she knew not to go in there.

And Harriet had said she wouldn't be back today. If anyone else had opened the door and gone into that room, they would have turned around the second they entered. The smell would have warned them. But not Harriet, no sense of smell meant she wouldn't have noticed the acrid scent of pest spray on the air.

The cupcake that Harriet had bitten into had nothing to do with any of it. That was just a silly little gift left in the letter box from an arsehole boy who was trying to lure his daughter out of the house.

No, for Harriet, the pesticides wouldn't have been toxic enough to kill her, but they might have been strong enough to disorient her. And maybe if she hadn't been choked up and coughing, then she would have seen it coming. Maybe she could have ducked.

Because that's when the second thing must have happened. The timing lined up. He put two and two together the moment he saw it lying on the floor by her body.

Her ridiculous driftwood sculpture.

The thing she'd insisted on hanging from the ceiling. He'd told her those hooks weren't strong enough to hold it. And to be honest, he'd thought it was a bit much, a bit overbearing, the huge, twisted hunk of wood seemingly levitating in the centre of the room.

It probably happened when he, Farrah and Tallulah dropped the couch upstairs. The living room was directly above the flat. The couch was heavy enough that he'd worried about the tiles, but he didn't even think of it reverberating through to the ceiling of the flat. Heavy enough to cause one of the hooks to come loose. As the hook was pulled out of the soft plasterboard of the roof by the weight of the driftwood, one side must have swung down in a beautiful arc and struck her from behind.

It was the police who explained the final pieces of the puzzle.

'It looks like the other side of the fishing line snapped, just here,' said one of the officers, pointing the frayed end out to Malek. 'That's how the whole thing landed next to her. Made it seem like her murderer had tossed their weapon to the floor and run. A terrible accident, but we will still need to investigate further to clarify the events.'

So that was it. They had the answer.

A perfect storm of catastrophes. One after the other. Like a Rube Goldberg machine in flawless sync.

With Harriet as the final domino at the end.

Harriet

You're out of time.

You really did always want a surprise party. You just never imagined it would end like this.

Do you think your parents will come to your funeral? It sounds like a funny thing to wonder, doesn't it? Why wouldn't they? But they weren't going to come to your fortieth. And they didn't come when your daughter was born. The last time they showed up was at your wedding. And that ended up being the worst mistake they ever made, as far as they were concerned. Not that they blamed themselves for the mistake. No, they blamed you.

It hurt when they moved to America with Eddie while you were in the middle of doing your HSC. You knew he had rare talent. You knew that eventually he would outgrow Australia and need to go somewhere else to really make it. You just didn't know that your parents would go with him. You knew right then that Eddie would always be more important to them.

That's why you pushed so hard for them to come to your wedding, right when Eddie had an important tournament. You picked that date on purpose, didn't you? But it was because you wanted them to show that they loved you. For once in their lives, you wanted them to put you first.

You've always wondered if Eddie overdosed to spite you. The six-year age gap between you had always felt like a huge ravine. You looked up to him, but he looked down on you. Your parents believe if only they'd been there, they would have been able to protect him.

Will they feel the same way about you, now?

The first time you met Malek's family, you were so … mystified by how different they were. They're such a close family. So different from yours. With their huge, rambunctious events and their cluttered home that is full of warmth and noise and cousins and aunts and pets and food. If you're being entirely honest, you've always been a little jealous. The amount of intense love in that home. It was in every plate of food and in every warm handshake and in every tight hug and even in the way they teased or scolded one another.

You tried to fit in with them, you really did. But you could never quite pull it off. It was like you were only ever playing the part … like you never knew how to love in the same way they did. You tried to call Malek habibi once in front of his family and his sisters laughed at you. It was probably because of the stilted way your voice sounded, like their language was unfamiliar on your tongue.

You can feel the end now. You're hallucinating faces. Malek. Karen. Victoria. They're all here with you. They all want to say goodbye.

There are so many things you wish you could say.

You desperately want to tell Victoria the truth about Dion, but how would you even begin to explain?

And Karen … you owe her an apology for the way you treated her, but it would never be enough.

Finally, Malek. You always knew how infatuated he was with you and you let that power go to your head. At least now he'll be free of your hold on him.

He always did deserve better.

PART FIVE

the aftermath

CHAPTER THIRTY-SIX

Malek

He'd honestly forgotten how much fun the early stages of a new relationship could be. At first he'd worried what people might think: was he moving on too fast? It had been just over a year since they'd lost Harriet. Should he still be sitting at home, grieving his wife, not going out on dates? He'd realised he was done caring what other people thought. And he could only hope that Harriet would have wanted him to be happy. If it was the other way around, he knew he wouldn't have wanted her to be alone. Harriet never would have been short of partners, though; hadn't been even when she was married to him. He could look back at his marriage now and see where he went wrong. Honesty, that was the issue. Harriet was always open with him, but he wasn't honest with her.

For some people, being in a throuple, or an open or polyamorous relationship might be perfect – exactly what they needed. And if Harriet had married a different guy, maybe she, Victoria and that guy could have lived happily ever after. But it wasn't for him. It never had been. And he should have spoken up sooner, told Harriet that it wasn't what he wanted. Although, to be fair, he was pretty sure it wasn't what Victoria had wanted either.

He took hold of Karen's hand, traced the tip of his fingers along the lines on her palm. He was regretting suggesting they come to this café for a coffee after the movie. He actually really wanted to take her home, but he'd been putting off inviting her back to his place – they hadn't taken that next step yet.

Karen leaned forward, resting her elbow on the table and her chin on the hand that Malek wasn't holding. She held eye contact for long enough that Malek felt a shiver go right through his body.

'Hope they hurry up with those drinks,' she said.

'Oh, yeah? Why's that?'

'Because Tallulah might have mentioned to me that Farrah is having a sleepover with her aunt tonight. And I'm wondering if that could mean you're going to extend the invite to your place after coffee.'

'Want to skip the coffee?'

'Hell, yes.'

*

Karen

Separating from Robert had been the hardest and simultaneously the most wonderful thing she had ever done in her life. It was so strange to realise that a marriage that appeared perfect on the surface was in fact broken underneath.

There were so many things that added up to make her realise they were no longer meant to be together. The decline of intimacy and chemistry between them should have been the first clue. Karen had tried to chalk the change up to normal relationship progression, but it had slowly become clear that it was more than that.

And then, of course, the confirmation that he had been cheating on her.

Ariella had been a lot easier to crack than Robert. Karen had gone to her place and cornered her the day after the party. There were too many unanswered questions. Too many clues that something was going on.

Ariella had broken down and confessed that the affair with Robert had been going on for six months. She claimed that Robert had told her they'd been having marital problems, and at first, they were just talking – she thought she was helping him work through it. But then it had turned into something else altogether. He'd made her feel special, made her feel like they had some kind of true love and what they were doing was pure and honourable rather than wrong and deceptive. He kept promising that he was going to come clean to Karen, but of course he never did.

One of the best things about leaving Robert was selling her business. Sure, she'd been good at spruiking those cleaning products, but it wasn't her passion – it never had been. It was only ever meant to be a temporary job when the kids were little. But she'd been so successful at it, Robert kept encouraging her to stay.

For now, she was taking a break from work while she figured out what she wanted to do next, but in the meantime, she was loving getting back into singing and wondering about using her business skills to open up her own music school.

Tallulah had helped her set up a TikTok account and she'd started sharing videos of herself singing and playing the guitar. She already had a decent following and at least one video had gone semi-viral after an influencer had commented on it, *Slay!*

*

They were both breathing hard, sheets tangled between their legs.

'That was spectacular,' said Malek. '*You* are spectacular.'

'You're not so bad yourself,' she replied.

He traced a finger down the long scar on her left arm. Karen rolled over to face him. 'I like that you're touching it,' she said. 'Most people pretend they don't notice it, which is ridiculous, because it's so obvious.'

'How did it happen?' he asked. 'If you're okay to talk about it.'

'I don't mind.' She lay back again and focused on the ceiling. 'Happened at a New Year's party almost eighteen years ago. We were all out on the balcony watching the fireworks when it collapsed underneath us. I was one of the lucky ones, coming out of it with only a broken arm ... I mean it was a *bad* break, a compound fracture, my radius bone was literally —'

Malek had sat bolt upright and was staring at her, his eyes wide.

'What's wrong?' she asked, sitting up next to him.

'Was this the townhouse on Wentworth Drive?'

'Yes! You heard about that?'

'I didn't hear about it! I was there! I left right before the accident happened.'

Karen shook her head in disbelief. 'You're kidding. No way.'

'Hundred per cent. It was my mate's party.'

'Simon,' they said at the same time.

'Holy shit,' said Karen. 'I can't believe you were there. How did you know Simon?'

'Uni? You?'

'I didn't even know him that well. He was friends with the guy I was dating at the time, I was more of a tag-along. But I ended up staying in contact with a lot of them. I guess I got to know them after being in hospital together. But then ... if Simon was your mate, why don't I see you at the yearly catch-ups?'

Malek looked the other way. 'You're going to think I'm awful,' he said.

'No, I won't,' she said, touching his arm. 'Talk to me.'

'It's ridiculous. I wasn't even there for the actual accident. But I started having panic attacks afterwards. And I felt so guilty for not being there for my friends ... In the end, I just couldn't face them anymore. I'm a complete coward. I know they must all hate me.'

'My God. You're the guy whose girlfriend saved him by convincing him to leave early. But Malek, they don't hate you! They talk about you. They miss you! Not one of them resents you for not being there when it happened, they're just glad you weren't hurt.'

Karen paused. She stared hard at Malek and that strange sense of déjà vu she'd felt at Harriet's fortieth party when she'd glanced across the room at Malek was back. Her skin tingled.

'Malek,' she said. 'I remember you.'

'No way,' said Malek, 'that place was packed … you probably just think you do now that you know I was there.'

'No, I'm serious. The guy I was dating … I wasn't really that into him, we didn't last. But I remember there was another guy there that I was checking out. Tight T-shirt, great hair. All night I was trying to decide if I should go over and talk to him. But then this stunning girl turned up late and I realised he was taken. She saw me peeking too. I remember she did *not* look happy. Next thing, they were gone. Wait … that was Harriet, wasn't it?'

'Yep, that was her.'

'I can't believe I didn't recognise her sooner. I mean, I clocked how beautiful she was, you'd think I would have.'

'Not necessarily. It was a long time ago and sounds like you only saw her very briefly.'

'I guess. And I suppose the balcony collapse kind of overtook my memories of that night.'

'We'd only just started dating, but that night changed everything for us. I always thought we were meant to be, like it was fate or something, because she saved my life by asking to leave.'

'Or maybe it has nothing to do with anyone else's actions

that night, Malek. It was just pure luck that you left when you did and it's no one's fault, and no one deserved to live or die. It just … happened.'

*

Victoria

Victoria clicked on the Instagram notification absentmindedly as she rolled up her yoga mat under her arm.

Hamish recently added to his story.

She smiled at the photo of Hamish and Aarnav taking a bushwalk together. Hamish still looked a little gaunt; it would be a while before he was back to full health. But, God, she was happy he'd made it. Thankfully, he was no longer in any danger from his old 'mate' Damien. While the police hadn't been able to catch him, it didn't matter – a rival gang had. Damien had been found dead two weeks later.

Technically, she shouldn't be following Hamish on any kind of social media. But he wasn't officially her parolee anymore, so she figured it wasn't that big a deal. And the lines between her job and friends had blurred a lot over this past year. But none more so than the line she'd crossed on the night of Harriet's fortieth.

It had been later in the night, after the truth of Harriet's devastating accident had been revealed. The sound of a dog barking next door had sparked something in Victoria's memory. As she'd stood to the side while the police asked Malek questions, the dog had let out a long, low howl, and for some reason, an image of Dex's Staffy had appeared in Victoria's mind, almost immediately followed by a realisation.

A Staffy had been mentioned in one of the police reports they had on file.

Suspect claimed he was trying to retrieve his Staffordshire terrier from his partner when he breached AVO …
Subsequent investigation found that the rightful owner of the animal was Shailene Pearson, and suspect had no legal claim to it. Ms Pearson expressed concern that he would try to steal the animal again in the future …

A sick feeling had swirled in Victoria's stomach, recalling when she'd dropped around to Dex's place and he'd brought the dog out of a back room. If Dex had the dog, that meant he'd been to see Shailene. And Shailene wouldn't have allowed her dog to go without a fight.

Her gut told her that there was another woman in trouble that night. She hadn't been able to save Harriet. But she could still save Shailene.

On the road, she'd called Barb's mobile to get a welfare check on Shailene, and had her worst fears confirmed when Barb called back: 'I'm sorry, love, but your instincts were spot on. I've just heard that Shailene's place was a mess. Clear signs of a struggle. And Shailene is missing. The police are headed for Dex's place now.'

The roads had been wet but at least the rain had finally stopped, so visibility had improved. And there'd been no traffic, so Victoria had only been five minutes out.

'Then I guess I'll see them there,' she'd replied.

'Vic, no. You need to stay back and leave this to them. I don't want you anywhere near that house.'

'It's okay, I'll wait for them to go in first, I promise.'

Technically it wasn't a direct lie. Victoria *had* intended to let the police go in first … if they beat her there. But when she'd arrived at Dex's place, she couldn't even hear their sirens. She'd tried to wait in the car, but as the seconds ticked by, she couldn't help herself.

The window she'd left unlatched earlier that day was heavy, but she'd been able to slide it up with minimal noise. She'd climbed through and dropped to the floor on her hands and knees, certain that, at any moment, Dex's bulky figure would loom above her. That he would grab hold of her and slam her against the wall.

She'd crept through the living room and down the hall, wondering which of the three closed doors off the hallway she should try.

That's when she'd heard it: the mournful whine of a dog from behind the last door.

When she'd twisted the handle and opened the door, for a split-second she'd felt like she was walking in on Harriet all over again. But the woman on the floor had much shorter hair than Harriet's – dark hair that was matted with blood. A ceiling fan spun slowly above her, a poster of Alfred Hitchcock's *Psycho* was pinned to the wall and a line of ants led to a half-eaten cupcake on the bedside table. A Staffy had been by Shailene's side, pawing at her arm.

'Shailene?' Victoria had whispered. 'You're going to be okay, help is on the way.'

There had been a soft murmur from Shailene in response, enough that Victoria had known there was still hope.

Victoria had been reprimanded by Barb, but only mildly. The ambos who'd arrived soon after the police said she'd probably saved Shailene's life that night. Thankfully, Dex had been fast asleep in the other room and woke to several officers standing over him. He'd never even known that Victoria had broken into his home and found Shailene first.

*

Victoria scrolled away from the photo of Hamish on her Instagram feed, closed her eyes for a moment and touched the fingertips of her other hand to her temple. Remembering everything that had happened that night at Dex's place still made her stomach dip at how rash she'd been. But then again, was it any wonder she hadn't been thinking clearly? Her best friend had died in her arms. But the phone call she'd had with Shailene a few months later – when Victoria had called to to check up on her – had made it all completely worthwhile.

'I just heard you moved into your new place yesterday,' Vic had started. 'I wanted to see if it all went well.'

'The new house is gorgeous,' Shailene had said. 'It has a huge yard for Monty to run around.'

'Good. Hope I'm not bothering you by calling ...?'

There'd been a short pause from Shailene and then a small laugh. 'Of course you're not bothering me, Vic. I always love hearing your voice. Every single time I hear it, it reminds me of the moment I knew I was going to be okay.'

*

Malek

'Do you ever feel weird being down here?'

Malek straightened up and leaned his pool cue against the table. He nodded. 'Sometimes I do, yeah. Do you?'

Farrah picked up the chalk and dusted the top of her cue. 'Yeah, a bit. But I think it helps that it looks so different now, and I'm glad that we didn't have to move.'

'Me too.'

Malek gazed at the room that used to be Harriet's project. The granny flat she was going to rent out. They'd stripped it completely and knocked out one wall, which now had huge folding glass doors opening out to the swimming pool. It wasn't a man cave like he'd once thought he might like, instead it was the perfect teenage hangout for Farrah and her friends. But thankfully Farrah seemed happy to share it with Malek on occasion.

They had discussed moving. They'd talked about whether or not the memory of losing Harriet here made it too hard to stay. But they'd ultimately agreed they weren't ready to leave. Malek had also been campaigning for a new bridge over Wilson Road to their estate so that access could never be cut off by flooding again. It wasn't going to be an easy fight, but he was enjoying the challenge and he was considering running for the local council, as he seemed to have a knack for this kind of thing. The estate might have been built in a poor choice of area originally, which Malek had known right from the bloody beginning, but if they succeeded in getting permission for the bridge through council, then their house would end up being a decent investment in a growing area.

'Lina should be here shortly. You can order pizza if you like.'

'Sounds good. You know, eventually you'll have to start leaving me home alone again, right? I'm fifteen now, I don't need a babysitter. I'm old enough to *be* a babysitter.'

'She's not babysitting you! She wants to hang out with her niece!'

'Yeah, sure. But eventually you have to trust me again, okay?'

Malek was about to take his shot, but instead he put down his pool cue and took three quick strides around the table to put his arms around Farrah. 'Sweetheart, of course I trust you. I trust you completely. It's the other jerks out in the world that I don't trust.'

Farrah hugged him back. He felt her crying against his chest.

'Shit, I'm sorry, I shouldn't have brought it up.'

'No, no, it's fine. Sometimes I feel so stupid for sneaking out that night. And I've heard Serge's case has gone to trial, so it's always on my mind lately.'

'Here,' said Malek, guiding her to the couch and sitting her down. 'It's okay to cry, cry as much as you need. You've been through a hell of a lot over the last year. We both lost your mum and I have a bloody good idea of what it would have been like to lose you too. I mean, my balcony thing isn't the same as yours, but I get it. I get that feeling of "what if?" I'm here for you, okay? Want me to stay home tonight?'

'No! Definitely not. I'm glad you're going to finally see those friends. I think it's going to be really good for you.'

'Yeah … I'm nervous though.'

'That's okay.' Farrah wiped her eyes and then gave her dad a smirk. '*Karen* will look after you.'

Malek laughed. 'You sure you're okay with that? With everything that's happening between the two of us?'

'Yeah! Are you kidding? Karen's so nice! I know she's not like Mum … I mean no one could be like Mum! But Tallulah's my best friend, so it's epic that we might even end up, like, stepsisters or something. I hate that I thought Tallulah was trying to break me up with Serge 'cause she liked him … She was only ever looking out for me and I was being such a bitch to her. I still can't believe Mum got it all wrong and thought she was the bad influence on me.'

'I know, I wish your mum had told me about the photo of you two with the bong that set it all off.'

Farrah winced. 'I know, I know … I'm sorry. But think of it this way … I crammed all of my teenage rebellion into, like, one week and then I got over it. Dad … can I ask you something?'

'Sure.'

'Do you … do you still miss Mum? I mean I know you did love her … but I also know that you two didn't have the best marriage, and so sometimes I wonder. You're not … happy that she's gone, are you?'

'Farrah, no. God, no. I absolutely still miss your mum and I always will. I can admit that if she hadn't died, then perhaps we might have split up, but that doesn't change the fact that I loved her and that I'll forever be glad she was in my life, because, apart from anything else, you wouldn't exist if she hadn't been.'

'Okay … Sorry, Dad, I shouldn't have asked that.'

'Don't be sorry, it's natural to want to talk about these things and ask these questions. You can always ask me anything.'

'Thanks, Dad.'

'Alright, if you're sure you're okay, I better get moving. Karen's swinging by to pick me up soon. Mind if Lina takes over the game for me?' he added, gesturing to the pool table.

'Yeah, sure.'

Malek headed upstairs to change his shirt. He wanted to make sure he made a good impression tonight, the first time in so long that he was seeing his old group of friends again for one of the yearly catch-ups to remember the mates they lost. At least he felt like his clothes were fitting him better around the stomach lately. Taking up boxing classes had been a good call, both for his fitness and his mental health; it was great to take out his aggression on the bag whenever he started to feel angry or anxious about everything that had happened. Whenever those tough memories started creeping in: Farrah standing on that picnic table surrounded by flood waters; Harriet lying lifeless on the carpet, the sunflowers scattered across the floor next to her; the faces of his friends that night when he made it back to the party after the balcony collapsed. Whenever that happened, he would pound his fists into the bag and the tingling in his feet would slowly dissipate. The images would be replaced with brighter pictures: Farrah giving him a hug; holding Karen's hand; his sisters standing on his front doorstep with a pot of food day after day during those first few weeks after Harriet had died. Lina kept bringing food for several months. She was filled with guilt about her bad relationship with Harriet and confessed that she'd always been jealous of the way their mother had taken to Harriet. Malek didn't bother telling her that that was always completely obvious.

They'd been through a lot, but there were much better days to come.

*

Victoria

Victoria sucked her vanilla protein shake through a straw as she watched a video of Karen on her phone. Karen was strumming her guitar and singing a stripped-back version of 'I Don't Feel Like Dancin'' by Scissor Sisters. That woman really could sing.

It had been a weird moment when Victoria had realised that Karen and Malek were falling for one another. And at first, Victoria had wondered if she should remain friends with Karen – she'd had enough of awkward love triangles for one lifetime – but Karen was different. She had no interest in taking things anywhere beyond that one spontaneous kiss at

Harriet's party. She just really wanted to be Victoria's friend. Her real friend.

'She sounds amazing,' said a voice from behind Victoria.

Victoria tapped on her phone to pause the video and saw Yumi her Pilates instructor peering over her shoulder.

'Sorry,' Victoria said. 'I shouldn't have my phone playing so loud.'

'Nah,' Yumi said, 'it's a gym café, not a library. You're fine. Do you mind if I sit? All the tables are taken.'

'Of course.' Victoria pushed out the other chair.

'I'm glad to get the chance to talk to you, actually. I think you ought to try one of the advanced Pilates classes. You're getting too good for mine.'

Victoria's mouth twisted. She had to admit, she'd been thinking the same thing for some time now. But she could hardly tell Yumi that the reason she hadn't switched to the other class was because Marg ran the advanced course, and Marg didn't look nearly as good in a pair of yoga pants and singlet top as Yumi did. The aim of Pilates was strengthening the body, not checking out your instructor.

Then again, it was probably time Victoria stopped entertaining crushes on women who would never reciprocate her affection, and Victoria had heard Yumi had been dating Blake, the gym's male receptionist.

'You're right,' Victoria said. 'I should. I've been procrastinating because you're a great teacher and I didn't want to give up your classes.'

Yumi's lips twitched. 'What if I told you I had an ulterior motive?'

'What do you mean? Have I done something wrong?'

'God no, hun, it's the opposite. Look, I'm just going to say it because I prefer to be direct. I've wanted to ask you out on a date forever, but management doesn't exactly approve of instructors hitting on people in their classes. I kept thinking eventually you'd progress to advanced Pilates, and I'd get the opportunity ... but ... here we are.'

Victoria did a double-take. 'Wait, you want to ask me out? But I thought ... I mean, aren't you straight?'

Yumi tucked a loose strand of dark hair behind her ear and there was a note of amusement in her voice when she replied. 'Ah, nope. Last time I checked, I was one hundred per cent gay. And don't take this the wrong way, but I've noticed you perving on me in class. You're not as subtle as you might think you are.'

'I heard you were dating Blake – the guy who runs the front desk.'

Yumi laughed. 'I was dating Blake. The *female* boxing instructor.'

'Oh my God. I can't believe I just assumed.'

'I can't believe you've never picked up on any of the signals I've been throwing your way. I mean, I know I don't stare at your butt the way you check mine out but —'

Victoria blushed. 'Stop! I'm so embarrassed! I swear I'm watching you because you're *teaching* the class!'

'Sure, sure, you keep telling yourself that. So, what do you think? Are you ready to graduate to advanced Pilates?'

Victoria bit her lip and considered the question Yumi was really asking. Was Yumi's playful confidence too reminiscent of Harriet's self-assured manner? At the same time though, Yumi was somehow completely different to Harriet: more down to earth; no confusing games.

She was probably exactly what Victoria needed.

Victoria locked eyes with Yumi. 'Yeah,' she said. 'I'm ready.'

*

Karen

It still felt so strange to be in an empty house on the weekends when the kids were with Robert. Sometimes she loved the peace and quiet, sometimes she missed the noise desperately. But she had to admit, having this space from Tallulah every second weekend had really improved their relationship.

She felt her watch buzz with a notification as she was gathering her keys, phone and handbag to go and pick up Malek. She glanced at her wrist. Instagram notification. She paused to open up the account on her phone.

Tallulah liked your video.

She smiled then closed the app on her phone and gathered up her things again. She looked up at the shelf by the front door as she headed out.

'Bye, Harriet, be good,' she said to the small ornamental hippo on display.

*

Colleen

Rise & Grind Espresso Bar

'These are gorgeous,' said Sammy, tapping her finger on the glass case to point out the various pastries on display. 'Such intricate designs.'

'Thanks!' said Colleen, resting her hands on the counter. 'Ever since I hand-painted the macarons for Malek's wife's fortieth, I've been right back into my artistic baking.'

Sammy's face turned solemn. 'That's so sad, isn't it? What happened to Mrs Osman. Have you seen Malek lately?'

'Not too recently, he doesn't seem to come in so much anymore.'

'That's a shame. Um, like, I know it might not be right to say it when someone's wife has recently died … but I did always think you two would make a really nice couple.'

Colleen nodded. 'Yeah, I used to think that too, actually.'

'Can I ask … How come you never asked him out, then … after?'

'Oh, I figured I'd always wonder if he was the one who really did kill her. I mean, the story is it was an accident, but you just never know, do you?'

*

Tallulah

Sometimes she wondered if everything would have been different if someone had known that Farrah's mum was

369

downstairs in that room sooner. And sometimes she wondered if Farrah's dad had spotted his wife running down the side of the house, too, or if she just imagined him looking out the window at the same time.

It was right before they'd tried to move that couch that Tallulah had glanced out the window and noticed Mrs Osman hurrying around the side of the house, carrying a big bunch of flowers and eating a cupcake. She still remembers thinking, *Why didn't she come through the front door?* But something about the way Mrs Osman was moving had made Tallulah feel like she didn't want to be seen, so she didn't say anything out loud.

Then a few minutes later, as they were moving the couch, curiosity had got the better of her and she'd whispered to Farrah, 'I think I just saw your mum sneaking down the side of the house ... weird, right?'

That's when Farrah lost her grip and they dropped their end of the couch.

Later, upstairs, Farrah had told Tallulah to forget about seeing her mum. 'Don't worry about it. She's always doing weird stuff.'

'But didn't you say your dad said no one should be down in the room under the house 'cause he set off that stuff for the cockroaches? Do you need to make sure she wasn't going in there?'

'Nah, she'll be fine.'

Harriet

So, you're gone. You're dead. You've ceased to exist.

Okay, so if you're dead, why are you still here?

It's because you still owe something. You need to share one final secret.

Remember your two truths and a lie? 'My hair is blonde. My eyes are blue. I recently slept with the husband of one of the women here tonight.'

Victoria probably already picked up on this, the fact that you wear coloured contacts. Honestly, they all should have, because you mentioned it during one of your other turns of the game that night.

Which means we come back to this being one of the truths: 'I slept with the husband of one of the women here tonight.'

No, you never slept with Robert. However, you had your reasons for letting them all believe it was him.

You first met Ariella out the front of Karen and Robert's house. Farrah had left her AirPods at their place when she'd spent the afternoon hanging out with Tallulah. The next day, you were passing by on your way back from a job and you figured you'd knock and see if someone was home.

You realised pretty quickly that Robert wasn't happy to see you. The way his face changed when he opened the door because you clearly weren't who he'd been expecting. The distracted way he was looking around you. The hurried way he grabbed Farrah's AirPods and sent you on your way. And no, Karen wasn't home.

You understood only a few minutes later, when you were walking away from the house and the woman pulled up across the street. She was suspicious from the moment she saw you. You understood. If a married man is cheating with you, at the back of your mind, you're always wondering if he might be cheating with someone else too. You could tell that she wanted to ask you who you were, what you were doing there. That she wanted to be reassured that she was the only one.

What can you say? Curiosity got the better of you. You gave her a look, slipped her a business card, raced off and waited for the call.

God, it had been a shock when it turned out to be Karen's sister!

Ariella really did think it was love. Well, she did until she met you and she started to think she wasn't the only one. But you underestimated his hold over her. Even with you telling her he was a sleaze and an arsehole and that he was never going to leave his wife for her, she kept going back.

The entire time you were thinking that Karen deserved better – much better – from her husband and her sister.

But when you lost your temper with Karen at the karaoke night, you decided to find another way to let her know her husband was a cheat. You were doing her a favour, planting the seed that her husband was up to something.

Do you regret what you did to Karen that night? No. You don't. But you do regret taking it back, trying to cover it up.

Because don't you think Karen deserved to know?

Don't you think she deserved to find someone who would truly make her happy?

Now, one final question. If you were telling the truth when you said you'd recently slept with the husband of one of the women there that night, but it wasn't Robert, who was it?

Well, you were one of the women there that night, weren't you?

And you slept with your husband quite regularly.

ACKNOWLEDGEMENTS

Every time I write a new book, I tell myself that I will keep track of anyone and everyone who has been kind enough to help me out with tips, advice and answering questions *while* I'm writing the book. And every time... I do not do this. This means that when it comes time to write the acknowledgements I *panic*. I hate the idea that I might leave out someone very important. (I have also misspelt names in the past – I still have nightmares about this). Therefore, this time, I've decided to keep it short and sweet and just focus on a few key people.

First, there is absolutely no way I would have been able to write Victoria's character without the invaluable help given to me by Justine Codd. She answered endless questions about her work in community corrections and was so generous with her time. Through talking with Justine, I came to know how greatly she cares about her work and her parolees and I'm in awe of what she does day-to-day.

I have however, then taken some poetic license when writing about Victoria's work life, so please note, any inaccuracies regarding community corrections are completely my own.

Another person who was extremely generous with their time was Joey Grima, who was working with the Parramatta

Eels when I randomly accosted him in a café and asked for his help. Joey was kind enough to let me visit him at the Eels' training facility and interview him about his career as a professional rugby league football coach. I apologise for not being impressed enough when you kept introducing me to famous Eels players on account of the fact that I prefer soccer. So sorry.

I also had some help from several other people regarding questions on police procedure, SES flood rescue, Arabic translations and all sorts of other topics, as well as early readers and general love and support. So, a huge and heartfelt thank you to Paul MacNamara, Bosco Tan, JPM, Pete Mawad, Ally Prowse, Mum, Liane, Jaclyn, Kati, Fiona and my entire family, Anna Valdinger, Shannon Kelly, Kylie Mason, Meaghan Amor and the rest of the team at HCP Australia, Pippa Masson and everyone at Curtis Brown, and Maxine Hitchcock, Hannah Smith, Rebecca Hilsdon and the rest of the team at Penguin UK.

As always, much love to Steve, Maddie and Pip. You guys rock.

Loved *Every Last Suspect?*
Read these next …

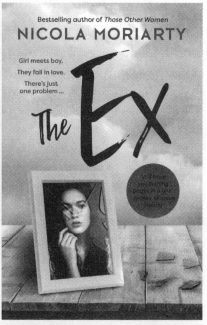

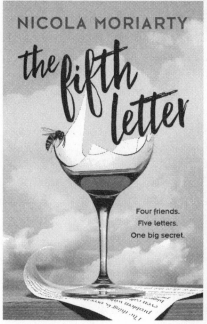

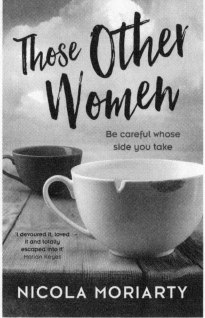